The Bun Also Rises

JANE ELZEY

Scorpius Carta Press

Eureka Springs, Arkansas

*"Find something you're passionate about and keep
tremendously interested in it."* — *Julia Child*

CHAPTER ONE

"Vivianna Lee!"

Her eyes shot up and she glanced around the restaurant to see if anyone else heard her name. No one seemed the least bit disturbed. She looked down at the three faces staring back from the yolks of her fried eggs. Earlene, Clara, and Floyd. Two aunts and an uncle from her mother's side of the family. All of them long, long dead.

She avoided the eggs and scooped a fork full of grits.

"Never enough salt," Earlene declared, her stiff bouffant bobbing. "Not enough butter either. If you can call that stuff butter."

"I have never met a Northerner who could make a decent pot of grits," Floyd said with a drawl.

"Any cook worth her larder knows if you don't add salt to the boiling water, your grits will taste like wet sand," Clara announced, her bangs curled like a sausage in a bun across her forehead.

Vivianna swallowed a mouthful of wet sand. "It's a Denny's," she whispered. "It's my only option. And why are you here now?" She glanced at the next table over. Yep. The kid with a smear of jam on his cheek was watching her whisper to her plate. She smiled thinly and he went back to his stack of pancakes.

"We're here because there's another rustle in the ethers," Floyd said, bobbing his head. He wore a pompadour hairstyle made popular by Elvis Presley. Floyd had mentioned to Viv more than once that he'd met his idol at the barbershop when Elvis was in Florida shooting *Follow That Dream*. "I think it might be gossip about you, Viv."

"Those are angel wings rustling," Earlene replied. "Honestly, brother, your hearing is suspect even on that side of the realm."

"My hearing is just fine," Floyd retorted. "It's my bunions that pain me. They're ghost pains." He laughed at his own joke and Vivianna found herself chuckling along with his infectious, high-pitched snicker. Glancing at the boy now eyeing her with cautious curiosity, she wrinkled her nose. He stuck out his tongue.

Earlene exhaled loudly. "You got bunions because Mama's high heels were too small for you. You should have borrowed Clara's. Her feet are as big as yours."

"Hush up, the both of you," Clara warned. "We're not here to discuss old habits. But if there is a rustle in the ethers, it could be angels rushing to choir practice or it could be something else entirely."

"Like what?" Viv whispered, wondering why angels needed choir practice.

"Like someone whispering a charm," Earlene answered. "Or somebody's ex getting turned into a toad. Or it could be just a witch sneeze."

"Sneeze or not, you need to watch your peas and cukes, Vivianna. There is something strange going on. If Floyd is right," Clara added, "that gossip could lead us right to the point of origin."

Viv smiled at the mix-up. Peas and cukes. Her entire existence was strange. "Point of origin?" She mumbled into her coffee cup.

"That's the moment when a specific magic is cast. That place in time when magic is called into being. The point when a spell is muttered behind the veil and…"

"Just say it already, Earlene," Clara scolded. "She means the reason we came to be. That magical moment when we popped into this side of the living. Not so much the when, but the why. I think we all remember as to when."

Viv sat back and stared at her plate. She hadn't ever thought about why the gourmet ancestors, as she had come to call them, had become pop-up ghosts and gastronomy gurus. She had wondered if anyone else had ancestors who showed up at the meal—actually *in the meal* and *only* in the meal. No one she knew ever volunteered that detail.

A year ago, if someone had asked her if she believed in magic, she would have said, no. Maybe with an indignant exclamation point! But opinions can change, and the appearance of the gourmet ancestors was definitely some kind of magic.

It was during her last semester of culinary school when it happened. When *they* happened. She was torching a tray of crème brûlée in pastry class. One second she was coaxing the sugar into a glossy caramel with the patience of a saint—and the next minute the torch was spewing green sparkles like a Fourth of July sparkler. Viv had watched wide-eyed as the flame turned red, then purple, then chartreuse before emitting a sound like a Champagne cork.

Pop. Pop. Pop.

Three faces appeared in three ramekins in front of her.

"Maybe a bit too much nutmeg," one of them had said. "It can make the tongue go numb, you know."

Viv had looked up, started, and glanced at the student working in the station next to her. "Did you say something?"

The student wrestling with a piping bag didn't even look up.

"I said: too much nutmeg can make the tongue numb," the voice repeated.

Viv blinked at the miniature, slightly translucent face floating above the custard like a marshmallow puff. The voice was definitely not inside her head. It sounded like any normal voice speaking, although full of Southern drawl and a slightly impatient snip that reminded Viv of her fifth-grade teacher.

"I think the vanilla bean adds just the right *oomph*," another voice said with encouragement.

Viv blinked, wondering why she was hallucinating.

"Watch your fingers," the last voice added, appearing over the custard like a tiny portrait of Elvis Pressley. "I believe you're about to set yourself on fire."

Viv looked down at the torch aimed dangerously at her fingers on the ramekin rim.

"If the flame consumes the cook, the meal feeds no one," he added. "Isn't that true, sister?"

"Any disaster is a learning process," she replied.

"A worthy quote from Julia Child," he said. "Or was that the Galloping Gourmet?"

"Cooking is like love. It should be approached with abandon or not at all. *Ibidem*," the teacher-voice added. "Another wisdom from our great gourmet guru, Julia Child."

And then, just as quickly, they were gone. Viv thought she was losing her mind. But then they appeared as meatballs in marinara sauce a few days later. As pineapple rings shortly after that. The more they appeared, the more her panic about their presence eased. She wasn't losing it. The gourmet ancestors were real. As real as any specter can be.

"I'm sorry we couldn't be much help in your kitchen last night," Earlene offered now, drawing Viv's attention back to her grits. "I'm glad the flames didn't reach any higher than they did."

Viv frowned. The steak she attempted to broil for supper that Earlene seemed determined to bring up yet again had sputtered and sparked into flame. Her kitchen had filled with smoke thicker than a fog machine. The alarm shrieked until she managed to fan the smoke out the back door. It was another kitchen-fire disaster. Accident number twenty-five. Or maybe twenty-six. She was losing track.

"Eat your eggs before they get cold," Clara said, and the three of them disappeared from her plate.

Her eggs were cold when she dug back in and scooped the last bit of yolk with a piece of buttered toast, remembering the last time she tried to fry an egg which promptly burst into flame. Somehow, her stove was always catching things on fire.

In the three months since graduating culinary school and moving to Crystal Bay, she had discovered that she could chop raw vegetables, pour cold cereal, and make a sandwich. When she added heat, dramatic and devastating things happened. Mostly, fire happened. Flames would shoot up seemingly out of nowhere. Little explosions blew out appliances. Sparks set food on fire even when the pan sat on low heat. The first microwave disaster merited a 911 call. She'd already been through three toasters. The crock-pot experience had been incredibly messy.

Something in the ether, Floyd had claimed when he popped into her breakfast. A rustle. Could that be gossip about her? Gossip about a chef who couldn't cook? Or more accurately, a chef who couldn't apply heat. A chef who created a firestorm when she turned on the stove. It wasn't because she was a terrible cook or a sloppy chef, or even an unlucky one. This problem was other-worldly. And the gourmet ancestors were as confused as she was about what was going on. For someone who had dreamed of becoming a chef since childhood, this was a lump in the béchamel. An enormous lump.

One day Viv was the top student in her culinary class with plenty of praise from her favorite professors. Job guarantees when she graduated. A few envious glares from her peers. The next thing she knew, the stove was exploding at her fingertips.

It had been the middle of a class bake-off. It started with a familiar little *ding!* from a timer she definitely didn't set. Then the stove let out an odd little gurgle, and—*boom!* It wasn't like a gas explosion; it was more like a riff on a timpani drum when danger rolls in on a movie screen. The smoke had been saffron-colored, and it puffed out from the oven door like a mushroom cloud. And yet, despite all the heat and crackle, Viv and her peers standing nearby remained completely unharmed. Unfreakingbelievable!

The memory still made her skin crawl. The incident could have been overlooked as an unusual and strange occurrence. Except. Except that it kept happening. That or something similar. Every time she touched anything that produced heat in the kitchen, heat produced flame. Or sparks and smoke. Or all three. Incident after incident plummeted her grades to the bottom and her spirits right along with it.

Viv returned her thoughts to the present, drained her orange juice and tucked her napkin under her plate. If not for the gourmet ancestors popping in when they did, she would have dropped out of school before the semester was up, too discouraged to continue. She would have packed her passion away in a box and taken up a sensible career like her mother, Charlotte, wanted. A job with prestige. A career with clout. Something with good pay and banker's hours. Not the long hours, sweat, and pores reeking of chopped onion that came with working in a kitchen. Even if Viv did push her chef dream aside and do something practical, she couldn't compete with her sister, the plastic surgeon, or her other sister living the country club lifestyle with teens in tennis camp. The way the gourmet ancestor saw it, Viv needed to follow her own path or none at all. A chef with credentials, despite the odds.

Viv paid her breakfast bill, chatted briefly with Bree the cashier, who she was getting to know since she ate breakfast at Denny's most days now. Bree had two kids in grade school and a no-good husband who she felt certain was cheating with someone from the bowling alley where he worked.

"That bimbo blonde is the most likely candidate," Bree said, and Vivianna nodded in full agreement.

"A no-good husband and a bimbo blonde," Viv repeated. Neither term seemed politically correct, but who was she to challenge anyone's point of view? Especially when her own perspective had gone off in another dimension like an episode of the *Twilight Zone*. Everyone had problems.

Feeling every ray of the Florida sunshine on the top of her head, Viv walked the three blocks from the restaurant to her house, a little square concrete block structure painted bright yellow. The front yard had a palm tree, an orange tree that made fresh-squeezed juice in the winter, and a tangerine tree with fruit so sour it would curl your tongue all the way to the roof of your mouth. The house was a recent inheritance with impeccable timing. And for that she would overlook the abundance of concrete statuary that dotted the lawn and were much too heavy to move. She patted the weather-worn mermaid statue as she walked up the chipped concrete walkway and opened the door she hadn't bothered to lock.

CHAPTER TWO

Viv sat on the velveteen couch, circa 1972, she guessed—like everything else in the house—and scrolled to the calendar on her phone. A new Greek bakery had opened, and Viv was asked to write a restaurant review for the local newspaper. A trial run, the editor said. A test to see if she had her writing chops *mise en place*. The editor claimed a position was open, and if she did well, she could write both a food column and a restaurant review to be published weekly. Asked to submit both for consideration, she would cross her fingers.

Professor Brown at the academy was behind the offer with the *Citrus Times*. He seemed to have connections everywhere. In culinary school, Professor Morris Brown, known as Chef Mojo, had been kind to her when things started going wrong. Make that horribly wrong.

She smiled at the thought of him bustling around the kitchen, hands on his hips like he was stalking the runway during fashion week. Professor Mojo was a playful and unnervingly knowledgeable chef turned professor. He loved sharing his passion for folkloric cooking from his Cuban roots. He instilled in his students the idea that every flavor tells a story. That every technique was a ritual. That nothing should be in the dish or on the plate that didn't have purpose. He encouraged them to experiment with unfamiliar ingredients and flavors with his culinary school versions of *Chopped* and *Top Chef*. Viv had won one of those competitions using fresh guava in a salad with endive, arugula, and Manchego cheese.

She had enjoyed all of her classes with Chef Mojo. As an instructor, he seemed to have a sixth sense for a roux about to burn or a student whose confidence was about to crack. Well regarded in the local community, he and his partner hosted fundraising dinners he called "Feast Blessings" that featured exotic fare and a table full of big money. He claimed his special menu included a dish Chef Mojo said was guaranteed to make a critic forgive anything and a rich man open his wallet. Viv had been lucky enough to go to one of them. Not because she had big money, but to help serve the feast. Exemplary service was a skill that Chef Mojo said all chefs needed to learn.

Since leaving school, she had received two encouraging emails from him. *"Stay in touch. Stay focused. And remember what I said: don't take shortcuts, don't cook when grieving, and always give an offering to the culinary gods when making bone broth."*

The second email had come shortly after the last 911 call to her kitchen.

No, she would not get hired in a restaurant kitchen anytime soon. That was an absolute given considering this predicament of making fire spark and sputter. Until that was resolved, she could at least lurk behind the scenes. She wasn't qualified to be a restaurant critic, but writing about food felt like a second chance.

This newspaper gig looked like a solid plan, anyway. If everything went off without trouble, she would write for the newspaper. Maybe she would earn her place as Crystal Bay's rising culinary star with an appetite for dining Michelin star. Except she wasn't actually a rising star. Her career was as flat as a sunken soufflé. And, if she was being honest with herself, there wasn't a Michelin star restaurant within a 100-mile radius. Today, she'd settle for writing about Greek-style donuts. Writing about food wasn't cooking, but it felt close enough. For now.

She decided she would clip her first column in the *Citrus Times* and send it with an old-fashioned thank-you note to Chef Mojo. There was a drawer full of unused cards in the desk. She had riffled through them, noticing their old-fashioned vibe, and yet, that's what made them appealing.

The house inheritance—and everything in it—had been unexpected. An aunt on her father's side of the family never had children, and as her namesake, Vivianna found herself the home's new owner. She hadn't known her Aunt Viv well, but her father had always spoken fondly of his sister. She wasn't sure why the property had come to her, not exactly, but she was grateful it had.

And, it had come at the best possible time. After that last culinary school fiasco, she barely graduated from the program. Fifty pounds of expensive protein slated for a fundraising dinner had burned to a crisp in a roasting oven that mysteriously jumped to 500 degrees when she wasn't looking. She did graduate but not top of her class as she expected. Her joy was zapped. Her aspirations deflated. Her job prospects vanished. She graduated with nothing but a certificate that said she had passed the curriculum.

She couldn't move home and face her mother, who would most likely say, *I told you so.* And mean it. Crushed by disappointment, disillusioned with her dream, and angry that everything caught fire, Viv couldn't face Charlotte's glare of disappointment.

She didn't have anywhere else to go.

Then suddenly, she did. Her own little house in Crystal Bay.

Viv touched her fingers to her laptop keyboard. No one could ever claim that Vivianna Marston was anything but optimistic. Maybe not always enthusiastically optimistic because sometimes circumstances really sucked. But she could always look for the rainbow sprinkles. Stay focused, she kept reminding herself. One day she could make a feast without it going up in smoke.

Rainbow sprinkles.

"I don't know what to write about," she said aloud, wondering if the ancestors were listening. "A food column. There are thousands of foods to write about."

Grandmother Mimi's voice drifted into her thoughts.

Recipes are just stories waiting to be told, Viv—add your own spices and make it your own recipe.

Tea-Time with Mimi

By Vivianna Marston, The Snooty Foodie

My love for food started early. My grandmother, Mimi Grace, is the one who gave me this passion. She lived in a creaky old house on a little homestead in North Florida. She always had a big garden, a yard full of chickens, and giant magnolia and pecan trees shading the old tin roof.

I spent holidays and summers standing barefoot on a stool beside my grandmother, obediently following every instruction to the letter. I spent a lot of time stirring grits with a wooden spoon worn smooth from decades of use.

Dinner at my family home was tuna casserole and peas from a can, a Little Debbie Swiss Roll right out of its cellophane wrapper for dessert.

Dinner at Mimi's was roast with rice and gravy, fresh picked field peas and giant sliced tomatoes from her garden. We could count on coconut cake or pecan pie for dessert. And sweet tea. There was always fresh brewed tea.

Mimi believed food should never be rushed. She believed the more one sweated over the meal, the sweeter it would be. We did sweat. Her kitchen was sweltering. Summers were spent canning. Winter was spent baking. Spring and Autumn were about feasts.

My favorite memories, though, are of Tea-Time with Mimi. She taught me how to make tea cakes and scones, shortbread cookies and molasses crisps. We made pimento cheese sandwiches, fresh sliced tomato and cucumber toast with homemade garlic mayo and pepper. Our tea parties were just for the two of us since neither my sisters nor parents were interested. Mimi would set the table for four, with lace napkins and delicate teacups that came from Japan. When I asked who would be joining us, Mimi would say, "No one who isn't already here."

When I was old enough to write cursive, it became my job to record the recipes in Mimi's recipe book. Every recipe needed a summary at the top and she left this task to me. This experience gave me the confidence to sample food with a curious appetite, a willing tongue, and an idea of what a busy cook might be hunting for when turning the pages to find inspiration.

Mimi's special recipe book has since been lost, but I hope someday to recreate those recipes, adding my own twists, of course, because she would want me to.

Her food was not fancy gourmet, but all good food is the nectar of the spirit and sharing it feeds the soul.

This is my first column as the Snooty Foodie for the *Citrus Times*, and hopefully not my last. My hope is that you will take a culinary journey with me every week, exploring the ways in which food makes us who we are.

My grandmother taught me much more than how to cook grits or fry a green tomato. She taught me that love and passion are added to every meal as sure as a pinch of salt and pepper, sugar and spice.

I would love to share this journey with you.

CHAPTER THREE

Satisfied with her column for the paper, Vivianna attached the file to the email and off it went. Nothing like the familiar *swoosh* of an email being sent to test one's confidence for a job well done. She wiped at her tears that had gathered along with the memories and then put away her laptop.

Pulling out her shoeshine kit and Louboutin heels, she buffed the toe box and heel with the soft bristle brush, then turned the shoes over to examine the sole. The lacquer was wearing thin in a few places. She grabbed the red nail polish she kept in the shoebox for just that reason, noticing the bottle was nearly empty. She covered the thinning spots on the sole, blowing gently to help the color set.

Even though the shoes were a bit worn—starting with their original owner—she wasn't ready to give them up. She had almost choked with astonished glee when she saw them in the resale shop. They were the right size. The right price. An incredible bargain at $85. Charlotte—her mother—would approve. The red sole of the Christian Louboutin black pumps said everything she wanted to say. They said she had style. They said she had means. They said she had the confidence of a woman who knew her place in the world and had the moxie to claim it. In snooty-tooty Orlando, where she went to culinary school, everything was about how you looked, and a pair of shoes like these were an absolute must. Cocktail parties, job interviews, networking events. A must for any occasion that needed a little pretentious *a la mode*.

It was all about the rainbow sprinkles, she reminded herself. Fake it 'til you make it.

She tapped the sole of the shoe lightly with her fingertips. Satisfied the lacquer was dry, she set them on the floor beside her. Putting on her pencil skirt, which was also a resale find, she studied her reflection in the mirror. Professional. Check. Successful. Check. Ready for action. Check. Viv pulled her hair into a bun on top of her head and then let it back down again, her chestnut brown locks falling full and straight to her shoulders. Although a bit slack on makcup as a routine, Viv added a stroke of mascara to make her blue eyes pop and a swish of blush to accent her Florida sun-kissed glow.

Lokol Made Bakery & Brunch was only a few blocks away. The walk took her through an abandoned garden center, past the historic church, and then on toward her destination. A bicycle would be a good investment, she thought, as she mopped the sweat beading around her hairline. Although, pencil skirts and high heels didn't fit a bike. But then, walking on sandy sidewalks in high heels was a bit troublesome, too. She crossed the street near the downtown square, noticing the jasmine and hibiscus and coral-red ixora blooming on the side of the road.

As with most cities in Florida, suburban sprawl had pulled business to the outskirts of town, to shopping strips with big parking lots and boring big-box fare. But there were several shops left for tourists in downtown Crystal Bay, with its tree-lined street and crushed-shell sidewalks. The buildings were painted in pastel seaside colors and decorated to catch the eye. On one side was a wine and cheese shop, a shipwreck museum, the town's first post office, and a clothing store she thought smelled like her grandmother's cedar chest. The opposite side of the street had a bar that served beer and fresh oysters, a real estate office, and a bookstore that also sold nautical charts and tide maps.

The Lokol Made Bakery & Brunch was next door to the bookstore. Viv smiled as she approached the front door painted Aegean blue with canvas awnings to match. Matching umbrellas helped shade a sprinkling of tables outside for tourists willing to endure the eternal presence of sunshine and bugs.

As Viv approached the counter, she was aware of every scent that rose to greet her. She inhaled deeply and caught the clean, slightly sweaty perfume of warm yeast and spices. Cinnamon and nutmeg for sure. She sniffed at the cheese baking, feta she guessed, and the tangy tart punch of tzatziki that was probably made by the bucketful. The overarching smell of hot grease bubbling away in the fryers said a new batch of donuts was about done.

"I'm Vivianna Marston," she said. The woman coming to the counter wrung her hands dry on a blue apron, her brow doused in sweat. "I'm here to write a review for the paper."

"Perfect timing," the woman said with a Southern accent tinged with something else. Greek roots, Viv supposed. "I just brought out a batch of loukoumades. There's nothing like it in the world. Piping hot dough, sweet and gooey honey, sprinkled with toasted coconut and pecans." She smacked her lips for effect.

"I can't wait," Vivianna said with a smile. "I've never had loukoumades."

The woman extended her hand across the counter. "Zoe Diamante, proprietor."

Vivianna shook her slightly damp hand.

"Sit," the woman commanded with hospitality and a smile, motioning to a table near the window. "Are you a coffee or a tea person? Might as well get down to business."

"Coffee, please," she answered.

Her eyes widened when the coffee and plate arrived, heaped and still steaming. The dish had three compartments. In one section, the little round, puffy donuts sat in a chocolate sauce. In another, a scoop of vanilla ice cream was slowly melting over the top, and the third was in a puddle of gooey honey with a sprinkle of shredded coconut and toasted pecans.

"I always say, life is too uncertain not to eat dessert first," Zoe said, handing her a fork as if she were handing her the keys to the city, a broad smile on her tanned and slightly wrinkled complexion. A weathered soul, Vivianna thought, and a happy one. Zoe was not thin, and Vivianna had always heard that the best-in-class bakers wore a few pounds as proof.

The bite was glorious, and she closed her eyes to savor it. She could taste every molecule that made the donut what it was. A perfectly proofed dough with perhaps a pinch of nutmeg. A crusty exterior that gave way with a puff of steam to a tender bread center. Doused in chocolate was good. Covered in ice cream was delicious. But the best bite was the puddle of sticky honey and toasted pecans.

"Good, yes?" Zoe asked and nodded. "It's a family recipe. The honey comes from a cousin's beehives. Orange blossom, of course. The pecans from a cousin in Georgia, just over the line. My family is all a bit scattered now. We couldn't all make a living diving for sponges."

"Sponges?" Vivianna said with a mouthful.

"You never heard of the Greek sponge divers in Tarpon Springs? It's about two hours south of here on the Gulf of Mexico. We're four generations deep. My family migrated to Tarpon Springs from the island of Kalymnos in Greece." She grabbed one of the donuts and popped it into her mouth. The gesture looked like a habit.

"Let's see, I left Tarpon Springs about thirty years ago. Gosh, it's been a while, hasn't it? Drifted around a little. Chased after a man not worth the effort." She grinned with humility. "Sometimes the stubborn in us has to learn by trial and error. He's history now, that's for sure."

Vivianna nodded. She wasn't sure if that meant he was deceased, but it sounded like he was out of Zoe's life for good.

Zoe clasped her hands in front of her. "What's next? More dessert like baklava or a homemade pita sandwich with shaved lamb, sliced cucumber, and tzatziki on top?"

Vivianna inhaled with pleasure. "Yes, please," she said, beaming. She didn't care in what order the dishes arrived.

While Zoe was busy behind the counter, Vivianna took out her notebook and began making notes. She jotted down her initial impressions—the colors, the smells, the tastes, the hospitality that made everything seem like a visit to a favorite relative. Just as she was reaching for another loukoumades, she heard a familiar little *pop*. She looked at the plate in front of her and three faces looked back, perfectly rounded into the surface of the donut.

"Jiminy crispies," Floyd exclaimed. Vivianna thought she saw him lick his lips. "I'm going to put on ten pounds just being around these things. I might split my britches."

"They look delicious," Earlene said. "Did you catch that subtle pinch of nutmeg, Viv? Although honey puffs are supposed to have a sprinkle of walnuts, not pecans."

"It's a twist on the family recipe," she defended in a whisper. "She has a cousin who grows pecans."

"What's that you said, dear?" Zoe called from the counter. "I didn't catch that."

Viv hid her lips behind her coffee cup. "I guess it's an all-in-the-family thing," she whispered and smiled to herself at the coincidence. Here she was having a conversation with three characters "all-in-the-family" who were long gone and still apparently among the living.

Viv knew the gourmet ancestors' knowledge of food came from experience. Back in their day, the three of them owned a popular cafe near the Florida-Georgia border. The cafe sat between an alligator zoo and a wampum trading post. The gourmet ancestors weren't all that clear on history, time being different once you live in the clouds, but Viv guessed it was in the 1950s or '60s, when politically correct had yet to be invented and everybody dreamed of a vacation to the beaches of Florida. Their cafe sat on the Florida side of the highway on the way to either coast. No matter where tourists were coming from or going to, the cafe was the perfect stop on the way.

"Personally, I'm looking forward to a slice of lamb," Clara said now, ignoring Earlene's critique of the donuts. "No one ever makes a good leg of lamb anymore. Mama used to make the best."

"Our specialty was meatloaf and mashed potatoes," Floyd said. "It was the best you ever sat down to eat, but I don't remember eating lamb."

"We told you it was pot roast," Earlene said and giggled. "You had this thing about Mary and her little lamb. Mama thought it was best for you to remain innocent of what she set before you."

"I ate it?"

"And you asked for seconds if I recall rightly," Clara added. "We made a good meatloaf because you didn't have to disclose what went in it—last week's lamb, yesterday's pork sausage, a little of this and a little of that, and it certainly didn't have to be this gluten-free razzamatazz." Clara popped out of one donut and into another. "Now, Viv, when your lamb arrives, be sure to take note of the temperature at which it was put to rest. That's the ticket to good lamb. None of this cooked until it's boot leather nonsense."

Viv chuckled under her breath. Boot leather and razzamatazz. That would have to make it to a food column in the future.

Zoe returned with a plate. Viv glanced at the chef and then back at the dish of leftover loukoumades. Her gourmet ancestors were gone, but she knew Zoe would not have seen them even if they were still there. A pop sounded near the counter, and she watched Floyd appear in the water dispenser on the counter. He floated around with the lemon slices and then was gone. Viv bit her lip to still her laughter.

"So, at what temperature do you let your lamb rest," she asked as she chewed through her second bite full of flavor and crunch and creamy yogurt sauce.

"What temperature does the lamb rest? You're kidding, right?" Zoe laughed, and Viv was struck by her ease.

"This is wonderful," Viv said, wiping the sauce from her lips. "I don't think I've had lamb so tender."

Zoe nodded, obviously pleased with her review so far.

"The spanakopita is just coming out of the oven," she said. "And you'll have a sample of my baklava for your second dessert."

Vivianna shook her head. "I don't know if I can eat any more, but I would love to hear your story. How did you come to Crystal Bay? How long have you been cooking? And what made you want to open a restaurant?"

"How about I make you a to-go box and pour you another cup of coffee?" Zoe said. "You really should try the spanakopita hot out of the oven."

"Okay," she agreed. "Just one. And I will take you up on that to-go box." Leftovers meant another kitchen disaster avoided. Maybe she could warm the pastries without catastrophe and smoke alarms.

While Vivianna crunched her way through flaky layers of puff pastry stuffed with spinach and feta cheese, Zoe relaxed into the conversation.

"My parents wanted me to pursue a reasonable career," Zoe shared. "I wanted that for myself, but college wasn't for me. I found it boring. Besides, there were cute guys everywhere and none of them were my cousins!" She laughed lightly, but Viv could imagine that was a big deal. Dating would be challenging in a town where everyone was related.

"One guy I liked was in a band and they dropped out of school to play their music. I wasn't musical, so I bought a little camper bus with a kitchen. I drove it to concerts and made food. The band went where the money was. So, that's where I went. I loved the freedom. And the adventure. The money wasn't bad either."

She sipped her coffee and Viv thought she smelled licorice in the steam, making her wonder if there was a shot of ouzo in the coffee.

"I cooked. I traveled. And then I met a sorry excuse for a boy-friend—although no one could tell me otherwise—and I spent a decade trying to get him to notice me.

"Well, to be honest, he noticed me just fine, but I wanted to get married, settle down and have kids. That was the absolute last thing on his mind." She paused and sipped her coffee. "He was a diver. Not a sponge diver like my family. He worked on sunken treasure crews. If that's not a Peter Pan red flag I don't know what is." She stopped for a moment, her mind obviously elsewhere. "Have you ever been married?"

Vivianna shook her head.

"You're wise."

"I haven't found the right guy."

"Good luck with that," Zoe frowned.

"How did you wind up here?" Viv asked.

"I ran out of gas. Literally and figuratively. I was on my way to cook for a festival down near Tampa when I ran out of gas on the highway in the boonies outside of town. That's when I knew I needed to stop moving." She drank her coffee and then smacked her lips in appreciation. The scent of licorice wafted across the ta-ble.

"I spent the winter here before I packed up and moved on, but something about this place never left my heart. I can't say I felt that way about any other place I've been. And I have been places. There are only three states I have not been."

Viv nodded and waited to hear which states, but something drew Zoe's attention. Zoe glanced out the huge store-front window and frowned, pushing a curl away from her eyes as if to get a better glimpse. Vivianna noticed the gray in her hairline starting to take over the jet black of her curls. It made her think of her own mom.

Charlotte would never let gray peek through her crisp bob.

Zoe brought her attention back to her coffee. "When my parents passed I inherited a little share of money, and I came back here. I bought a house and a boat and a bunch of fishing poles. I thought I could make a living taking families out in the Gulf." She smiled and shook her head. "That got old quick. Some people don't manage a rocking boat particularly well, and I am no Nurse Nancy."

Vivianna chuckled.

"Next thing I know, friends were telling me I should resurrect my old food truck. I was a food truck queen way before food trucks were a thing. Now, food trucks are all tricked out in stainless steel and serving gourmet grub. My old rusty rig was history, and the more I thought about buying a new one, the more I had that been-there-done-that feeling. Cooking for others? Yes, I would do that again in a heartbeat. But in a food truck?" She patted her hips. "I've gotten too wide to maneuver in a tiny little galley. No matter how shiny and picture perfect."

She opened her arms to motion to her bakery at large, and Viv could see pride and satisfaction spread across her face. "That's how I got here. The lease on this building came up. I grabbed it. Sold my boat for cash and here I am."

"I love the name," Vivianna said. "Lokol Made."

"I thought it was a clever twist on Greek loukoumades," Zoe said. "The Greek language doesn't roll off the tongue for most people. Few would ever get the pronunciation right anyway, so why not go with the flow? Besides, I think it puts a fun spin on our local vibe. It doesn't really matter how they say it; it's the look on their faces when they taste my loukoumades that counts."

The word did roll off Zoe's tongue, and Vivianna scrambled to write down Zoe's comment. It was perfect for her review.

Viv was under the impression that food reviewers preferred to do their research incognito to avoid special treatment, but the newspaper editor had laughed that off in the first few minutes of the job interview. Small town, she said. Anonymity was impossible. Special treatment was part of the landscape. Besides, how would you get a good printable quote from the chef or owner? The point, she said, was to draw in business—both to the restaurant and to the newspaper's advertising department. She warned her against making review comments that were harsh. There's always something good to say, she said. Viv wondered if that would be possible always, especially if the gourmet ancestors got chatty. How they could taste and smell as a vapor in the ethers was still unknown, but there were a lot of things about this magic beings and fire and broken dreams situation that offered no reasonable or rational explanation.

She looked up from her notebook to find Zoe staring out the window again. The look on her face said she didn't like what she saw. Viv followed her gaze to see a young man with dark curly hair leaning against the palm tree in the Lokol Made courtyard. He was wearing a bright orange Hawaiian shirt; the kind found at any tourist shop, and a tattered green backpack slung over his shoulder. His gaze was on Zoe. Viv moved slightly to get a better look, and when he realized they were both looking at him, he disappeared behind the trunk.

"Uh, well," Viv stuttered, now feeling awkward. "I guess that's all. I think I have what I need. I would like to take a menu with me to be sure to get all the Greek words spelled correctly."

Zoe nodded absently, and Viv could sense the change in her demeanor. Zoe gathered the takeout items, bagged them in a paper bag with handles, and added a menu. "Thank you. If you need anything more for the review, just call me."

Viv nodded. "Let me settle my bill," she said and pulled out her debit card.

"Oh no! No charge," Zoe said. "It's on the house. You had to try at least one of everything, right?"

"That's so generous."

"I really need this review to make a big splash," Zoe said.

"I should get a photo."

"Oh, no!" Zoe said again, this time patting her cheeks. "I look awful!"

"You look beautiful," Viv offered. "Here, let's take one near the window with the courtyard and umbrellas behind you." She arranged her subject, moved a few items out of the frame, and shot the photo with her phone.

"The review will be in Saturday's paper, I think," she said, shaking the woman's hand. "I don't control that, but I believe that's the schedule."

"I'm counting on success," Zoe said. "I'll make an extra-large batch of everything and expect a crowd. I like feeding crowds."

CHAPTER FOUR

"Well look at you making the front page of the newspaper," Clara said as an orange fruity loop floating in almond milk. "I like seeing your name in print."

"I like your turn of the phrase, Viv," Earlene said popping into a green loop. "'Lokal Made will make locals happier than a dog with two tails.' Although I don't quite see the juxtaposition. You could have swung for a food metaphor."

"Kid in a candy store is cliché," Floyd said, making his floating appearance last, choosing to manifest in a pink loop.

The bowl seemed a bit crowded all of a sudden.

"Mama never let us loose in a candy store," he added. "We each got a quarter to spend at the Sears candy counter. I bought malted milk balls with mine. You bought hot cashews, Earlene. Remember?"

"I saved my quarter," Clara said in a rather reproachful tone.

"Yeah, and then you mooched off of us."

"I seem to remember you offering to share," Clara retorted.

"I seem to recall a stern reminder that sharing was caring," Floyd countered. "Along with that big-eyed puppy dog look at my candy bag."

"And we're back to the puppy dogs," Earlene said. "Maybe it wasn't as thin of an analogy as I thought at first."

"I can't eat my cereal with y'all in the way," Viv said. "There's not enough room for the three of you and my spoon."

"Well, we don't want soggy cereal on a spoon, now do we?"

Earlene said, as if not expecting an answer. "I only wanted to say how proud we are of our young aspiring writer."

"Have you heard any more gossip?" Vivianna ventured through a mouthful of cereal. "Any gossip from the rustle in the ether?" She felt silly just saying it. "Have you had any luck figuring out what's happening to me? This eating out is getting expensive."

"About that," Clara said. "We're following the trail of some dark magic, which, as you might guess, is not our forte. We're simple kitchen magic. Helper folk. The kind that Cinderella had at her behest, I presume."

"Yes, dark magic does have a certain odor to it, doesn't it?" Earlene asked. Again, no one expected to answer. "It smells like a kitchen match right when it sparks."

"Do you have any idea what the problem is?" Vivianna asked.

"It's a hex," Clara said matter-of-factly. "That's clear enough. But as to who put the hex on you and how we get rid of it is something we're still hoping to figure out. It bears repeating, we don't deal in hex magic, and so we don't have much experience."

"We don't have any experience at all," Earlene added to support Clara's point of view. "But we want to help. That's why we're here."

"A hex?" Viv echoed. "You think someone put a hex on me? But why?"

"Some folks cook with heart. Others stir the pot with something darker," Clara said.

"Mimi used to say that!" Viv exclaimed.

"That's the gist of it," Clara returned. "We're as stumped as you are. That's why we're looking for the point of origin. It could tell us what we need to know. Floyd's got a keen sense of smell, so we're hoping he can sniff out the culprit, sooner or later."

"I hope it's sooner than later," Viv grumbled. "The fire department is sick of my 911 calls. And I would really enjoy a plate of homemade pasta carbonara."

"Oh, yes!" Floyd exclaimed. She thought she saw a little splash in the milk. "That makes my taste buds tingle."

"You don't have taste buds, brother," Clara warned. "And take that silly bun off the top of your head, Vivianna," she added. "You look like a Choux pastry bun rising in the oven. Your mama gave you a beautiful head of hair. Show it off while you can."

And with that, they were gone.

Vivianna spooned the last bright-colored soggy O from her bowl. She picked up the newspaper and read the review again. The review really was a good one, as her gourmet ancestors had said. That felt good, and she hoped that both the editor and the restaurant would benefit. She pictured Zoe with customers lining the sidewalk outside her shop, all waiting for a plate of fresh loukoumades dripping with honey and pecans.

The picture of Zoe wasn't the best. She should have moved her away from the window. Not only was Zoe's face shadowed, but somebody had photobombed Zoe outside the restaurant window. The man in the bright orange shirt.

A reminder dinged on her phone as she was reading her review for the nth time. Earlene was right, she should have searched for a better metaphor. A dog with two tails was not particularly food-worthy. It was a good review, but she could do better. She hoped it was good enough to get her the job.

She checked the phone reminder that claimed her bank balance was low. Again. Although apprehensive about what she might find, she logged in to her account, anyway. It wasn't great news. The house might be paid for, but the rest of her life wasn't. Utilities, insurance, taxes, food—they all took a big bite. Money was going out and not coming in. It was all this eating out that was hurting her dwindling bank balance, but there was only so much cereal and milk a person could tolerate.

She needed a full-time job. Even if she wrote two columns a week, that wasn't enough to keep her afloat until … well, until she got rid of this hex and could start working her way to the top.

Viv paused. A hex. Had Aunt Clara really said it was a hex? Clearly. Could a hex really be why this fire thing was happening?

What the heck was a hex? Who would do such a thing? Why would someone do such a thing?

She dived into the search bar, passing up all the black witchy pages until she found a page that felt safe.

Hexes and curses and what to do about them.

That sounded useful.

Hexes, according to this source, were a short-term brand of harmful magic. It wasn't as bad as a curse, which was something that could last a lifetime. They could be passed down through the generations. A hex was invoked to cause someone to suffer difficulty in some part of their life. It wasn't all-encompassing, but rather about creating frustration and setbacks in a very specific aspect of their day-to-day existence.

A hex. It was beginning to make sense although not at all. Her world wasn't a witchy world, with the exception of her gourmet ancestors. Her world was a plain old get-up-and-go-about-your-business kind of world. A world where you manifested through hard work and maybe a pinch of good timing.

A hex was beginning to sound feasible. If she could believe in magic; if she could believe in ancestors popping into her food, she could believe in hexes.

She scrolled on.

What to do about a hex?

Find the source and create a remedy.

Well, that wasn't particularly helpful. How do you find the source and what's the remedy?

She read on.

Create a decoy.

A decoy was something that represented the hexed victim. It could be anything, but the most successful would be a homemade doll adorned with locks of hair and personal effects. It was called a poppet, but it sounded more like a voodoo doll. Transferring the hex to the poppet took a little magic unto itself, but once transferred, the poppet could be destroyed. By fire.

Viv blew out stale air.

That didn't feel right. Too close to the truth. What if she went up in flames along with the hex?

The next suggestion was to bury the hex in the ground. The description claimed that this was a simple process. Using a string and a bottle and a little incantation, she could trap the hex and then bury it in the ground. It didn't say where to bury it, and that seemed chancy. What if someone else dug it up? What if the hex then transferred to them? That would certainly make bad karma kick in.

The last suggestion was of no use whatsoever. It required that you take a picture of the person who hexed you and place it in a box of mirrors. With any luck, the hex would reflect away from you and onto them. If the gourmet ancestors succeeded in finding the point of origin as they suggested they might, they may also discover who was behind this horrible thing that was not the least bit funny. If they did, the mirror idea was worth a try. Maybe Floyd really could sniff out the culprit. She had no clue how to do that herself.

In the meantime, cold food would have to do. That and a less than occasional dinner out. Her bank balance demanded it.

She read her review one more time, then noticed the advertisement in the paper. The Saturday Market had farm-fresh fruits and vegetables, homemade jams and jellies, fresh cheese, bread and pastries, and locally grown mushrooms. The market took place in downtown Crystal Bay, at the old garden center parking lot. She remembered walking through the parking lot on her way to Lokol Made.

She glanced at her watch. Perfect timing.

~~~~~~

The bay part of Crystal Bay was a mesmerizing expanse of blue water. Like most Florida lakes, the water flowed from the freshwater springs underground. The Florida natives called them boils because the water boiled up from the spring with a great deal of force. Millions of gallons of water filled the bay hourly before ebbing through a network of man-made canals that joined tidal waters in the Gulf.

Viv's little yellow house sat four blocks from the bay, and she detoured along the path that led from the quayside where the fishing boats were moored. The sun burned golden in a blue sky, a brisk but gentle wind reminding her that it was winter and at least 75 degrees. The wharf and bay were quiet for a Saturday. No one was swimming, not even the snowbirds who could tolerate the 72-degree water temp constant all year 'round.

Tempted to test the water with her toes, Viv walked down to the beach, noticing a set of tracks that swerved one way then another in the sand. A pair of turtles, she thought, making their way to the water. Or maybe a fat lizard swinging its tail in the sand. Or maybe just a beach chair being dragged by a winter sun worshipper. She bent down to untie her shoelaces and curl her toes in the
~~~~~~

sand. A glint in the sunlight caught her eye as it glittered in the grass near the shore. A wishbone. No, not a wishbone. She bent to pick it up. It was shaped like a chicken wishbone, the kind she'd made wishes with at Mimi's supper table, hoping for a second dessert. This was bigger and it was made of metal. Some old apparatus used for fooling fish, she thought, seeing a bony carcass of some kind nearby. Turning the wishbone over in her hands, she felt the wet of the morning dew still clinging. And then she noticed the dew on her hands was red.

"Gross," she said aloud and dropped it back onto the grass, her hands now speckled with what looked like flecks of blood. Fish blood, she thought, glancing again at the carcass left behind by a careless fisherman.

A chip wrapper lay in the grass a few feet away. She grabbed the wishbone with the bag and walked it to the trash can. A takeout napkin lay on top of the heap, and she grabbed it to wipe her hands. Better someone's dinner germs than old fish blood. The lesser of two evils. Fish prep was the one of the lesson in culinary school she hadn't enjoyed. Slimy business, fish. She wadded the napkin and tossed it back in the trash.

A sharp sound caught her attention then, and she turned to see a seagull tugging at something egg yolk yellow a few feet away. A balloon left from a kid's party in the park, she thought. Not something a bird needed to eat.

As she stepped toward the bird and its prey, the bird stepped aside, squawking over the invasion of its territory. As she picked up the deflated balloon, she realized it wasn't a balloon, or at least not a typical one. This looked more like a tube made of rubber with the circumference of a rope. Neither was good for wildlife. People were too careless with their trash, she thought, especially around water, inadvertently killing wildlife mistaking it for food. She pushed the rubber tube into her pocket to dispose of it at home, away from the birds in the park and their curious beaks in the park trash. The bird raged for a moment, pecked at a shred of paper on the ground and then joined the flock of fellow seagulls. Viv picked up the paper the bird left behind and stuck it in her pocket.

The gray and white gulls caught her attention again as they squawked at something in the center of the park, their cackling sounding like raucous laughter. One bird let out a loud hoot and cry. Then the rest of them joined in, as if the bird had told a joke that was exceptionally funny.

Viv noticed the bronze placard nearby, and something was stuck to the sign. She leaned in and squinted. It looked like an airline ticket stuck with a wad of gum. Someone was going to miss their flight.

She moved closer to the anchor now covered with birds. The seagulls on the ground warily sidestepped before breaking into another round of bird-style comedy. As she looked more closely, her breath caught in her throat.

The birds were not laughing at something funny. The gulls were cawing at someone dead. A body hung across the arms of the anchor, a harpoon piercing the back of an orange Hawaiian shirt.

Viv stared at the sight. A flutter filled her stomach. She clenched her jaw and her fists. The urge to reach out and help rose, but it was obvious he was dead. And something about him was familiar. She looked away from the corpse, but all she could see was the image in her mind. She looked back, tentative but curious. If she wasn't mistaken, this was the same man she captured in the photo behind Zoe Diamante. The same man who photobombed the picture as he peeked out from behind the tree.

She hesitated a moment and then, with trembling fingers, dialed 911. They would recognize her cell number. She was sure of that.

CHAPTER FIVE

The cop in uniform found her on the park bench facing the water two hundred feet from the statue and its laughing gulls. The other officers were still circling the body draped on the anchor. She had washed her hands in the water fountain, shook them dry, and then took a seat and waited.

"Are you the one who called it in?" he asked, his voice deep and gentler than she expected.

She nodded.

"Not a pretty sight."

She shook her head in agreement.

"I gotta get details from you."

She looked up at him, but his face was shadowed by the morning sun directly behind him and she blinked at the bright light.

He motioned to the bench. "Care if I sit down?"

Without waiting for an answer, he sat heavily on the other end of the bench. He pulled out a notebook and turned to face her. "Are you a tourist or a local? Is this anybody you know?" He motioned with his head.

"I just moved here. And no, I don't know who he is."

"Ever see him before?"

Viv hesitated. She remembered the look on Zoe's face as she peered through the window at the man leaning against the tree, and now, she questioned if the photobomb was accidental at all.

"I took a picture of Zoe Diamante at the new Greek bakery on

Wednesday. I didn't notice it until it was published in the newspaper, but this guy was standing behind her in the photo. I thought it was accidental."

"Well, this definitely was no accident," he said flatly. "Somebody harpooned this man and left him to hang across that anchor."

Viv squeezed her eyes shut. The image wouldn't go away. "I meant that capturing him in the photo was accidental, but maybe he was trying to catch Zoe's attention."

His pen raced across the page of his notebook. "Zoe Diamante," he repeated. "Did she say who he was?"

"No. She didn't say anything about him." She could tell the officer about Zoe's strange expression and that maybe Zoe recognized him, and that she wondered at the time if Zoe didn't like the fact he was there. But those details were totally subjective, and she wasn't about to throw suspicion at a new acquaintance. It was his job to uncover the details. His or somebody else's in the chain of command in the Crystal Bay police department.

They exchanged details. She gave him her name, address and phone number, and a summary of how she came upon the body. He jotted it all down before adding, "Anything else you want to add?"

"I found something odd in the grass, and I threw it in the garbage," she said. "I think it might have had blood on it. I wiped my hands on a napkin and put that in the trash, too."

He glanced around and pointed. "That garbage bin?"

Viv nodded.

"Well, don't plan any out-of-town trips," the cop said with an authority he didn't sound all that comfortable with. "We're not done until we're done. Until we get this matter settled, you need to make yourself available for further questioning. The detective will be in touch. He's retiring in a couple of months." His mouth curved into a wry smile, as if amused by the afterthought. "He'll be raring to wrap this up, pronto. I never known him to be one to leave a fish dangling on a hook. So, to speak." He snapped his notebook shut. "The detective will be in touch," he added, and his weight lifted from the bench.

Viv felt queasy, as if experiencing a delayed reaction to how the morning started and how it would end. One thing was for certain; the photobombed man's morning couldn't have ended any worse.

Her feet felt numb as she walked the path toward the town square. Her head felt fuzzy. She wasn't freaked out. Or grossed out. She hadn't panicked. Was that because she was experiencing shock? Was this what shock looked like from the inside looking out? She didn't know, but it wasn't often a person came across a scene in a park like that.

She considered returning home and putting herself back to bed, but there wasn't much in her fridge, and the farmer's market was open on Saturday only.

By the time she finally made it to the square, the sun was hot, and the vegetables picked over. She bought the last loaf of sourdough and a tub of herbed farmer's cheese at one stand, chose a guava jam at another, and loaded up on salad items at the last. She eyed the fresh eggs, wondering if she might coddle an egg in a bowl of hot water. Hot tap water. She wasn't willing to turn on the burner to bring the pan to a boil. She needed a workaround for this no-cook hex business or find a remedy quick.

"You're new in town, right?"

She glanced at the young man in shorts and flip-flops nearly invisible in the shade of his umbrella. He smiled and beckoned her to his stand. His cart was painted sea blue with a splattering of bright colored shapes. She eyed the shrimp and the jalapeño, the lemon and the scallop shell painted on the side of his cart.

"You live here, right?" he asked, a smile opening a thin face with bristly sun-bleached hair. "Over on Dolphin Street. Yellow block house?"

Viv felt startled. "How do you know that?"

"Volunteer firefighter," he answered simply and opened the lid on his cart. "You seem to have a knack for catching things on fire."

She grimaced, and he smiled.

"You like ceviche? I make the best in town." She watched as he placed a sample in a cup, grabbed an avocado, and in a couple of quick moves with a sharp knife, added avocado chunks on top.

Viv's eyes widened at the sight. She spooned a bite with a tortilla chip. "Yum!" She mumbled with a mouthful. "This tastes amazing!" She fanned her lips. "And hot."

"Yeah, my jalapeños were a little hot this year. Sometimes they're hot and sometimes they're not."

Viv nodded, her attention greedily focused on the ceviche in the bowl. Her lips were on fire and her taste buds were humming. "Dang, that's good," she said finally, blowing the heat from her mouth. She looked at the bowl. "Shrimp, scallop, tomato, onion, cilantro, jalapeno, but not lemon, it's … something else."

He nodded. "Tart tangerine. It adds the right bite of sour. It would be a secret ingredient if everybody didn't know it already." He grinned and nodded in her direction. "Jake. Short for Jacob Palmer. Farmer, fireman, and owner of SeaViche a la Cart."

She grinned at his puns. "I get it," she said, chuckling. "Ceviche. On a cart."

"Gotta have a gimmick," he said.

"Vivianna Marston," she said, smiling back. "Viv for short. Recent transplant, aspiring chef, flame thrower. Although I would give up that last moniker in a heartbeat."

He cocked his head. "I know that name. Vivianna Marston. You're writing for the *Citrus Times*. I read your food column and your restaurant review for Zoe at Lokol Made. You're the Snooty Foodie. Now that's a good gimmick."

She blushed in the heat.

"You don't look all that snooty to me and I had you pictured a lot older. With an upturned nose and a pompous attitude. I'm glad to see that's not true. Besides, I've seen you in your PJs."

"I haven't had a fire in two weeks!" Viv exclaimed and then felt silly.

"Weirdest fire I've ever seen," Jake said. "Lots of smoke, not much flame. A lingering smell I couldn't identify. I thought maybe you had a candle burning or something. Maybe one of those hocus pocus candles."

He laughed and Viv found herself drawn to this stranger with his wild, sun-bleached hair and baggy shorts. She didn't recognize him, but he must have been one of the firemen who came to douse her last kitchen blaze.

"You actually read a newspaper?" she asked, a bit incredulous. "You actually hold it in your hands and everything?"

His smile faded and she was filled with regret for asking. She didn't mean it as an insult.

"I know it's old-school," he said, his tone light. "I read it to my mom. She's not in great health right now, so reading the newspaper is something we do together. I read it cover to cover, even the ads and the classifieds. I always learn something I wouldn't have known about."

"Oh," Viv said. "I'm sorry your mom's not well."

He didn't seem to hold offense by her comment, but a silence passed between them. She thought of Charlotte, who refused to be called Mom in public. She had been Charlotte since Viv was a kid. Charlotte wouldn't stand for such sentiment, like the two of them reading a newspaper together. No, Charlotte was strict, practical, and perpetually worried about what other people thought. By contrast her father was a cheerful man who worked long hours and tried his best to play peacemaker among the "girls" in the house. He wasn't a doormat, more like a welcome mat, always giving in to Charlotte's hang-ups to keep the peace.

It didn't sound like Jake's father was in the picture, but that wasn't any of her business to ask.

"How long does ceviche last in the fridge?" She asked instead, spooning the last bites from her bowl. Maybe this was a solution she could live with. She needed more protein in her diet. Peanut butter was getting old.

"It needs to be eaten the same day it's made," Jake said. "The shrimp and scallops aren't cooked by heat, you know. It's cooked in the citrus acid. So, you can't let it sit long." He pointed to his cart. "My rig is refrigerated, and the ceviche is on ice," he added. "I can't take any chances of it spoiling, and I almost always sell out. Today was slow for some reason. I got here a little later than my usual and I missed the early crowd."

Viv nodded. She had reached the market late, too. She glanced at Jake, wondering if the news of the body in the park had spread this far yet. She wondered if the news had reached Zoe Diamante. She couldn't think of a way to launch into that conversation and not feel weirdly creepy, so she didn't. Instead, she focused on the ceviche. "If I make this for myself, where would I buy fresh seafood?"

Jake narrowed his eyes playfully. "You're going to compete with the best? Game on!" She could tell he was teasing her.

"If you won't sell me enough ceviche to live on all week, I may be forced to compete. My stove is out of commission for now."

He laughed, and she noticed the little chip in his front tooth. "The market over on the docks is the best place. It's not very snooty, but the fish is fresh."

She watched as he spooned the ceviche into a container, added a handful of chips and a ripe, uncut avocado to the bag. "You promise you'll eat this today?"

"I promise."

"Then compliments of SeaViche a la Cart," he said and handed her the bag. "Welcome to Crystal Bay. And watch that stove, will ya? You don't need to burn the town to the ground to get noticed."

She heard a familiar little *pop* and looked around, but she didn't see the gourmet ancestors. She opened the bag and peeked in.

"*Ooh, la la,*" Floyd chanted as the avocado. "Now that's the fresh catch of the day."

"Don't be vulgar," Clara said as she materialized onto a tortilla chip.

"Oh, don't be a prude," Earlene said. "Viv needs a little hormone chili today, hot tamale."

"You mean Hormel," Clara corrected.

"I do not," Earlene countered with a smirk.

Viv grinned at the interior of the bag. When she glanced up, Jake was watching her intently.

"Thanks for the grub," she said awkwardly and snapped the bag shut.

"See you next week, maybe?" He lifted his hand in a wave.

"See you next week," she agreed. "Unless my ceviche is better."

"You're a tough crab to crack," he said, grinning.

She could hear him laughing as she walked away, thinking Crystal Bay might be an okay place to settle after all.

CHAPTER SIX

As Viv put away the groceries, dodging the gourmet ancestors crowding the top shelf of the fridge, she ignored their banter about where things should go, and instead pondered the morning behind her. She had launched the day with a bowl of fruity loops and a murder. She had made news—and obviously at least one fan—with her first column and review in the newspaper. She had met the farmer's market vendors, including Jake and his SeaViche a la Cart. And, she had found a new food group she could make without heat and disaster.

An unusual Saturday by all comparisons. Had she not been carrying the container of ceviche that needed refrigeration, she would have stopped in to see Zoe. She was curious how the review went and whether it had brought in business. And, she was curious whether Zoe had been interviewed by the police. She was eager to find out what the relationship between Zoe and the dead guy might be. Even though it was absolutely none of her business.

As if by osmosis—and maybe a pinch of magic—Earlene picked up on her thoughts.

"If you don't ask, you will never know," Earlene said. "And really, Viv, I think investigating might do you some good."

"What?" Viv slammed the fridge door and then opened it again.

"Here's what I've been thinking," Earlene continued in earnest. "The more people you meet, the more suspects we have on your hex list. Under the guise of a friendly murder investigation, you might be able to oust this hex culprit into the open."

"A friendly murder investigation," Floyd echoed with a sniff. "That's an oxymoron."

"Do you think the person who put this hex on me is living in Crystal Bay?"

"Maybe they followed you here. Maybe they're keeping an eye on you. Maybe it doesn't work unless they stay nearby."

"That's a really creepy thought," Viv said and shut the refrigerator door.

"Can you remember what happened right before the stove blew up?" Floyd asked, now shifted to the candy dish on the table. "The stove at the school, I mean."

Viv sat down at the kitchen table and pulled a glass of tea toward her. Sun tea. Brewed under the rays of the Florida's sun. At least the sun wasn't catching things on fire in her kitchen. "I've been thinking about that. You three came first. And then a few days later, the stove fiasco happened. It was right after I made one of the highest scores on a class project," Viv said. "It was another one of Chef Mojo's Culinary Competitions. The highest score won a paid gig with a high-brow catering chef in Orlando. The winner won money in her pocket, a little resumé experience, and a great networking opportunity."

"But the catering gig didn't happen," Clara suggested, settling in next to Floyd.

"No," Viv said, trying her best to remember. "Not for me. It's all a little hazy, but I think there was a tie score. I can't remember what happened exactly, but I do remember feeling really weird all of a sudden. I had a splitting headache, so I left class early. Maybe there would have been a tie breaker competition if I hadn't gotten sick. But the very next time I touched a stove, it blew up. That's about all I can remember."

"I understand," Floyd said. "Things get hazy on this side, too."

"This is the very reason why I conclude you've been hexed," Clara announced. "It has all the fat and trimmings of someone who was jealous of your talents. Someone with access to magic."

"Someone I knew at the academy?"

"That would be my guess," Clara added. "Someone who couldn't tolerate you being a better chef. Someone with a bad attitude and some black magic."

Viv sipped her tea, browsing through the faces of her classmates in her mind. No one stood out as fitting that description. They were all young, eager, and aimless in their pursuit of culinary excellence. They were all untrained, unskilled, and nearly unmanageable as a class of upstarts with more passion than skill. At least, that's how they started out. For most of the students, their skills caught up with their ambitions by the end of the year.

"I really can't think of anyone in particular," Viv said finally. "I don't think anyone was jealous of me. I don't know what access to magic looks like."

"It does take a discerning eye," Earlene said as if to soothe Viv's inadequate observations. "I can't say we knew we had any magic in us when we were living."

Viv grinned. She wasn't sure popping in and out of food was any great form of magic, either, but it was something. "Is there anyone else in our family with access to magic? Did anyone in your family have magical kitchen helpers? What did you call yourselves? Helper folk. The kind from the fairytales."

"Well, mother was known to talk to herself," Floyd said. "Especially when she was in the kitchen. I just thought she was getting a little batty, but maybe she wasn't talking to herself. Maybe she had magical helper folk like us."

Viv laughed. "Same with my grandmother, Mimi. She was always mumbling under her breath in the kitchen. My oldest sister claimed Mimi was talking to the pots. Charlotte claimed Mimi was just babbling to herself, but then, the two of them were night and day, oil and water. Charlotte was timid. Mimi was bold. They never agreed on anything."

"I think I would have liked your Mimi," Earlene said. "Our grandmother was gone early in life. We never knew her."

"Mimi was the most important person in my life," Viv said.

"Did she have a long life?" Clara asked.

"Not long enough," Viv said, feeling her chin tighten and her eyes grow hot. "She had a stroke. There were complications. I... I was going to stay with her that summer, but I went on a camping trip with friends. If I had, if I had just ..." Her voice strained and faded away.

"You can't blame yourself for that, Viv," Clara said. "Everyone has a time. Everyone has a place. To everything there is a season…”

“Turn, turn, turn,” Earlene added.

“I know,” Viv said quietly. “I know. But I can’t help but think that if I had been there, I could have saved her.”

The gourmet ancestors were quiet for so long, Viv wondered if they were still in the room.

“This is why investigating this murder would be a good thing,” Earlene offered, breaking the silence as a butter mint in the candy dish. “You were the one who found the body in the park, you know. I won’t say finders keepers, but that has to have some soul-sticking power. Like old grease in a pan that never goes away no matter how hard you scrub. The goo just keeps on getting gooier. Stumbling upon a murder is sticky business, too.”

“What reason could I have for investigating a murder when I have no experience and nothing to gain?” At this point she realized she was talking to the air. The gourmet ancestors were somewhere in her kitchen, but she couldn’t see where.

“I’ll give you five reasons,” Earlene said, appearing as an ice cube in her glass. Viv set the glass on the table. “Somebody put a hex on you to make your life a hot mess. You took a photo with a dead man in it. Well, he wasn’t dead then, but you know what I mean. And then you found that same dead man in the park. There’s a napkin in the park trash with your fingerprints on it, and that rubber thingy is still stuffed in your pocket. And five, the detective is going to pin this murder on someone so he can retire in good standing. All things considered that makes you the A.1. Sauce suspect.”

Viv gasped. She had forgotten all about the yellow rubber thing in her pocket. She pulled it out and dropped it on the table. What the heck was it? She pulled the shred of paper from her pocket. It had been on the ground near the anchor in the park, one of the gulls tugging at the damp end. It was a piece of writing paper; something ripped from a notepad. She stared at the message, her brow furrowed.

“Find the statue and you find…” The last words were blurred by morning dew and bird beak.

Uh, oh, Viv thought. Earlene might be right. She might become the A.1. Sauce suspect if her morning misadventure caught the detective's investigative eye. Especially if there was a chance that the hex and the murder were connected. She needed answers.

"I have an idea," Viv offered. "The newspaper editor mentioned they needed sales help. If she would hire me to sell advertising for the newspaper, I would have an excuse to talk to people in town."

"The perfect excuse to grill them like oysters over flame," Floyd added. "With a little heat, they'll pop open and reveal their secrets."

Viv laughed. "What do you think? I could sure use the money."

"I think it's a plan ready for action," Clara said. "Do you need our help? We could put a good word in her ear. Or maybe in her tuna salad sandwich."

"You can do that?" Viv asked. "You can pop into other people's food for a chat?"

"I don't know," Clara answered. "We've never had cause. I don't guess it would hurt to try."

Viv shook her head. "I think it's better if I get my own job, but thank you for offering. I'd like the three of you to work on finding a solution for this hex. Is there a book or something? Like a record of bad deeds? A directory of hexes?"

"Dial X for Hex," Floyd said and giggled.

Viv looked hopeful.

"Don't count on it, kiddo. It's going to take some leg work and a little teamwork. We're Team Viv," Floyd added with a splash in her glass. "We're on it like gravy on rice." With that, the three of them disappeared from the kitchen.

~~~~~~~

Left to herself for the first time in what seemed like hours, Viv sat in the winter sun on the patio like a turtle on a rock. The air was crisp, and she zipped her hoodie closed, but the sky was blue, and the sun was hot and before long she found herself drifting off, dreaming of food and Mimi's kitchen.

She awoke with a start, brushing at something tickling her face.
~~~~~~~

A dragonfly had settled on the end of her nose and even after swatting it away it hovered nearby. Iridescent blue and green sparkled in the sunlight, the lace-like wings looking too fragile to carry anything with weight. It zipped and dipped and then landed on the toe of her shoe.

"Hello, dragonfly," she said quietly.

Its wings seemed to shimmer in the light.

She watched it rise and land, bank a curve and then land again. She had read that dragonflies were magical creatures that delivered messages from other realms. A year ago, she would have dismissed that belief without a second thought. A year ago, she didn't have the gourmet ancestors. A year ago, she wasn't hexed. Now she wondered if this dragonfly might have a message.

As a symbol of transformation, the dragonfly was known to speak of the soul's calling. Or so she had read. The dragonfly symbol called for transformation. For a leap of faith. For new beginnings and a fresh start. Wasn't that what she was trying to do? Why was everything so difficult? Was she being punished for having a dream? Had she run afoul of some karmic debt?

The dragonfly fluttered its wings, and she sighed with a sense of peace. Everything was going to be okay in the end. Right? The wings shimmered.

A thought landed as the iridescent wings settled.

Look beyond the obvious.

Nothing seemed more obvious at present. She was in hot water. In steam up to her ears. No real job. No real prospects. Probably hexed. A murder on her doorstep.

Well, not actually on her doorstep, but close enough.

How in the world had she gotten here? Was this the hex at work? Was there really a magical influence bringing about this bad luck? Was she doomed or was she careless?

She moved her shoe, and the dragonfly darted off, zipped and zoomed around the hibiscus and then landed back on the toe of her shoe.

She remembered an assignment at school. They were assigned partners, and each had to prepare a three-course meal for the other to critique. She felt a twinge of regret in her stomach. She had been too honest with her review. Too forthright. Too critical of the food she had been served.

The bouillabaisse *had been* salty. The salad *was* over dressed. The dessert *did have* more vowels in the name than it had taste. And, last but not least, the student had crackle-popped her gum in Viv's ear when she leaned in with the plate.

Maybe the gourmet ancestors were right. Not only was she hexed but the hex seemed to be spreading. Like flame fed by oxygen and fuel. The more she struggled, the deeper the mess. Someone didn't want her to succeed. Not as a chef. Not even as a law-abiding citizen of Crystal Bay. Because now she was going to be a person of interest in a murder investigation!

How dare someone do such a thing!

Anger rising, she stomped the ground with a foot that had fallen asleep. The dragonfly darted off then returned. She watched as it landed on the back of her hand.

Look through the illusion, she heard in her head. *Rise like the steam from the kettle and settle into the tea.*

Hadn't Mimi said something like that once? She pushed through her memories. Mimi had at least said something very similar. It didn't make any more sense now than it did when she was a child in Mimi's lap crying about something that seemed soul crushing. Probably after being teased by her sisters who would never let her hang out with them unless her parents insisted.

One thing was certain. Earlene and Clara were right. She was going to be the A.1. Sauce suspect in a murder if she didn't watch her peas and cukes. She couldn't do anything about the hex just yet, but she could hunt the killer before the police tried to arrest her for the crime. She only stumbled upon that body in the park. Maybe in the same way the victim had stumbled into that picture of Zoe. But the way things were leading, she was connected to the photobomber's murder. Whether that murder was connected to the hex or not, that was an unknown. She felt like things were getting hotter. Things were about to boil. Things were about to blow off steam.

The dragonfly's wings shimmered again.

"Not going to happen on my watch," Viv said out loud. "This Vivianna Marston is not going to take any of this without some kind of a fight." She stomped her foot. The dragonfly rose again and then zoomed away.

Marinara in the House

By Vivianna Marston, The Snooty Foodie

One of the unsung heroes of the cook's kitchen is the humble marinara sauce—something every home chef can aspire to make. It's not difficult and it can make the difference between a blah lasagna and a blue-ribbon dish.

Quick, versatile, and deeply satisfying, marinara is the superhero on the plate. Big flavor. Little effort.

My memories of making marinara in my grandmother Mimi's kitchen are some of my favorites. I never tired of tending the sauce on the stove, washing canning jars, or sopping up leftovers in the pot with a slice of fresh baked bread.

Mimi's garden was a showplace for tomatoes. She grew a dozen heirloom varieties, and each had its place at the table. Her favorite for sauce was the Italian San Marzano that thrived in the muggy heat of Florida, but any ripe tomato on sauce day was fair game for the pot. By the end of a hot day, quarts of thick, rich, red sauce would be lined up and cooling.

The wonderful thing about marinara is that it can slather a pasta or meatballs, shrimp and chicken, veggies, eggplant

Oh, and the ways you can customize that delicious tomato-zing. Add chili flakes for a little heat. Add cream for velvety richness, add sautéed anchovies for salty pleasure and depth. The marinara is a deep, bold splash of color on a never-ending canvas of culinary art.

Don't be shy showing it off.

Another one of the beginner-friendly sauces, marinara is not much more than tomatoes simmered in garlic, olive oil, and herbs, but the flavor is rich and ready when you are.

Immerse ripe tomatoes in hot water and then immediately in cold to remove the skins. Add the tomatoes to a pot and simmer, crushing them gently with a fork or potato masher as they stew. Add a pinch of salt and pepper. A pinch of sugar, too, if you are a fan of a sweeter sauce.

A gentle simmer for 30 to 40 minutes is all you really need. But the loner it cooks, the richer the sauce becomes.

When summer tomatoes weigh in plump, juicy, and abundant at the market, that's the time to forgo ready-made and stew your own. You can store marinara for up to five days in the fridge or freeze for up to a year.

While today's cook may be prone to grab a jar off the shelf, the Snooty Foodie is here to encourage you to take another route. The homemade route. You will taste the difference.

Find tomatoes at the Citrus Bay Farmer's Market every Saturday. Remember to grab a crisp loaf of fresh bread for mopping up the excess sauce.

Be sure to get there early or miss out!

CHAPTER SEVEN

Viv breathed a sigh of relief when the newspaper article didn't mention her by name. A passerby, it said, found the body on an early morning stroll. The police identified the victim from his wallet. His name was being withheld pending notification of next of kin. The story seemed sketchy on details but that was probably because the police were sketchy on details to the press. A male, age twenty-five, probable victim of a homicide, was found in Anchor Park. An investigation was underway.

There was no mention of Zoe Diamante at Lokol Made. Maybe the police hadn't gotten a chance to visit with her. Or maybe the officer Viv talked to had written that detail off as nothing more than coincidence.

Maybe the editor had something to do with that. Appearances and all. The editor seemed preoccupied with appearances. She was enthusiastic about Viv selling advertising in addition to writing columns and reviews. Maybe the editor was a little too eager, Viv thought now. Maybe she'd been too quick to accept the first offer. She doubted a line of applicants was waiting for that job because most people hated selling anything.

Now, looking over the list of advertisers who would be her clients, she perused the paper. Zoe had taken out a big ad touting her upcoming grand opening, promising free loukoumades all day. Viv wasn't sure how Zoe would manage that, but that wasn't Viv's problem.

The other shops downtown were on her client list, but she

didn't see ads in the paper. Reason to stop in and introduce herself. she thought. And, while she was asking questions about their business, she could slip in a question about the victim in the park.

She took out her pencil skirt and Louboutin pumps and then did a double take on a cute little romper in peach colored gingham. Her tennis shoes beckoned. If she was going to walk, she needed to be comfortable. Besides, pencil skirts and high heels stood out in Crystal Bay like ketchup on a hot dog. Anything other than mustard and trimmings was a sin in the eyes of hot dog enthusiasts, a tidbit she had learned from a culinary classmate born and bred in Chicago. Ketchup on a dog was a true crime.

That meant her Louies could last another year.

She ate her last piece of sourdough bread slathered in peanut butter and mango jam, downed a glass of milk and headed out. Today, she decided, she would avoid Anchor Park altogether.

~~~~~

The Corks and Curds Charcuterie was about as adorable as a wine and cheese shop could get. Two walls were covered floor to ceiling in wallpaper that depicted an underground wine tunnel, and Viv thought the effect gave the tiny shop a cavernous feel. Somehow, it felt both adventurous and cozy. She could smell the sharp tang and brine of the cheese, the earthy scent of barrels and crates being used for decoration, and the hearty, pungent aroma of cured meats. Her taste buds quickened as she eyed the deli cooler and contents.

"You're just in time," the woman said brightly, appearing from behind the counter, looking as if she were coming out of the cellar from the mural on the walls. "I was just opening a bottle of Prosecco for us to taste this morning. It pairs so nicely with a bite of Brie and walnut."

Viv licked her lips. "I shouldn't," she said, as the woman handed her a small flute still bubbling. "I'm supposed to be working."

"Oh? Working on what?" The woman moved to a clear cloche containing an array of cheeses.
~~~~~

"It's my first day on the job," Viv said, accepting a napkin with a tiny wedge of cheese topped by a piece of walnut. "I'm working for the newspaper and food is my jam."

"Mine, too," the woman said and smiled. "Every day is an adventure for the palate. That's our motto here at Corks and Curds. We say, *come explore the world you've not yet tasted.* Go ahead," the woman encouraged with a nod. "Explore. A little taste won't hurt anything."

Viv smiled and tipped her glass. It was crisp and fruity with hints of pear and apple and lemon dancing on her tongue. She could hear the effervescence in her glass. "Lovely," she said, and then sampled the Brie.

"Prosciutto is another good companion to Prosecco," the woman said. "Any one of our gourmet meats, as well. The peppered salami is my favorite. Do you want to try a piece?"

Viv nodded and the women moved to the deli case. She watched as she shaved a piece the perfect size for a cracker. "Artisanal cured without unnecessary additives. I, for one, appreciate its long shelf life, although it never lasts that long in my home. We all love it too much."

"Mmm," Viv mumbled. "Delicious." She pictured this new food group being added to her menu. She hadn't even thought of cheese and crackers as a meal choice and here was a world of gourmet cured meat and cheese flavors. "This really is a culinary world to explore."

The woman smiled with satisfaction.

Viv set the napkin and empty glass on the counter and extended her hand. "Vivianna Marston. New to town, new to the newspaper business, and very new to selling advertising," she added, with a shy smile. "I'm also writing a food column and restaurant reviews, but I'm actually an aspiring chef."

The woman's brow shot up. "That's quite the vitae for someone your age. I'm Gerry, as in Geraldine. I own this store and the one on the other side of the Post Office. The dress shop. It's been in my family a long time."

Viv grinned. She remembered the shop smelled like her grandmother's cedar chest.

"New to town," Gerry repeated with a smile. "You really must meet my nephew. He's single. He's handsome. And he's all about food."

Viv nodded absently and looked over the deli options.

"I'll take a half-pound of your three favorites," she said on impulse, the salty flavor still lingering on her tongue. "Match it with three of your best cheeses," Viv added. "I love a good cheese, and I love culinary surprises."

Viv placed a package of gourmet crisps on the counter while Gerry busied herself with the order. Wine would have to wait until she had more money in the bank. "I don't recall seeing a Corks and Curds ad in the newspaper this week," Viv said cheerfully, adding another package of crackers and a tin of imported sardines to the pile. "Or the dress shop, either. Is that something you would consider?"

The woman chuckled and cocked her head. "Well…"

"I wrote the review for Lokol Made across the street. Maybe you saw it?" She pulled the newspaper from her bag. "My first food column is in there." She handed her the paper and Gerry lowered her eyes to the page.

"Lokol Made is having a grand opening and I was thinking that all the stores on the square would benefit if they advertised at the same time. It could be a block party celebration. Everyone loves a party."

Gerry chuckled. "Everyone loves a party. And a party loves wine and cheese! I see where you're going with that."

Viv smiled again. "No pressure, of course. I just wanted to spin that idea. Maybe I can write a review about your store. I would love that! It really is like a restaurant. Well, kind of."

"I like the idea," Gerry said, glancing again at the newspaper in her hands. "And I will definitely have to read this review."

"Oh gosh, that's my only copy," Viv said, "I should have brought more with me. I didn't think about that. I could bring you a copy. Could I stop in tomorrow?"

"No bother," Gerry said. "I already have a subscription. Can't say I always read it, but, I have it. Vivianne Marston," she added with reflection. "Why is that name familiar?"

"My aunt, maybe? She lived here a long time."

"Viv Marston! My goodness, I didn't add two and two together. She's passed if I remember."

Viv nodded. "She left me her house."

"Oh, dear, I am sorry," Gerry said, then added quickly, "Well, not sorry about inheriting the house, but for your loss."

"I didn't really know her," Viv said.

Gerry wrapped the goods and put them in a kraft bag with handles. "I'm not sure anybody did. I remember her being a quiet person who kept mostly to herself."

A person who kept to herself and her statuary, Viv thought, then wondered how she could move off this topic and onto another with grace. She motioned to the paper still in Gerry's hands. "Do you know that man in the picture by any chance? The one standing behind Zoe Diamante in the window."

Gerry pulled the paper closer. "No. But you're not the first person to ask. The police were here asking if I had seen this man. I told him I had."

"You saw him?" Viv felt the energy flood to her toes.

"It would have been around the same day this photo was taken, I imagine. He was in the square. Going in and out of the shops with a certain swagger about him. He came in wanting to know where he could find Zoe Diamante. He said he had a message to deliver. A rather brash young man, I thought, and I was hesitant to say anything, given his demeanor. But I didn't want him in my shop, either, drinking free wine and bothering my customers. So, I sent him over to Lokol Made. You know," Gerry paused, "he mentioned Viv Marston, too, but he must have been talking about your aunt. I'm afraid it went in one ear and out the other."

"Did he say where he was from?" Viv asked. "Or why he was here?"

"He said he had unfinished business. That he was here to collect his due. I didn't know what he was talking about, and I didn't ask. What is it about this guy that has everybody so curious?" Gerry demanded.

A slow beat passed before Viv answered. "He's the one found in Anchor Park. The one that was dead."

Gerry's brows arched. "He's dead? That guy is dead?"

"And I'm the one who found him," Viv said. "It was in this morning's paper, but it didn't mention my name, thank goodness."

Gerry reached for the bottle and poured another splash into both of their glasses.

"I shouldn't," Viv said, knowing that she would.

"Go on. Tell me what happened?"

"I was walking through Anchor Park, and the seagulls were all laughing at something sprawled across that anchor. It turned out to be this guy. I recognized him from this photo. He photobombed the picture of Zoe and then wound up harpooned in the park."

Gerry swallowed hard. "Harpooned? Are you saying someone shot him with a harpoon?"

Viv nodded and Gerry tipped the glass to her lips. A slight twitch started in her right eye, and Viv noticed Gerry pressed her fingers against her eyelid.

"Isn't that an unusual weapon?" Viv asked. "I mean, who carries one of those around in their backpack?"

Gerry smoothed her blonde hair, which was cut short, framing a face that looked familiar with cosmetic routines and maybe even a surgery or two. She looked younger than Viv thought she was and that seemed certainly on purpose. The twitch stopped and Gerry's face smoothed into composure.

"I can't say that I know," she said at last and swept up the glasses from the counter. "We are a fishing community. I would guess half the men in town have a speargun in their garage somewhere. We might even have one in ours. It's illegal to spearfish in Crystal Bay."

She turned away and placed the used glasses in a small tub on the counter. Viv thought she saw her mouth working as if she were talking to herself. Something about the harpoon had landed. It wasn't clear what. Other than the obvious.

"Is a harpoon the same thing as a speargun?" Viv asked.

"Well, I just assumed…" Gerry said, turning toward the cash register to ring up Viv's goods. "I just assumed you meant a speargun. Horrible things… horrible."

"Can you think of anyone who might know?" Viv asked as she swiped her debit card.

"Might know what?" Gerry asked, her brow creasing slightly. "I have no idea why he was here. Obviously, he stuck his nose where it doesn't belong. And look where that got him." The twitch started again. "If you're smart, you won't be doing the same thing."

Viv felt a bit put out by the implication that she was sticking her nose where it didn't belong, but she wasn't offended enough to lose a new client over it. "I guess you're right. I didn't have any-thing to do with it. I accidentally took a picture, and I accidentally found the body. My aunt says that's suspicious."

Gerry eyed her carefully. "Your aunt? I thought she passed."

"Oh, a different aunt."

She heard a *pop* and out of the corner of her eye, she saw Earlene and Clara blinking frantically from the sausage case, two fat links with faces.

"Time to make like a fig and leave," Earlene whispered with a hiss. "We've got a lead on a suspect."

A murder suspect? Or a hex suspect? She couldn't ask with Gerry still giving her that look.

Viv glanced at the sausage and then back to Gerry.

"I love your shop, and I promise to come back with a proposal for the block party ad."

"I will look forward to it," Gerry said, guiding the handles of the bag into Viv's hands. "And thank you for shopping at Corks and Curds."

~~~~~~~

"What was that about?" Viv asked when they were on the side-walk and out of earshot. She opened the bag and two faces plas-tered on the box of crackers looked back. "I thought you were go-ing to roll right off the shelf with all that gesturing and gesticulat-ing. Was it really so urgent that it couldn't wait?"

"Urgent if you're planning on drinking your way to lunchtime," Clara said in rebuke. "One should never imbibe be-fore noon."

She thought Earlene gave Clara a dirty look.

"I wasn't imbibing," Viv said in defense. "I was deal-making. I was trying to win friends and influence enemies."

"Speaking of enemies," Earlene said, "Floyd is on the trail of something particularly stinky. I told you hex magic has a certain smell."

"What is he after?"

"We won't know until he returns from wherever he went. I hope he didn't have to go all the way to h-e-double hockey sticks."

Viv looked up as a young woman approached on the sidewalk,
~~~~~~~

her face down as she stared at her phone screen. Dark hair fell in long strands that obscured her face. She bumped into Viv and looked up, startled.

"Hey, watch it!" the woman exclaimed.

"Amelia?" Viv asked. "Is that you?"

"Hey!" Amelia exclaimed, brushing the hair from her eyes. "OMG. It's Chef Flame Thrower! The one who *almost* took the top chef spot. The one who almost set the school on fire." Amelia grinned impishly. "*Almost*," she said drawing an air quote with one hand. "That counts everywhere but the bake, right?"

"Yep, that's me," Viv said, forcing more cheer than she felt. Did all her classmates call her that behind her back? Or just Amelia? She felt the sting hit her cheeks.

"I heard something about you getting a dumpy little house up here."

Viv laughed lightly, hoping to cover her embarrassment. "I don't think it's so dumpy. But it is mustard yellow. And how did you know about that?"

"Oh, you know how things spread. Kind of like wildfire." Amelia looked up at Viv, a good head taller, and grinned. "You're not the first one to set the kitchen on fire, you know. I guess that's where the expression came from. *If you can't stand the heat, stay out of the kitchen.*"

Viv flinched. Amelia's dark eyes darted to Viv's hair, her gingham outfit, then down to her shoes. Viv brushed an imaginary crumb from her colorful romper.

"That's cute," Amelia said, pointing to Viv's bag. "I had one like it *last* year. Only in *black*." Amelia wore a black dress, black Doc Martens and a very red lip. Viv remembered this same look at school. Amelia might have had one black dress or fifty. Who could tell since they all looked the same?

"What are you doing in Crystal Bay?" Viv asked.

"Me? My cousin has a guru shop. I'm going to run it while she's having baby number three."

"A guru shop?"

"Yeah, incense and crystals and woo stuff for tourists. Something wrong with that?"

Viv shrugged. "No, I'm just surprised to see you here."

"Really?" Amelia said and shifted the backpack on her shoulder. "Surprised? That's cool, I guess. But we weren't really friends in school."

"No, we weren't," Viv agreed. "We were both too busy with the chaos in the kitchen."

"Chaos," Amelia echoed, nodding. "What I remember most about you was that you were the teacher's pet. The top student. The one to beat. Everybody noticed. *Everybody*."

"Top student? I don't think so. Weren't you the one who nailed the soufflé? Mine looked like the smashed crown of a chef's hat."

Amelia laughed and slipped her phone into a patch pocket on her dress. "Yeah, and I also took top bake in Chef Mojo's chocolate bake-off. Remember? You mixed up the sugar and the salt. Simple mistake."

Viv cocked her head. "Someone swapped the containers at my station."

Amelia's eyes widened. "They did? Man, that's too bad." Her impish grin returned. "You always nailed the knife work, though. I still have trouble keeping my fingers away from the blade."

Viv noticed a bandage on one of her fingers. "At least there's not much knife work in a bakery. How's that going? Is it up and running, yet?"

Amelia shuffled her feet. "No."

"Oh, no, what happened? That was your dream. Your passion!"

Amelia exhaled. "Yeah, well…" She let the words drop. Viv thought she understood. They had all made big plans for the future.

"You were so pumped about opening your bakery. You said that with all your family connections you would rise to the top. What happened?"

"It didn't work out, okay?" Amelia snapped, her dark eyes flashing.

Viv heard Earlene hiss from inside the shopping bag and her ears started ringing. Maybe Clara was right. Two glasses of Prosecco were one too many. She shuffled the bag in her hand.

"I'm not doing what I thought I would be doing either," Viv said.

"What happened to you? I thought you'd be cheffing in some award-winning kitchen by now, clawing your way to the top. Although Crystal Bay isn't exactly gourmet avenue."

"I, uhm…" Viv stammered.

"What *are* you doing?" Amelia demanded. "What are you doing with *your passion?*"

Viv blanched at the question and the inflection behind it. What was she doing with her passion? Not much. She pulled the newspaper from her bag. It was still folded on the page featuring the new Greek restaurant. "I'm writing for the local newspaper. Food columns. Restaurant reviews. You know. That kind of stuff."

Amelia glanced at the newspaper and frowned. "Restaurant reviews? That kind of sucks for you."

Viv inhaled. The faintest trace of something foul filled the back of her throat. It was an acrid taste. Like smoke from a spent match. Maybe the sausage from the charcuterie shop was coming back to haunt her.

A silence fell between the two of them standing on the sidewalk. It was the kind of awkward silence that happens when a conversation has run its course, and no one knows what else to say. She was surprised and even a little excited to see someone she knew from culinary school, but that spark sputtered out. Amelia didn't seem that happy to see her, and she definitely wasn't happy her bakery plans hadn't gone as hoped. Viv knew that feeling. A heaviness settled between her breastbone and belly.

"Hey, look, I gotta go," Amelia said. "Nice chat."

Viv nodded. "Maybe we should get together sometime."

"Sure," Amelia said. "You should stop by the shop. It's the Willow Wood Witch. Cool stuff. And I'm really good at tarot cards."

"Do have my number?"

Amelia nodded and waved, phone back in her hand. "Oh, yeah. I got your number."

"Did you smell that?" Earlene asked after Amelia sprinted down the sidewalk and was gone.

"Something stinky," Clara said.

"Yes," Viv said out loud. "Something very stinky."

CHAPTER EIGHT

Meet Florida's Most Famous Treasure Hunter!

The faded sign sat slightly crooked on the wrought iron easel outside. The sign did nothing to keep the Sunken Treasure Museum from looking like a dark and stormy place from the outside. Maybe that was the intention.

Two round windows surrounded by coquina rock resembled portholes on an old ship. The portholes flanked either side of a heavy wooden door that weighed a solid ton as Viv pulled it open.

The air inside felt cool, and somehow also damp, as if misted by the sea. She peered into the musty darkness, so different from the vibrant wine shop next door.

"Hello?" she called, her eyes adjusting to the dark interior. "Are you open? Is anyone here?"

The low-hanging lights sprang to life and a swishing sound came up beside her. She nearly yelped in surprise.

"Of course we're open," a voice croaked, sounding as dry as sand. A man appeared and rolled his wheelchair beside her and then stopped. Looking up at her, he added, "I'd have the door locked if we were closed, now wouldn't it?"

She caught the sarcastic grin in his wizened cheeks before he flashed a smile full of pipe-stained teeth. He clenched the stem of his pipe Popeye-style in the corner of his mouth.

Viv tried not to stare.

"So, you're here to meet Florida's most famous treasure hunter," he said, wheeling the chair ahead a few feet. "It is I! Famous and never to be forgotten," he said, turning to face her once again. "Let the quest for treasure begin!"

Was this guy for real? Viv wondered if he was half mad or just terribly theatrical.

"It began one blustery day when the gales of winter blew across the Great Exuma Sound. Due north was the tiny island of New Providence. To our west, the great island of Andros and her tiny islands and cays." He flipped a switch close to his hand, and the floor flooded with an eerie blue light. Viv glanced at her feet. The floor had become the ocean, with blues and greens of every shade creating the landscape beneath. From somewhere in the dark the sound of sea waves crashing and ship lines creaking crackled over a speaker.

Despite the over-the-top delivery, Viv found it captivating.

The light beneath her feet dimmed. Another flared. She could see the room was designed to resemble the inside of an old ship. Wood planks covered the walls, every inch showcasing sailing and diving devices complete with creaking timbers, slapping waves, and ship bells ringing in the night.

He pulled the pipe from his mouth. Even though his hands were gnarled, they looked strong and capable as they rested on the wheels.

"We must protect the treasure from the pirates at all costs! Why, we had a pirate try to breach the ship the other day. I dispensed with him forthwith!" He clamped his jaws on the pipe.

"We've no time to waste. The crew has been at sea for many weeks and provisions are low. Still, we have no treasure in our hold. The divers are restless. A mutiny threatens to have them all swimming the tides to Andros Town for rum and dancing!

"No! They will obey their captain. They must obey! They will guard the night against thieves or die trying!" His voice rose. The quick grin surfaced once more.

Viv looked at him with concern. Was he serious, loony, or acting a part? She glanced around, looking for an escape route if she needed one. The heavy door behind her seemed the only way in or out.

"But, lass, you haven't come for a story about pirates and rum, have you? You've come for a tale of the sunken ship and her treasure of gold and diamonds. I shall not disappoint you. I will tell you that story. A story you've never before heard. And perhaps, never will again."

He looked at Viv expectantly. Was this where he took her money for the tour?

"I'm not really here for a tour of the museum," she said. "Although this is all fascinating and worth the price I'm..." She stretched her hand toward his, stepping into the spotlight overhead. "I'm Viv Marston. I work for the newspaper."

His grip was unyielding.

"Viv?" he squinted up at her. "Viv Marston? As I live and breathe!"

"You must be thinking of my Aunt Viv," she said quickly, hoping to quell any confusion that could send him off on another salty tirade. "Maybe you didn't know she passed. I inherited her house."

She thought his face fell in sadness. He squinted up at her again. "You look nothing like her," he said. "Well, maybe that topknot business you've got flopping around on your skull. She wore hers the same way. All swept up like a tidal wave about to crash to shore."

The image made her smile.

He spun the wheelchair again and rode toward a dimly lighted case a few feet away. Viv followed. He reached beside the cabinet and as if by magic, the case lit up like a stage. Her breath caught in her chest as a rugged piece of coral encrusted with jewels winked in the light.

"Behold," he said. She could hear the awe in his voice. "I give you the famous Bella Dona Jewels. Lost at sea in 1675. Lost in the waves not much more than 100 nautical miles from this very spot." He tapped the arm of his wheelchair.

"A journey of a lifetime," he said wistfully, his eyes watching the jewels sparkle in the case. "And a lifetime ago."

"Is this the treasure you found?"

He squinted up at her and clamped the pipe between his teeth. "I did. No thanks to that lazy crew who claimed to be divers and seafaring men. The lousy, thieving lot!" He grabbed the pipe once again and his eyes glistened. Tour or not, he had captured her attention, and he knew it.

"I was certain the ship was there. Not exactly where, mind you. But somewhere buried in centuries of sand and coral." His voice was raspy and yet surprisingly full of vigor.

"We sailed where stormy skies and shallow waters will cast a ship asunder. Where waves and shoals roll a ship until she breaks before the great King Neptune like tinder under an axe."

Viv could tell he was back in his rehearsed theatrics.

He coughed lightly, briefly, and then went on.

"I knew she was there, the Bella Dona. I knew she was sunk in the reef off the southern tip of Andros. I knew it. And she was."

"In the Bahamas?"

He nodded. "And that's where I got this!" He pulled up the cuff of his pant leg to reveal a deep scar hollowing his leg near the ankle.

"Shark bite?" Viv asked.

"Moray eel," he corrected and laughed with a hoarse cough. "Like Tolkien's dragon Smaug, she was. All twined and nested in her jewel-encrusted coral. Ten full feet of slimy eel. Ten full feet of vengeance. She latched onto my ankle with her jagged bite. The moray death bite, they call it. The moray: they don't let go."

Viv glanced at his leg, now once again covered by his pants. "How did you get free?"

He turned to the wall above the cabinet. Implements, knives, spears, and tools of an underwater trade she knew nothing about hung mounted with short pieces of rope. He cocked his head as if looking for something and then pointed.

"With that very spear," he said.

Viv followed his finger to where he pointed. It looked much like a shotgun with a dangerously sharp point at one end.

"It was to be either the eel or me," he said. "Neither one of us was going to give up that treasure without a fight to the death."

"Wow," Viv breathed. She couldn't imagine coming face to face with something that dangerous. He was a real-life underwater Indiana Jones.

"Why are you here, Viv Marston, if you are not here to take my tour as you say? Which you have enjoyed, I gather."

"I only wanted to introduce myself," she said, taken aback by the quick turn of his attention. "I'm new to town. I want to get to know all my advertisers."

"Advertisers?"

Viv nodded.

"We haven't advertised in that rag in a decade! Bah! That paper is just another pirate after the spoils!" He rolled the chair forward. "Back in the day I was the one who made the news. I was the news. I was Florida's most famous treasure hunter. I gave it all away." He glanced around the museum. "This is all there is left to that story," he said, but his tone did not seem bitter. "The government of ownership claims its share first, you see. I don't blame them. Treasure hunters keep a small share for their efforts, and the rules for disobeying are stern. Sometimes even jail time."

"Wow," Viv said again. "Then treasure hunting is not about the money. It really is about the hunt."

He nodded. "Even now, I would still dive if I could."

Light interrupted the dark interior as a door opened at the back of the museum and daylight filtered in.

"Dad?" A tall, lanky woman came through the door and scanned the room. Her eyes landed on his wheelchair, and she crossed the room, then tapped him on the shoulder with tenderness.

"I thought we agreed you would not open the museum today. I was looking everywhere for you. I was worried something had happened."

He tapped her hand with the same tenderness.

"Bah," he said. "What could happen to an old man except meeting that lone rider on his pale horse? I'm not afraid of death. I'm not afraid of these ghosts from the past rearing their heads. The Grim Reaper can't come too soon, my dear," he said, and then added, "Viv Marston, meet Katarina Becker, my daughter."

"What?" The woman stepped beside the chair and glared at Viv.

"Your father was just telling me about the moray eel," Viv said. "What a story."

"One of many," Katarina said, eyeing Viv with caution. "You've never heard of Florida's most famous treasure hunter?"

Viv shrugged. "Not until today. This is fascinating."

"Come by often enough and you'll hear all the stories. Buy the book and take Captain Fred's stories home with you. Stories I've heard at least a hundred times."

She could sense impatience behind the woman's words, and she wondered if it was meant to be disrespectful or just sounded that way. How many times had she listened to her own father's stories and jokes and repertoire that never changed? It did get tiresome, that was certain, but there were some things you endured with love and kindness. And patience, too, as often as you could muster it.

"Do you dive?" Viv asked.

"No."

"Oh, Katarina, will you never let that be?" He spoke slowly. It was a throaty whisper that spoke of weary caution, like a parent admonishing a child for the umpteenth time.

The sound Katarina made in response seemed familiar in return. The sound was not acquiescence. Not discord. It struck Viv as something private and personal between the two. An exchange so ingrained in their history that they knew it line by line, breath by breath. For a moment she felt embarrassed to be a witness, but the moment passed quickly. Maybe the angst between father and daughter was more common than she realized.

"I was planning to clean the museum today since you were going to be out," Katarina said. "Everything desperately needs a good dusting. Swab the deck," she added with a gentle laugh and another touch to his shoulder. "Floor to ceiling. Bow to stern."

"Bow to stern," he repeated, and patted her hand.

"I'm working with the *Citrus Times*," Viv said brightly, hoping to once again offer her reason for being there. "I see this might not be the time to talk to you about advertising, but I would like to come by again." She smiled at the old man. "And I'd love to hear more of your stories, Mr. Becker."

"Frederick," he said. "You must call me Frederick. Captain Fred would suit me even better."

"Captain Fred," Viv repeated. She glanced at Katarina, but the woman was staring at the wall above the lighted case, her teeth raking her bottom lip. Viv followed her gaze and now saw what she hadn't noticed before. Something was missing from the wall on the wall. A light patch on the old paint outlined where something had once hung. Hung long enough to cast a shape on the wall. A shape that looked to Viv like a harpoon.

CHAPTER NINE

There was a line at the counter at Lokol Made when Viv entered, and without hesitation she turned and went back out into the courtyard. She was glad to see Zoe had customers, but she wanted to talk to her without interruption. She'd wait until the rush was over.

There were other stores on this side of the street to explore, and potential advertisers to meet. Maybe someone knew who the harpooned victim was. And maybe someone knew if the harpoon in question could have come from the Sunken Treasure Museum.

She poked her head in the bookstore next door to the restaurant, the electric door chime announcing her entrance. A middle-aged woman stepped out from behind a shelf of books. Viv noticed she had two pairs of glasses on top of her head and another pair hanging from a decorative cord around her neck.

"Hello!" the woman called with a smile. "It's Bookworm Day. Everything is 25 percent off. Cash and carry. What kind of reading adventures are you looking for?"

Viv laughed. "Well, I like cookbooks. And a good mystery."

The woman clasped her hands in front of a generous bosom printed with a bright green bookworm, who, Viv now noticed, was also wearing a pair of glasses.

"Cookbooks! We have an entire collection of cookbooks. Old Florida. New Florida. Gourmet Florida. Bed and Breakfast Florida. Church lady recipes for the newlywed." She was already weaving her way through the stacks as she talked. "You name it, we stock it."

Viv wondered how such a tiny space could hold so many books. "Do you have anything on raw foods?" Viv asked as they came to a stop.

"Raw foods?" The woman's eyebrows knitted into a well-worn crease on her brow. "Well, let's see." She turned to the shelf with her pointer finger extended.

Viv noticed a colorful spine in bright yellow. "Cooking with Lemon," she read, as she pulled the book from the shelf. "101 creative uses for lemon."

"Oh, that's perfect," the woman said. "I'd forgotten about that old book. Written by a local over in Steinhatchee. There's got to be a raw food section in there."

Viv thumbed through the pages. It was more than a cookbook on the use of lemon in the kitchen. It was laid out like a story book of old Florida customs, with ornate hand-drawn illustrations of ingredients and herbs. And lemons. Lots and lots of lemons.

"If I may ask, what is your interest in raw foods? Are you doing that macrobiotic thing?" The woman pulled a spiral-bound book from the shelf and swept the cover with her fingers.

"It's a new direction I'm taking," Viv said, realizing she was being coy. Honest but coy. "I'm trying to avoid using heat in my kitchen."

"That's interesting," the woman answered. "It gets so hot here that anytime you can forgo the stove, the more comfortable the kitchen will be."

Viv nodded. The woman didn't know how true that was. "I'm Viv," she said with a smile. "I'm new to town. I'm a wanna-be chef and I've just launched the Snooty Foodie food column in the *Citrus Times*."

The woman clasped her hands again and the bookworm on her chest wiggled excitedly. "You're the Snooty Foodie! Well, I'll be a monkey's uncle. I read your article about Mimi's Tea. I read your review on Lokol Made next door. You've got talent."

Viv blushed. "I don't know if I have any writing talent. I do hope I have chops in the kitchen. Right now, I'm focusing on raw foods." She waved the book in her hands. "And things you can cook with lemon."

The woman laughed and the pleasant sound was broken by radio chatter blasting from the front of the store. The woman cocked an ear, listening.

"What is that?" Viv asked as the chatter continued.

"Police scanner," the woman answered with a slightly embarrassed smile. "It's weird, I know. My ex was an EMT, and I got in the habit of keeping tabs on what he might be up against. We've been divorced for ten years, but I can't kick this habit. I like knowing what's going on behind the scenes. I do a little ham radio also. SARnet. Statewide Amateur Radio Network. Sure is helpful during hurricane season."

Viv paused to listen. It was difficult to understand the lingo with the static, but maybe once you listened long enough you'd understand. She grinned to herself. If she mentioned that she lived on Dolphin Street, this woman might have new understanding about her not wanting to cook with heat.

They made their way to the counter and Viv dug for cash in her purse. She picked up a business card from the holder. Martie Grim. Owner of Tropical Tomes. Any time is tome time. Specializing in Florida authors and lore.

Viv pocketed the card. "Did you happen to hear the call about that guy they found in Anchor Park the other day?"

"Boy, did I!" The woman exclaimed. "That was the most excitement I've had all week. 10-54d. 10-107 on site." She glanced at Viv's confusion. "Possible dead body. Suspicious person on site."

Viv gulped. She was the 10-107. "Did they say who he was?"

The woman shook her head. "Tourist. I don't remember the address they coded. Somewhere out of state. White. Male. Suspicious person ended up being the bystander who found him."

Viv pulled the newspaper from her bag. It was still turned to the review of Lokol Made and she handed it to the woman.

"I recognize this," she said, nodding. "I know Zoe was happy with it because she said as much."

Viv poked a finger at the man in the picture. "That's him," she said. "That's the guy they found in the park."

"How do you know?" the woman asked, suspicion narrowing her eyes.

"Because I'm the one who found him," Viv said. "I was the 10-107. Only I wasn't suspicious. I was just walking by and there he was."

"That was you?"

Viv nodded. "I'm almost one hundred percent certain this is the same man. And I think Zoe knows who he is."

"I'll be a monkey's uncle," Martie Grim said slowly. "I always wondered what secrets Zoe was hiding. I reckon this could be one of them."

CHAPTER TEN

She could smell the oysters popping on the grill, the salty brine sizzling over the heat. The Oyster Bar, simply called that, was a little tiki hut bar with a big grill and a sweaty chef. A young man in thick rubber gloves was shucking oysters at a chipped porcelain sink.

Viv grabbed a seat and put her elbows on the damp bar.

"Beer?"

Viv glanced at her watch and nodded. Close enough for Aunt Clara. Five minutes to noon.

He plopped a sudsy beer in front of her and stood expectantly.

"Raw or steamed?"

Viv hesitated.

"That's all we got. Fryer's down today. You can try one of each if you like. See which one slides down better." He dragged a wire basket of hot sauces toward her. There were six different kinds. Four looked like they could eat the oysters themselves judging by the ferocity of the label, along with the old standby—Tabasco— plus a bottle of suburban cocktail sauce.

She dribbled a drop of Crack of Don on the raw oyster in the half shell, slurped it into her mouth, chewed twice and then swallowed it whole. Hot pepper and pineapple coated her tongue, elevating the salty brine of the oyster. She licked the heat from her lips and then grabbed a saltine from the sleeve. The heat built the longer it sat in her mouth.

She sipped her beer before choosing the Sam Sauce for the

second oyster. The label said it was made with Japanese black vinegar and Yuzu, with roasted tomatillos, jalapeños, and a hot pepper she had never heard of called 7-Pot Primo. She slurped the warm oyster into her mouth. It was tangy and citrusy and so spicy her eyes watered. But it was also delicious. Maybe she would dive into hot sauces in one of her food columns.

"Steamed," she said when he returned for her order. "A dozen will do."

She ate another cracker and sipped her beer as she waited.

From this vantage point, she could see everyone in the bar. There were six of them lined up at the bar, slurping oysters and beer. Four of them looked like locals. The others were tourists. There was no mistaking the newly acquired suntan and overly styled clothing meant to look like Jimmy Buffett fans. There were four tables against the wall, and they were full.

She turned to the guy seated next to her. She could tell he was trying to be mindful of his elbows.

"This is a great find," she said amicably. "Do locals come here a lot?"

He glanced at her, a dribble of sauce still in the corner of his mouth.

"Sure thing," he said. "Best oysters in town if you're not into harvesting yourself. Blasted things are sharper than a razor blade. Easier to pay someone else to do the hard work for ya."

Viv nodded. "You live here?"

"Sure thing," he said again. "And you?"

"I'm new to town."

"Cool," he said and picked up another shell.

She couldn't tell how old he was, exactly, but she guessed about ten years her senior. She didn't want him to think she was hitting on him, but she wasn't sure he would notice if she was.

"I guess everybody knows everybody?"

"I guess," he said, nodding in agreement. "If you want to know everybody, that is. Most of us grew up here."

"What's the deal with Captain Frederick and his daughter?" she ventured in a moment of daring. "Do they really make a living running the museum?"

He grinned. "Yeah. Like he needs to make a living. He dove treasure, you know. Back when there was still sunken treasure to dive for. He made a fortune on sunken gold.”

“He told me that treasure divers never got to keep much.”

“You can bet he didn’t give up everything he found, and he probably didn’t give up anything he didn’t have to,” the man said with a laugh. “Not our squirrely old Captain Fred.”

“What about his daughter?” Viv asked, wondering now if the old man’s comment was a lie or humble pie. “What does Katarina do? Doesn’t seem like there’s much for her to do at the museum.”

He glanced at Viv. “Apple doesn’t fall far from the tree, does it? Her highness Katarina,” he said, almost under his breath. “You’d think the sun rises and sets on her shoulders.”

“I think she feels the same way about her father.”

“I was being sarcastic,” he said. “She thought she was too good for any of us. Her father being famous and all. She’s gotten out of a number of scrapes with his fame. Nothing serious. Just a spoiled, bratty kid.”

“What do you mean? Scrapes?”

“She was caught shoplifting in a jewelry store once or twice. Was blamed for stealing a classmate’s watch and got herself kicked out of boarding school. Used a credit card that didn’t belong to her at the mall. The card belonged to some tourist in Ohio.

“That was a long, long time ago. Funny, that I still remember. But yeah, she helps Fred with the museum some. Mostly she runs a boat tour around the springs for tourists. A dive boat. Sort of.”

“Sort of?”

“You don’t need to be much of a diver to drop a few feet to see the manatee. They’re everywhere. But she is certified, and she does cater to tourists who want to dive. It just means they spend more money than they need to see a manatee up close.”

“She told me she didn’t dive.”

“Not the kind of diving her daddy respects. He’s hardcore, you know. He’s that ‘wild ocean, relentless hunt for the gold’ kind of diver. Not the kind that dives a quiet little bay with giant, gentle manatee. If you believe him, he fought off the Kraken of the Caribbean.”

“Really?”

“It’s a good story, ain’t it? He wrote a book about his adventures. I’m sure they sell it in the museum. Martie would have a copy. She specializes in Florida lore.” He grinned at her then.

"Martie's my sister. She's always been a bookworm." He said it with tenderness.

"They're a funny pair, those two. Both of them stuck somewhere in time. The old man's still reliving his days as a treasure hunter and Katarina's still trying to get his attention."

"And the mother? His wife? Is she around?"

He shook his head. "Not that I know. Always a little sketchy on the details, but she disappeared a long time ago. Back when Katarina was little. He never remarried."

"Katarina is what—forty? Forty-five?"

"Somewhere around there."

Viv's oysters appeared and she busied herself sampling the other sauces. The 420 Sauce with roasted peppers and hemp seed made for a rather unique taste. Good, but not the best. She went back to the Sam Sauce several times, but she just couldn't beat that tangy hot, old-school Tabasco. Her mouth was on fire. Just the way she liked it.

"Are you one of those Florida history buffs?" he asked abruptly, as if it struck him to reciprocate in the conversation.

"No, I'm a chef," she answered. "At least, that's what I want to do. Things are a little off right now, but I'm going to figure it out."

He nodded politely.

"What do you do?" she said, still making polite conversation.

"I own Citrus Lanes. The bowling alley," he added when confusion creased her brow. "You bowl?"

"Not since I was a kid." Viv was thinking of Bree at Denny's. Maybe he knew the bimbo blonde.

"It's good, clean exercise," he said. "I know it's a little old-school, maybe, but the snowbirds love it."

She heard a familiar pop and looked around the room. She could sense the gourmet ancestors were somewhere nearby. She grabbed a cracker to ease the burn in her mouth.

"Vivianna Lee Marston," Aunt Clara declared. "You're not going to believe what your Uncle Floyd has unearthed about that girl you ran into on the street!"

The face of the sun on the bottle of the Crack of Don sauce looked a lot like Aunt Clara and when she glanced at the bottle of Sam Sauce next to it, the two faces looking back were Earlene and

Floyd. She resisted the urge to laugh.

"I think your little school chum is a witch," Floyd said. "And I don't mean the B kind of Witch. I mean a full on, spell-casting, potion-toting witch. I read it in the *Book of Nines*."

"*Book of Nines?*"

The man beside her glanced over. "Book of what?"

"Oh, sorry," Viv said. "I was reading the label." She grabbed a bottle of sauce.

"The book is about an ancestral story about a family of women who sailed from Haiti," Floyd continued in his familiar I-told-you-so nasal whine. "They put down roots, spread their magic, and made a fortune. And guess where they lived?"

Viv bit her lip. It was obvious she couldn't answer.

"I'll tell you where they lived. Right across the Gulf of Mexico near New Orleans."

Haiti? New Orleans? Neither sounded plausible. She was dying to ask what all that had to do with Crystal Bay. Or her culinary school peer, Amelia. Or more importantly, with the kitchen hex.

The man beside her pushed his plate of shells away and rose. He nodded in her direction. "Hope all goes good for you. Doing that chef thing," he said, and Viv could tell he meant it. "Come bowl a game. On the house."

"Thanks."

"See you around?"

Viv nodded.

She paid her bill, and anxious to learn more from Uncle Floyd, she readied to leave. She was just about to give up her bar stool when Jake from the SeaViche a la Cart walked in. He caught her eye instantly and broke into a grin.

"*Ooh la la,*" Floyd said. He was still one of the faces on the Sam Sauce bottle. "Here comes that hot bod from the food cart. The one with the tan and tousled hair."

Viv heard Earlene chuckle.

"Hey, Snooty Foodie," Jake said as he approached and settled onto the bar stool. "I heard you were in town today. Drumming up business, are you?"

"From what little bird did you hear that?"

He grinned. "If I told you I'd have to…"

She waited for the cliched punchline … but it didn't come.

"…I'd have to ask you to dinner."

"Look at those muscles," Floyd whispered. "*Gurrl.*"

Viv grinned. Jake grinned back. "Is that a yes, then?"

"No. Wait. What did you just say?"

"We were talking about his muscles," Floyd encouraged. "Don't you want to squeeze them?"

"Ssshh," Viv whispered.

"Ssshh?" Jake pulled his fingers through his messy sun-bleached hair. "What do you mean? I said, is that a yes? Will you let me take you to dinner?"

Viv felt her face flush. There was no way she could hold a conversation with both Jake and Uncle Floyd who was apparently in a flirtatious mood.

"I just had lunch," she said finally. "A dozen steamed oysters with a ton of this Sam Sauce." She picked up the bottle and stuffed it, along with Earlene and Floyd, back into the wire basket.

"Oh, I didn't mean now," Jake said. "I meant next Friday night. It's shrimp and crab night in Homosassa. It's not fancy, but it sure is good. It's one of my favorite spots. Low-key. Good food. Sometimes good music worth dancing to. Sometimes not." He flashed a toothy grin, with that cute little chip in his front tooth. "What do you say?" he added.

"I say, yes," Viv answered. "I would love to do low-key, not fancy but good."

His grin grew wider. "Awesome. Give me your phone and I'll put in my number. Want another beer?"

Viv glanced at her watch. She wasn't through with her day, but she had business cards and contact information for the Corks and Curds wine shop, the Sunken Treasure Museum, Tropical Tomes bookstore, and a matchbook from The Oyster Bar. She hadn't discussed advertising with them, but she felt she'd made a good first impression. The rest could follow. She still wanted to talk to Zoe, but maybe circumstances—or fate—had put Jake in her path.

"Why not," she said finally.

"Why not," he repeated, and motioned to the bartender.

"You met one of my aunts," he said, when their beer arrived. "She liked you."

"Are you talking about Gerry at Corks and Curds?"

He nodded.

"I liked her too. She has a nice shop."

"She told me you were the one who found that guy in the park last Saturday. You didn't mention it at the Farmer's Market when we met. Seems like something you'd want to get off your chest."

Viv turned and looked at Jake. His eyes were blue. His skin was tan. And he had a fresh, sea-breeze air about him. But the way he studied her, she knew he wasn't a beach bum with air between his ears.

"I think I was numb," she said finally. "I was still processing it. Especially those laughing gulls and that ghastly harpoon. And I didn't know you. I mean, really, how would I bring up something like that? Hello, I'll take a carton of ceviche and some emotional support, please?"

He laughed. "You got me there. But you can talk about it now. Right?"

"Maybe," she answered. "I'm still trying to sort the pieces."

"What do you mean?"

"Gerry—your aunt, said that guy was in town looking for Zoe and Viv Marston. I guess he didn't know about my aunt. I don't think he meant me. Anyway, he photobombed the photo I took of Zoe Diamante not long after that if I'm correct in my timing. We both saw him through the window. I didn't think much of it at the time, except that I believe Zoe recognized him. I don't think she was happy to see him, either. Or, at least, she was surprised to see him standing there."

Jake's gaze was intense as he listened.

"I don't know what all that means, exactly, but I think Zoe has more information than she's sharing."

"Maybe your imagination is getting in the way. Seeing something like what you saw in the park could sure mess with your head. I know Zoe pretty well and she's about as above board as any of us."

Viv shrugged. "But then, when I was in the shipwreck museum, I noticed something was missing from the wall. Something the very shape of that harpoon that was poking out of the guy's back. Katarina noticed it too."

Jake whistled under his breath. "You sure get around. I don't think our detective on the job has gotten half the scoop you have.

And he's a few weeks from retirement. Been here most of his adult life." He paused before asking, "What were you doing in Anchor Park anyway?"

"Just part of my route. I was on the way to the Farmer's Market, and I thought it would be a scenic walk. The Bay is beautiful. Usually."

"Did you see anybody else?"

"No. And I remember thinking that was odd, although it was early. There wasn't anyone in the park and no one was swimming. It seemed quiet for a Saturday. Except for those laughing gulls."

"Are you sure you didn't see anyone? No one? You said it was early morning, right?"

She turned to look at him. "What are you getting at? Don't you believe me?"

"Of course I believe you. Why wouldn't I?" He drew silent long enough to sip his beer, but she could sense there was something left unsaid. She couldn't think of anything to add, and the gourmet ancestors were surprisingly mute. She glanced at the wire rack and the bottles. Just ordinary labels now. She glanced around the bar, but the gourmet threesome seemed absent. Maybe they were giving her space.

"I haven't heard Dolphin Street on the scanner lately." He grinned. "I guess you've finally got it under control." His grin deepened. "What is it with you and fire, anyway? Are you just accident prone? I mean, I'm not trying to fire shame you or anything, but it does seem to be a pattern."

She felt her cheeks grow hot. Fire shaming from a firefighter. That was rich. She wasn't ready to share any of that, and when and if she was ready to share, she'd have to figure out how to talk about the gourmet ancestors. They went hand in hand with the hex. One wrong slip of the tongue and he would think she was looney-bird crazy. For now, she'd have to let him assume she was accident prone. Bittersweet. Like too much coffee in the brownie batter.

"Do you know Amelia by any chance?"

"Amelia who?"

"Amelia Delatour. I think she has cousins here."

"I don't know any Delatours. I don't think I know any Amelias, either. Why?"

"Just trying to put people and places on the table."

"Sorting the pieces," Jake said.

Viv nodded. "Yep."

"I need to run," Jake said when he finished his beer. "I got some place I had to be about five minutes ago. Can I pick you up at six next Friday? It's better if we get there early."

"You know where I live," Viv said, smiling, and Uncle Floyd made a sound she could hear all the way across the counter. It was a cross between a cat call and a gurgle. Viv bit her lip and rolled her eyes. Oh, please don't let them pop in at dinner with Jake, she prayed silently, wondering to whom, exactly, she was making her plea.

~~~~~

"Back so soon?" Martie asked as Viv stepped into Tropical Tomes for the second time that day.

"Twenty-five percent off is hard to pass up," Viv said with a smile. "I was hoping you had a copy of Captain Frederick's book. I met your brother next door, and he said you'd have a copy."

"Which brother?"

Viv blushed. "Bowling alley. I forgot to ask his name."

"Doesn't matter," Martie said. "I only have four. Mitch, Morgan, Matt, and Mark…" she recited as she wove her way through the stacks. "And Martie. That's me."

Viv laughed.

"I know. My parents didn't spend much time looking at baby name books, did they?" She pulled a book off the shelf and handed it to Viv. It was a slimmer volume than she would have guessed, something put together on an ancient PC and printed at the local print shop.

"What about local history? Do you have anything on Anchor Park?"

"I have a book on the history of the county written by a local historian. She goes all the way back to Native Indian times. I also have this." Martie pulled a little booklet from the shelf. Again, from somebody's ancient PC.

"Captain Frederick donated the anchor to the city," she added. "This book tells all about that. The other book is all about his tales
~~~~~

at sea."

"Have you read it?"

Martie nodded. "Decades ago. But I think you'll find the stories interesting. He was a pretty famous treasure hunter back in the day, our Captain Fred. He even went to jail briefly over an antique necklace that authorities claim he pocketed. Something from a dive. He denied it and they've never found it. Worth millions, they said. It's all in there." Martie motioned to the book in Viv's hands. "There's even a story about an underwater creature he called the Slithering Kraken."

Viv grinned, and armed with her new purchases, set off for Lokol Made. If she had to wait for Zoe to get free, she'd dive into the adventures of Captain Frederick, *Florida's Most Famous Treasure Hunter*.

~~~~~

As it was, Lokol Made was empty when she stepped into what she could imagine the Greek islands smelled like on a warm spring day. The aroma was pungent and full of herbs.

Zoe was behind the counter, sprigs of damp hair plastered against her forehead. When she looked up and saw Viv, she smiled.

"You did good," Zoe said brightly. "I don't think anyone has ever said such wonderful things about me and my food."

Viv smiled. "It was well-deserved."

"I agree." Zoe wiped her hands on her apron and came around to greet her. "I know we've only met but I want to give you a big fat Greek hug." She reached out and pulled Viv toward her, and Viv folded into her arms like a long-lost kid.

"You did good," Zoe repeated, finally releasing Viv from her grasp. "You hungry? Are you thirsty?"

"Cup of coffee?" Viv asked. "Would that be doable?"

"Doable?" Zoe spread her arms and Viv wondered if Zoe was going back for a second hug. "It's doable," she said. "With a shot of ouzo or no?"

Viv shook her head. "I had wine at the wine shop and beer at the oyster bar. It's only two o'clock. I need some stiffening up. Just coffee black, please."

Viv sat at a table near the window and waited. Zoe returned
~~~~~

quickly with two steaming espressos, and Viv could smell the licorice wafting from Zoe's cup. The steam smelled delicious, but she knew better than to add liquor on top of everything else.

"So," Zoe said, after taking a sip, lips smacking with approval. "Where'd you learn to write like that?"

Viv grinned at the compliment. "I don't know that I write well so much as I write from the palate. I see and feel, taste and smell my way through the meal I'm writing about. Somehow the words flow onto the page like warm ganache over a freshly made cake."

Zoe smacked her lips again. "Whatever it is you do, you brought the house down. My restaurant has been full of customers ever since. After my grand opening next week, I'll be the talk of the town. Everyone will know about Lokol Made."

"I'm glad the review made a difference," Viv said. "That's all we can ever hope for. I wanted to let you know I'm selling advertising for the *Citrus Times* now, and I'll be handling your account." Viv made a little bow with her head. "I'm your ad babe. At your service," she said, now feeling a little tipsy.

Zoe laughed and sipped her coffee. "Good for you, Viv. You'll be the talk of the town. Everyone will know Vivianna Marston."

Despite how good that compliment felt, her cheeks flared with embarrassment anyway. Being in the spotlight was never easy.

"There is something I need to talk to you about," Viv started, watching Zoe over the rim of her coffee cup. "Have the police talked to you yet?"

"The police?" Zoe set her cup down with a thud. "Why would the police be talking to me? I haven't done anything illegal."

"It's about that guy," Viv said. "The one who was in the window the day I took the photo of you. The guy who was lurking behind the tree. He wound up in the photo we ran with your review."

"Oh, yeah," Zoe said, her voice lowered an octave. "Him."

"Him," Viv repeated. "Do you know who he was?"

Zoe shook her head and brought the cup back to her lips.

"I think you do," Viv pushed. "I think you may have recognized him when you saw him through this window. And the police need to talk to you about it, because, well, because he's dead."

Zoe gulped her coffee and sputtered. "He's what? He's dead?"

"Didn't you read the paper? They found him in the park by

the bay." Viv paused for a moment. "Correction. I found him in the park by the bay. He was dead, Zoe. He had a harpoon in his back. Well, that or a spear from a speargun. I'm not sure I know which is which."

Zoe was staring at her with eyes wide and full of unhappy surprise. "Oh, how horrible," she said, absently rubbing an object in her hands. Viv glanced down at her fingers working a heart-shaped keychain. "That's just horrible," Zoe repeated.

"So, if the police haven't talked to you about him, they will be, and before they get to you, I'd like to know who he was and what he was doing here."

Zoe shook her head. "I don't know anything."

"Really?" Viv looked doubtful. "Gerry over at Corks and Curds said he claimed he had unfinished business with you. A message to deliver. He knew your name."

Zoe blew out. Viv could smell the licorice.

"I believe he found you," Viv continued. "And that's why he was hanging out in the courtyard. You recognized him. I know you did."

"Look," Zoe said, her tone terse. "I don't know the guy."

"Then why did it look like you did?" Viv could see the muscles working in Zoe's jaw.

"He looked like someone I knew a long time ago," Zoe said finally. "A really long time ago. I knew it couldn't be him. He would be as old as I am. But for that moment when he first came into view, I thought it was my old flame. That guy I told you about. The one I followed around hoping he'd make me his wife."

Viv sighed and sat back. "Oh," she said simply. "I guess that makes sense."

"Well, of course it makes sense," Zoe said. "For that fleeting moment, I thought I was staring at an old lover. Thank goodness I was wrong." She closed her hand around the heart keychain, her fist balling tightly.

"What's that?" Viv asked. "A lucky charm?"

Zoe looked down at her fist, and Viv could see her knuckles were white where she was clenching the metal. She opened her hand again and Viv saw the red heart with a key attached. "Oh, it's nothing," she said, closing her hand around the metal. "It's just an old keychain. I don't even remember what lock this key fits."

"You're going to have to tell the police when they ask."

"Tell them about this?" Zoe asked, her eyes wide. She dropped it back into her pocket.

"No, I mean you're going to have to tell them about your old flame. That you thought it might be him."

"Why?" Zoe shook her head. "No, it's not anybody's business. My reaction was just a misreading on my part. A moment of menopausal madness. Look, Viv, I don't know the guy. I hate what happened to him, but the police can't say I'm involved in any of that business because I'm not."

"Well, I am," Viv said quietly. "I touched the evidence left in the park. Bloody evidence. And then I wiped my hands on a napkin and threw it in the trash. I'm sure the police collected the refuse to sort for clues."

Zoe was staring at her again. "You touched bloody evidence? Gross!"

"I didn't know it was evidence," Viv spat back. "I thought it was a wishbone. And a balloon I stuffed in my pants. And the birds were laughing. And now I'm going to be a suspect if I don't get these pieces sorted out!"

"Whoa," Zoe said and held up a hand. "That caffeine is going straight to your adrenals. You picked up what? Stuffed a balloon where? Who was laughing? And what kind of a suspect?"

Viv shook the knob of hair on the top of her head.

"Back up a bit and take it a lot slower."

Viv sighed, and in a calmer tone, told Zoe what happened in the park. She didn't leave any of it out, and when she was done, she fell silent.

"Dang," Zoe said. "Bummer walk in the park. Like a bad trip in the '60s."

Viv furrowed her brow. "Dang? Bummer? That's all you've got to say?"

"Well, what do you want me to say? Give a hoot, don't pollute? You did your civic duty. You picked up trash you found in the park. How were you to know where it came from? Or how it had been used?"

Viv sat back and shook her head. "Ok. You think it's no big deal. You think I can waltz into the police department and tell them what I didn't tell them to begin with? Tell them this omission of fact, for which I have no good reasonable explanation, I might add. I don't know why I didn't tell them everything. I just didn't."

"You didn't think it was important," Zoe said. "Why would you think some trash in the park was evidence of a crime before you even knew there was a crime?"

"The blood, maybe? That was a sign."

"But you didn't think that, did you? Not until later. Not until you went all Magnum PI on yourself and now you've worked yourself into a tizzy."

"Maybe," Viv said quietly, her tension beginning to ease. "And you know what else? There's a speargun missing from the Sunken Treasure Museum. And Katarina knows it."

"Whoa," Zoe said. "Now that is interesting. She's an odd one. And Captain Frederick is a little creepy. Maybe a few sails short of a cruise if you ask me."

"You think they could be involved?"

Zoe shrugged. "I think anyone could be involved. Except me," she added. "And I guess you." She ran her eyes up and down Viv until Viv burst out laughing.

"I guess it is a little silly," Viv said. "I really was just picking up trash in the park. Give a hoot, don't pollute." She laughed again. "I haven't heard that since I was a kid."

The little pop she was now used to hearing caught her attention. She looked around the restaurant. There was no food out. The water container with its floating lemons was gone from the counter. Viv looked down at her coffee cup, the dregs of espresso staining the bottom.

"You better get home, young lady," Aunt Clara said as a smear of brown coffee sludge. "The police are banging on your door."

CHAPTER ELEVEN

Viv felt a little embarrassed by how abruptly she left Lokol Made, but it wasn't often cops were at her door. She wasn't going to run but she was definitely sprint-walking, caffeine and adrenaline flowing. She was headed in the direction of Dolphin Street when a big SUV pulled up beside her.

"Want a ride?" Katarina Becker asked, poking her head out of the window. "You're walking like you're on a mission."

"Well, sure," Viv said. "That would be great."

"I know we just met," Katarina said, when Viv was settled into the seat and buckled in, "but everybody can use a new friend in a new town. You have that enthusiastic sparkle everybody has when they first move here. It doesn't last long. Honestly, though, I think it's refreshing."

Viv smiled. "Yeah, thanks. I've only been here a couple of months."

"You'll fit right in eventually. Don't worry about that."

"Uh. Okay," Viv answered, not sure how to take that in.

"I'm glad you came by the museum to introduce yourself—although I think you gave my father a scare—he thought you were somebody from his past."

"My Aunt Viv."

Katarina nodded. "Weird that you have the same name. Why is that?"

Viv shrugged. "I really don't know why. Family dynamics, I guess."

"I know all about family dynamics." She tapped the steering wheel with her fingertips. "Other than his time at the museum, Dad likes to keep to himself. It's just the two of us." She turned and nodded at Viv, and it felt as if an invisible fence snapped into place. Captain Fred and Katarina Becker on the inside. Everybody else on the outside.

"He likes to take things over the top, doesn't he?"

"I thought he was fascinating," Viv said. "His stories were so, so… entertaining."

"That's a nice thing to say," Katarina replied. She glanced at Viv and smiled. "You're a chef, I hear."

"Where did you hear that?" Viv felt leery about where the conversation was going. She didn't want to talk about fire trucks and cold foods.

"Just around town," Katarina said with a thin smile. "I should tell you—this town likes to gossip. I want to say most of it is innocent, but there are those who don't have the facts and gossip anyway." She glanced at Viv briefly.

"One year Mrs. Callahan got caught nicking Roman coins from our museum. She was a docent. That was back when we used volunteers." Katarina glanced at Viv and shook her head. "Never again. Anyway, everybody got uptight about Mrs. C. turning into a kleptomaniac. I had to watch her like a sailor in the crow's nest." Katarina grinned. "Turns out she wasn't seeing well, and she thought she was pocketing Kennedy half dollars as a lucky find. Finders keepers, right?"

Viv laughed.

"I just wanted you to know you can't believe everything you hear." She put her hands obediently on the wheel at ten and two and then glanced over at Viv. "I'm sure you heard the gossip about that guy in the park."

Viv nodded. "I'm the one who reported it."

"That was you? How untimely," she added. "Dad said that guy came in the museum, and he chased him out the door in his wheelchair, hollering like a foghorn at midnight," Katarina grinned. "I bet you heard about that. I think *everybody* heard that. The Captain gets overly excited when he feels threatened."

"You mean the guy threatened him?"

Katarina nodded. "Dad thought he was going to steal something from the museum. Claimed he had that *look* about him. Called him a pirate and a thief and I guess this out-of-town guy took offense. I don't know what he said in response, but something that made Fred run him out the door." Katarina grinned. "I can sure see that happening." She glanced at Viv. "I wanted you to know that he's really harmless. Gruff, maybe. Theatrical for certain. He's just a cantankerous old man used to having his own way. Fame will do that to you."

Viv nodded again. "Hey, did you miss the turn?"

"No problem," the other woman said and shrugged, her hands still poised on the wheel. "I'll just drive around the block. "

Viv wanted to say she was in a hurry but decided that would be rude.

"So what happened in the park? I can't get anybody at the police department to tell me anything. That detective won't even return my calls. What did you see? Did they tell you anything?"

"Uh, no, not really," Viv answered, the park scene pushing forward in her mind. "The police didn't really say anything. I told them how I found him and what I did when I found him, and that was it. They took my name and number and said, don't leave town."

"Don't leave town?" Katarina repeated. "Did you know the guy?"

"No."

"Huh," she breathed. "Didn't you recognize him?"

Viv glanced at Katarina. "Sort of," she said slowly. "Did you see the review of Lokol Made in the paper? He was in the picture behind Zoe Diamante. He was standing by the palm tree in her courtyard."

Katarina whistled under her breath. "You took the last picture of this guy before he…" She heaved a quick sigh. "Well, you know, before someone gigged him in the back. What a way to go."

Viv frowned. Both were gruesome facts she preferred not to think about.

"The police must be interested in what you know."

"Not so far," Viv answered, thinking again about the cop at her door. "That will probably come a little later." Like in five minutes, she thought. "The weirdest thing was the airline ticket stuck to a sign. Like one of those serial killer calling-cards you see on TV."

Katarina turned in her seat. "Come on. Really? You're not one of those true crime junkies, are you? What did you do with it?"

"I didn't touch it. I left it for the police to find."

Katarina was quiet for a moment, and Viv wondered where she had disappeared to in her thoughts. She was getting antsy about getting to Dolphin Street, and she hadn't realized until now that Katarina had driven several blocks out of the way. She glanced at the woman driving—tall, thin, dark blonde ponytail pulled through the back of a cap. She was probably in her late forties now that Viv was looking at her closely. The dim lighting of the museum had played gentle tricks, and now Viv could see a woman battling the wrinkle war. She didn't see laugh lines, and she couldn't see her eyes behind the sunglasses, but she saw a seriousness that drew Katarina's mouth in a tight line against her lips.

"That makes me think of old Mrs. Callahan and her Roman coins," Katarina said finally. "*Veni, Vidi, Vici.* I saw, I came, I conquered. That's what Julius Caesar said to the Roman Senate." She glanced over at Viv. "You think someone was sending a message of some kind? What did you make of it?"

Viv shrugged. "I didn't know what to think. I didn't touch it."

Katarina nodded. "It could have been us to find him, you know. We go to the park almost every morning. Dad likes to shoo the birds from his anchor. It could have been us who found him," she repeated. "We didn't go to the park that day. Fred didn't want to go, and I couldn't persuade him otherwise."

"I guess those weren't Captain Fred's wheelchair tracks then," Viv said absently, thinking out loud.

Katarina turned to Viv. "Tracks?"

"Oh yeah, down by the water. In the sand. I thought maybe it was a pair of turtles or somebody's beach chair, but then I decided they were probably from your father's wheelchair."

"Down by the water? Wheelchair tracks? I think you're mistaken," Katarina said bluntly.

Viv nodded. "I could be mistaken."

Katarina nodded. Another moment passed. "Well, of course,

it could be from last week. You're right. We went down to the water that day. I just forgot. It hasn't rained in a while, so those tracks must still be there from Tuesday. I'm sure it was last Tuesday."

Viv nodded. "What's your thing?"

"I beg your pardon?"

"Your thing. You said, you drop him off and do your thing."

"Oh, duh," Katarina said and laughed again. "I run a tour boat in the bay. Manatee tours. You should come out. Suit up and you can swim with the manatees. I even make a spray that attracts them. Well, it doesn't really because manatees don't have a strong sense of smell, but the tourists don't know that. The spray keeps the bugs away. And if you want a big tip from the tour, you need to keep the mosquitoes off your tourists."

Viv grinned and sniffed the air. "Is that what I smell? It smells good. I thought it was an air freshener."

Katarina nodded. "You really should come on a tour. I insist. Nighttime is even better because the view at night is special."

"Here I am," Viv said as the car approached the corner near the yellow mustard-colored house. She didn't want the SUV to pull into the driveway and announce her arrival to the cop who was probably still banging on her door. "I'd like to walk the rest of the way. I need to stretch my legs."

Katarina frowned. "Okay." She slowed the car to a stop. "Right here?" She looked confused.

"Thanks for the ride and the chat," Viv said and tugged at the handle. The door didn't budge.

"No problem. I needed to talk to you, anyway."

"You *needed* to talk to me? About what? Advertising for the museum?"

Katarina nodded, her gaze steady.

Viv pulled at the handle again. "It's locked."

Katarina smiled. "Oh, right. Sorry."

The lock clicked open, and Katarina's mouth curved a little deeper, one corner lifting higher than the other—a smile that suggested she was amused by Viv's captivity.

CHAPTER TWELVE

Viv surveyed the unmarked car in her driveway and hid behind a palm tree to watch, uncertain what she was walking into. An older man in a brown suit two sizes too big stood on her porch ringing the doorbell. She could hear the chime from where she stood. The adrenaline drained and took her bravado with it, and for the first time she wondered if she was walking into something more troublesome than she thought. She hesitated a moment more behind the tree, wondering what defense she might need to offer, when he abruptly left the porch and walked around the side of the house toward her backyard.

She could sprint to the door and let herself in, she thought, and wait for him to ring again. Or maybe she should follow him around the back. She had one foot behind the palm and one foot out with indecision when a voice behind her spoke.

"Vivianna Marston?"

She nearly jumped out of her sneakers.

She whirled around to face him.

"Detective Smith," he said with no expression. "Crystal Bay. I wonder if I can have a few minutes of your time." It wasn't a question.

Viv stood rooted to the grass under the palm tree. It was as if her feet were part of the tree anchored in Florida soil.

"Okay," she said, her stomach starting to roil. Beer and oysters and hot sauce heating under pressure. "Is this about Anchor Park?"

He nodded.

"Could I see your badge?"

He nodded again and pulled a wallet-style badge from the breast pocket of his jacket. She couldn't read it from where she stood, but it looked official enough.

"It would be better if we went inside," he said, and motioned to the house. "More comfortable. More private."

The roiling ratcheted up a notch. She stood rooted like the tree.

"Shall we?" he motioned again toward the house. She could see the sweat beading on his forehead.

She felt the sting, then. A sharp, burning, piercing pain like a fire-heated needle. She looked down at her shoe, now dotted with ants marching toward her flesh. She screamed and stomped her feet, further disturbing the ant mound at the base of the tree. The grainy soil around the hill was now fuming with fat red ants rushing to battle the enemy. She was the enemy.

"Ow!" she screamed, stomping the ground. "Ants!" she yelled and stomped away from the mound, brushing at her legs with her fingertips.

"Move away!" he bellowed. "Take off your shoes!"

She felt the water before she knew what was happening, and she looked up to see that Detective Smith was holding the garden hose connected to the spigot on the outside of the house. He aimed the spray at the ants still marching up her legs. The water in the hose was warm from the sun, but it cooled quickly, the cool stream on the fire-y stings was a welcome relief.

Ants finally defeated and her clothing soaked, Viv left her shoes where they were and hobbled barefoot toward the front door. She could feel the pinch and burn of the stings that had landed and the red welts rising like an angry rash.

"Fire ants," Detective Smith said, a few steps behind her. "Worst thing on the planet." He had followed her uninvited into the house, but she would not say so. His quick thinking saved her from greater injury. She hurried to the kitchen, and he followed.

"Ice is best," he said, opening the freezer and pulling the ice bin from the shelf. He grabbed the dishtowel hanging on the sink and filled it with ice. All this he did as if he owned the place. As if he knew Viv personally. As if he were used to saving damsels in distress.

"It really hurts," Viv wailed.

"Got any Benadryl? How about hydrocortisone cream?" He wrapped the icy cloth around her ankle resting on the seat of the kitchen chair.

"It will be in the medicine cabinet if I do. Something left over from Aunt Viv, maybe."

He left the room and went down the hall, the only hall. There was only one way to go. All these block houses from the 1970s had one floor plan. She heard the old medicine cabinet door squeak open.

"Here," he said when he returned and handed her a tube of cream. "Put this on the bites and then keep icing." He filled a glass with water from the sink and handed her a sleeve of Benadryl. "Take one now and another when you wake up in the middle of the night."

"Middle of the night? What do you mean?"

"You'll know exactly what I mean when it happens."

He pulled up a chair at the table and sat down. "Bad luck about the ants," he said. "I wouldn't wish fire ants on my worst enemy. They are the scourge of the insect world. I guess God put them on Earth for a reason, but I've yet to see one." He grinned, a little lopsided, she noticed. "Mind if I get a drink for myself?"

"Be my guest," Viv mumbled, the oddity of the situation taking hold. Who didn't want a cop nosing around in the kitchen? But the cream and ice were working, and the burning was fading a little. She wouldn't have known what to do about the ant bites if she had been by herself.

"You are lucky you only got a few stings," he said, after noisily gulping down a glass of water from the sink. "I've seen people covered with stings so severe they had to be hospitalized."

Viv nodded, her legs numb.

"You can't do much about them, either," he added, shaking his head. He had flabby jowls and a smooth-shaved chin. "You can fight them in one place, and they pop up in another."

Viv drank the last of her water and watched as the detective glanced around the room, taking in the nuances of the owner. "So, you inherited Viv's house," he said. "I wondered what would come of this place."

"You knew my Aunt Viv?"

"Sure," he said and smiled that lopsided smile. "We were friends. At one time we were friends. She and my wife were pretty close."

"What did Aunt Viv do for a living before she retired? I never heard."

"I don't know that she ever retired. She was a bookkeeper. Ran her business out of her home here on Dolphin Street. My wife gave her a hand during tax season. I think that's how they became friends."

"Interesting," Viv said, although it wasn't.

"What happened? You said at one time you were friends. Did something happen to change that?"

He paused before answering. "Death happened. It's inescapable. My wife," he added, without further explanation.

Viv nodded, admittedly a little disappointed. She had been thinking maybe something more sinister broke up the friendship, like jealousy or a love triangle gone wrong. Detective Smith wasn't always an old beige bear.

"You found that victim over in Anchor Park."

Sly, she thought. He'd been wanting to ask that for the last half hour. She nodded.

"You ready to talk about it?"

She nodded again. Her head was foggy, and her leg felt numb.

He didn't seem surprised when she told him about the metal wishbone and the napkin in the trash. She pointed to a plastic bag stashed on top of the fridge. She had wanted to throw the yellow tube thing away when she pulled it from her pocket, but she had decided that it should be saved. It could be evidence. In fact, it probably was evidence. And she had taken it from the scene of the crime.

"You know what this is?" he asked, fingering the material through the plastic.

Viv shook her head.

"It's the force behind a speargun. It's kind of like a slingshot, only more deadly."

Her eyes widened. "Like the one that…" she let her words trail away, but he nodded.

"Yep, the murder weapon. Have you ever use a speargun?"

"No."

"I've seen these rubber slings take off a finger. If you got your finger in the wrong spot when the spear's released, that is. Not out of the realm of possibility if you don't know what you're doing. That might be where the blood on the wishbone came from. That's the other part of this apparatus."

"How far does one of those things shoot?" Viv asked.

"Ten feet max. At less than ten feet it would be devastatingly effective."

The image of the guy draped across the anchor surfaced. Very effective, she thought, remembering how permanently deadly the harpoon spear had seemed.

"Do you think whoever pulled the trigger stood that close? Close to that guy? Who I guess was walking away," she added and then glanced at the detective with a curious and hopeful look.

He nodded. "That would be my take on it."

"Was there any other evidence left behind?" She was thinking about the cop shows she watched when she was sick in bed with the flu. She wasn't a crime show junkie like Katarina had suggested, but she *was* thinking about the napkin in the trash with her own DNA on it.

"Like what?" he asked.

"Like signs of a struggle, or footprints in blood, or DNA. Or even wheel tracks."

"Wheel tracks? You mean from a vehicle?"

"Or a wheelchair," she said and looked up.

He shrugged but didn't answer.

"Why would someone use a speargun?"

Detective Smith shrugged again. "Why not? It's silent when fired. The only sound you'd hear is the snap of these bands. No one near the park would hear anything out of the ordinary."

Viv exhaled. Gigged in the back. That's how Katarina put it. Both silent and deadly.

"I'm not dense enough to think you pulled the trigger on this thing. But I do have to wonder why you think it's okay to go around asking questions about the victim." He paused long enough for Viv to answer, but she didn't have an answer.

"That's my job. At least for another fifty-eight days and counting."

He spun his empty water glass on the table. "Gerry over on the square says you had lots of questions about the victim and what we were doing about it. Katarina Becker says you were nosing around the museum."

"I was talking with them because I'm working for the newspaper," Viv said in defense. "I wanted to get to know them before I sold them advertising. It doesn't feel right to walk in with your hand out."

Detective Smith smiled. It looked like an uncomfortable habit meant to placate the unavoidable. "Martie at the bookstore said you identified yourself as the person who found the victim. That's not a great thing to advertise. There's someone out there with murder on their mind, and you sound like a person who could get in the way of their freedom."

Viv hadn't thought about that. She had been focused on the details to clear her name from the A.1. Sauce suspect list when and if she made the list officially. Earlene had been the one who brought that up, and now Viv wondered if it had been the wrong lead to follow. She was an innocent bystander. Innocent of everything but removing evidence from a crime scene. And that wasn't intentional.

"Did you know the victim in question?"

"No."

"Can you describe the scene as best you remember?"

"Do I have to? It was pretty shocking."

"Give it a shot."

Viv grimaced. Poor choice of words.

She went through the motions again, tracking her steps and her memory. This time she didn't leave out the wheel tracks at the water's edge, or the airline ticket on the sign, or that the spear in his back looked like the one missing from the wall at the museum.

"Did you touch anything?

"Just the things I mentioned."

"Okay," he said again in a mollifying tone, "you sound like you have theories. You tell me yours, and I'll tell you mine."

"Really?" Her interest piqued.

The detective nodded.

"My theory is that he was here to see Zoe Diamante," Viv said. "He had a message to deliver. I don't know what message. Zoe claims she doesn't know. She also claims she doesn't know who he was. But here's what I think. I think he looks like his father. And that's why Zoe thought she recognized him."

"I'm not following," he said.

"When he showed up at Zoe's restaurant that day, I was there, and he was in the courtyard. I saw the reaction on Zoe's face when she saw him, and later, just today actually, she literally admitted that she thought it was her old flame standing there. Someone she was in love with a long time ago. It couldn't be him, this guy was young, but he could've been his son. Judging from Zoe's reaction, I'd say he looked like her ex."

The detective cocked his head. "But it's not *her* son?"

"No, because the issue with that boyfriend was that he didn't want to settle down and have kids. That's what Zoe wanted. So, she moved on."

"Why was he in town?"

"That's where I lost ground," Viv said. "He told Gerry he had unfinished business. That he came to deliver a message. What message and what unfinished business, I don't know. That's what I was trying to find out."

Detective Smith was quiet for a moment, and Viv wondered if she had landed a seed in his thoughts. It made sense to her that if the victim looked like Zoe's old flame that he was probably his son. Now that she was thinking out loud, she realized Zoe had in fact responded to his sudden appearance with emotion akin to pheromones in a beehive. A pheromone rush. When they talked about the murder, Zoe had grasped that heart keychain so hard her knuckles went white. Now it seemed obvious that Zoe knew something she wasn't sharing. That would be something to bring up with Zoe next time they spoke.

The detective was watching her.

"Your turn," she said. "What's your theory?"

"My theory is that he was meeting someone in the park. It was dark. He didn't see what was coming."

"Wow," Viv said, thinking of the airline ticket stuck to the sign. "Any ideas who?"

"That's why I make the big bucks," he said and laughed. It was a pleasant sound. She knew he didn't make the big bucks. Not in a suit like that.

His cellphone rang at that moment, and he answered a beat-up Samsung about as old as it could be and still take calls.

"Smith," he barked and then listened. "I'll be there in a few minutes."

"Is it about this case?" Viv asked, hopeful for more details.

"I'm not in a position to share that information."

"I thought we were trading theories." She watched as he pocketed the plastic bag and then he motioned to the back door.

"You should keep that locked. Front door, too."

She looked at the kitchen door and then back at him. He was already making his way toward the front door. She was taken again about his ease in her home. Maybe he knew his way around Aunt Viv's house better than he let on.

Viv lifted the ice pack and surveyed the angry bites.

Fire ants. The irony was not lost.

CHAPTER THIRTEEN

"Do we trust him?" Aunt Clara asked. "That detective. Can we trust him? He seemed like a nice, helpful guy, but I watched him take something out of your garbage in the alley."

Viv's gaze landed on the wire basket full of fruit. "You can see that from here?"

"Let's just say we have access to whatever foodstuffs belong to you. Past and present."

"Gross. You were in my garbage can?"

"Somebody had to keep an eye on him."

"I don't see that we have any choice but to trust him to do the right thing," Earlene said. "What do you think, brother?"

"I think we need to focus on little Miss *Book of Nines* instead," Floyd said, his face a bright tangerine glow. "We need to focus on finding out if Amelia is the one who put this hex on Viv and how we turn it off."

"It's not like a sink faucet," Clara said. "You can't just turn it on, turn it off."

"Why not?" Floyd asked. "Everything else works that way. Black or white. Yes or no. On or off. What makes a hex any different?"

"Beyond me," Earlene said. "My familiarity with hexes is as deep as my understanding of algebra. Never did get the hang of X and Y."

"As I recall," Clara said pointedly, "you didn't get the hang of anything other than X and Y. Boys were your favorite curriculum."

Floyd cackled. "Speaking of," he added. "Did we overhear you accepting a date with Mr. A la Cart? Is there a little romance in your future, Viv?"

Viv blushed but didn't answer.

"I don't suppose you want us tagging along," Earlene said. "That could be a bit over the top if we tagged along on your dinner date. Do you feel safe with him?"

"Safe? Why wouldn't I?" The Benadryl was taking over, and Viv's eyes were so heavy she could barely keep them open.

"It was something he said at the oyster bar," Earlene said. "Let me think. My memory is a little glitchy today…"

Floyd let out a snarky snicker. "Only just today?"

Earlene ignored him. "He kept asking if you saw anyone else at the park. He asked several times. It sounded as if he really wanted to know who you had seen that morning."

"What? What are you talking about?" Viv sat up and the ice slid off her ankle.

"Jake said he was late to the Farmer's Market that morning. That's why he still had ceviche on his cart," Earlene recounted. "Now, I would like to know why he was late. And why he seemed interested in who you saw in the park. Is that coincidence?"

"Jake also claimed he didn't know anyone from the Delatour family when you asked him," Floyd put in, "but I don't think that's possible. The phone book has nine Delatours listed. There are nine. That can't be a coincidence, either."

"What is this *Book of Nines*, anyway," Viv asked, yawning. "You brought it up in that Oyster Bar but that's all I've heard so far."

"I'm still hunting its history," Floyd said. "From what I've gathered so far, the *Book of Nines* is a recipe book. Of sorts."

"A recipe book," Earlene repeated with guarded enthusiasm.

"A magic recipe book for spells," Clara added.

"In the realm of numerology, nine is the number of completion," Floyd went on. "Endings that begin and beginnings that end. You get the picture."

Viv blinked, willing her eyes to stay open. The antihistamine was making her drowsy, her head fuzzy, and she was struggling to comprehend the nuances of this mumbo-jumbo-voodoo lecture.

"This book holds the secret to unmaking and remaking history," Floyd went on. "But there's a catch…"

"There are many catches," Clara said, interrupting. "All of them are dangerous."

"The catch," Floyd continued, "is that the magic must balance. To change one reality, you must give up another. You must give up something of equal value."

"You mean a life for a life?" Viv's mouth went dry, and her stomach flopped over like a pancake on a griddle. Her eyes stung with unshed tears.

"Maybe not as extreme as that," Earlene said.

"What begins in nine, ends in nine," Floyd said, his tone grave. "In cyclical magic there must always be a completion of the loop. Every action comes full circle. Every spell requires a path of return. Nothing is linear. Nothing is free."

"I can't handle all this magic stuff! I can't deal with nines and numerology and that awful loop-thing." Viv heard her voice escalating higher until it broke. "I just want to cook!" she wailed, hot tears cascading down her cheeks. "What's going to happen to me? What's going to happen to me next?"

"Oh, dear," Earlene said. "We've frightened her, brother. I knew you were going to turn this into something like *Dark Shadows*. You were such a fan of those TV vampires and ghoulish whatnot."

"To put it more simply," Clara said, her voice soothing, "if that particular spellbook was used, whoever hexed you gave up something of equal value. To impose their Will, they surrendered their Freedom. If they wanted to bend Time, they gave up Time. If they wanted to wield Fire, they…"

"…they gave up Fire," Viv interrupted with a loud sniffle. "Are you saying they can't cook either?"

"It might not be as simple as that," Earlene suggested. "But perhaps close. In theory, anyway. Cyclical magic isn't linear. Neither is the logic behind it."

Floyd popped out of the tangerine in the hanging wire basket and into a bowl of unshelled pecans on the table. "All this is to say that the Delatour witches would be very familiar with this spellbook. The good news is that hexes are a short-term brand of magic. It's not as bad as a lifelong curse."

"Thank goodness," Clara whispered, now snuggled next to Floyd in the bowl. "A curse can last a lifetime."

"In your case, Viv, the hex is cooking with heat," Floyd announced, as if the idea had just come to him clearly. "You can't do it."

Viv wiped at her tears, now embarrassed by the outburst that had overtaken her. Floyd was right, she couldn't cook with heat and that was a real problem for someone whose heart and soul was in the kitchen, but if she had to be hexed by a magic spell, there was no better company than three dead but devoted ancestors who wanted to help.

"The remedies for such a hex," Aunt Clara put in, "are pretty widespread. We've identified three remedies we think would be most useful, knowing what little we do. The first thing we must determine is who put the hex on you. We really can't move forward until we figure that out."

"There's one more caveat," Earlene added, joining the others as a pecan in the bowl. "If we succeed in removing the hex from you, it is likely we will succeed in removing us as well. We are attached to your hex somehow. We are part of the circle magic. If we clear the hex, you will be able to cook. And we will be gone. "

Viv's heart dropped like a bag of flour hitting the floor. She could feel its weight pulling her shoulders down until the ache in her chest seemed unbearable. She was getting used to their popping in and out of her food unexpectedly. Like a surprise visit from family. She enjoyed their witty banter, all their semi-helpful comments, and their sibling rivalry that really was quite sweet. Her own sisters were so much older that she never really felt a part of their family. She was always excluded from their activities. Too young to play their almost grown-up games.

She was getting used to this family of four, ever how implausible that was, while feeling adrift in a new town. Just when she thought she could rise above her problems as long as the gourmet ancestors were there, here it was. The clincher. Maybe one of the biggest decisions of her lifetime. Give up cooking. Or give up the gourmet ancestors. Give up on her dreams. Or give up family she loved. Viv squeezed her eyes shut against more tears.

"It's not a decision you have to make today, my dear," Earlene said, as if reading her mind. "We have yet to identify the hexer."

"And that is the first step," Clara added. "Although we know where you need to start."

Viv blinked at the bowl full of pecans and gourmet ancestors. "You do?"

"Yep," Floyd said. "We know exactly where you need to start. And that's why I am nose-deep in the details. Everything begins at the beginning."

Floyd cleared his throat.

Viv yawned.

"Once every nine hundred and ninety-nine years," he began, as if reading from a document somewhere in his line of sight but invisible to Viv. "The *Nèf Sentes*, or Nine Saints, gather under the ninth full moon." His voice was full of cadence and singsong rhythm.

"It is then they give birth to their next generation, and when this genesis comes to power, they rule over fire, water, earth, and wind. They rule over the night, bone and shadow. When they speak, their language is of the spirits. When they dance, they dance on the edge of dreams, and they bargain for favors with the dead..."

Viv felt her eyes droop. Her chin dipped to her chest, and she heard no more of Floyd's tale of the *Book of Nines*.

<div style="text-align: center">~~~~~</div>

Viv awoke to a searing, throbbing pain in her ankle.

She didn't remember getting into bed, but she must have. She lay in a pool of sweat on top of her duvet, even though the night was cool and the window was open. Her ankle seared and itched. One moment she felt like a hot skillet was on her and the next minute the itch was overwhelming. The cycle was close to unbearable.

This is what Detective Smith was talking about, she thought.

In the middle of the night. She would know.

She dragged herself to the kitchen, retrieved the tube of hydrocortisone cream and generously slathered it over the bites, fighting every urge to dig at them with the dish towel. Or the vegetable brush. Or even the steel wool under the sink.

She grabbed an antihistamine tablet from the table and washed it down with a glass of water. Opening the freezer for ice, she nearly climbed in. Instead, she filled a plastic baggie and wrapped the soggy dish towel around it.

Five stings. Only five. She couldn't imagine a leg full of fire ant bites. They'd have to be hospitalized her like Detective Smith said. Drug her into a state of unconsciousness. She inspected her leg. The bites were several inches apart, and each was surrounded by an angry silver-dollar pancake of skin as tight and hot as any sunburn she'd ever had. In the middle of the fire-red pancake, a blistered knob of venom rose like a volcano ready to erupt.

She was hungry but not enough to bother with any food prep. Grabbing an orange from the wire basket, she made her way back to bed, flipping the lights off as she stumbled back down the hall.

She didn't remember dreaming, but something was poking at the back of her dream mind. Something about the earth, wind, and fire. And Floyd's gentle voice droning on and on. And on.

Now perched on top of the duvet so nothing but ice would touch the bites, she peeled and nibbled on the orange, forgoing protocol about the peels and seeds and juice on her pillow.

Her mouth felt dry and fuzzy, and for some reason she thought of Jake. She thought about his cute smile and chipped tooth and his tangy tangerine version of ceviche.

Why had he asked her who she saw in the park? Earlene had zeroed in on that, and now Viv couldn't shake it. Maybe he was in the park too. Maybe he saw the body and didn't do anything about it. Maybe he didn't call 911. Maybe he just put his head down and went on to the market.

Did that sound like Jake?

She didn't know. She didn't know him well enough to make that supposition. Honestly, she didn't know any of them well enough to make any suppositions. She was the newcomer in town. She was the unknown in the equation. It wasn't algebra, but it was certainly a confounding problem.

What had Detective Smith said? Something about her advertising that she found the body in the park. The newspaper had left that out. Maybe because they didn't know that fact. Or maybe because they knew better. But she hadn't known better, and she had gone around town telling everybody she trusted that she was the one who found the body.

Detective Smith had implied that the culprit could easily turn on her. "You're starting to sound like a person who could get in the way of their freedom." That's what the detective said. He was right. She had been foolish with her words.

Back to Jake. He hadn't paid much attention to her until Viv told his aunt about her discovery. Gerry muttered something over their used wine flutes, and now Viv wondered if her comment about everyone having a speargun handy was a smokescreen put up to throw Viv off Jake's trail. Maybe Gerry sent Jake to the Oyster Bar to spy on Viv. Gerry was chatty about that poor guy's attitude, but she hadn't seemed all that curious about why he was in town. She had every opportunity to ask, but she hadn't.

Or had she?

And Zoe. Was she really so oblivious? Viv put herself in Zoe's shoes. If she saw someone who looked like a long-lost ex, wouldn't she be curious? Wouldn't she invite him in for espresso and ouzo and a chat?

Maybe Zoe had invited him in for a chat. Maybe he delivered his message. Maybe he settled his unfinished business. Perhaps it got him killed.

Viv threw a pillow to the foot of the bed and propped up her ankle wrapped in ice. Detective Smith hadn't said how many nights she would wake in distress. She could only hope this night was the one and only.

Something caught her attention as she was slow breathing to shift her mind away from all this chatter in her head. It was coming through the window outside her bedroom, which was open to let in the cool air. She strained her ears to hear the sound. What was that? It was a shuffling sound. Like something metal brushing against something soft.

She rose up on her knees and peered over the windowsill above her bed. She could just make out a dark shadow on the lawn. Listening intently, she waited for the sound to repeat. Was someone digging up her yard?

She rose a little higher to peer into the darkness. The streetlamp across the road cast a beam of gray-blue haze across her lawn.

Zoe? Was that Zoe Diamante with a shovel? She couldn't see clearly, but there was something familiar about the figure in the shadows. Dark hair. A full frame.

Impossible. Did Zoe even know where she lived?

Her foot slipped on the bed, and she knocked her chin on the windowsill.

"Ow!" She yelped, and the digging stopped.

When she looked again, the shadow was gone.

CHAPTER FOURTEEN

"Does this have anything to do with your digging in my trash?" Viv asked hotly. She was seated across the table from Detective Smith, who was showing a different side of himself. No longer a helpful grandpa with jiggly jowls, his expression said he was intent on getting down to business. Police business. Murder business, even.

She awoke to him knocking at her door. Now she was seated in the interrogation room at the downtown Crystal Bay PD.

"And what are you doing about whoever was digging in my yard in the middle of the night? I woke up because these ant bites were on fire, but I could see somebody out my bedroom window."

"Digging? Did you report it to the police?"

"I'm sort of doing that now. Aren't I?"

He nodded and Viv thought he signaled to someone on the outside listening in.

"Did you see who it was?"

"Not really." Viv glared at the man in front of her. She didn't want to point the finger at Zoe any more than she had already. She didn't want a finger pointing back at herself, either.

"It was dark," she continued. "But they were looking for something. Over by one of the statues in my yard. Aunt Viv liked her statues," she added.

He nodded. "She did. She had a thing for statues."

"Tell me about it," Viv muttered. "And they are too heavy to move off the lawn."

"Could be that someone was digging for fishing worms and crossed your property line. It happens."

"In the middle of the night?"

"They don't call them nightcrawlers for nothing."

Detective Smith paused for a beat. "You know how to drive a boat?"

Viv looked at him and frowned. "No, but it couldn't be any harder than a car, could it? Easier, maybe. You don't have to stay in your lane."

"Someone rented a boat for an early morning fishing trip, but then never showed up."

"Well, that's interesting," she said. "What does it have to do with me?"

"The weapon was in the cabin at the bow. We can't run a ballistic test like we would run on a gun, but I'm going to say it's the weapon we're looking for. The harpoon is missing from the barrel. And so is the steel wishbone along with one of the two rubber pieces. Just like the one you had on top of your fridge."

"Isn't that good?" Viv asked. "Doesn't that mean you're closing in?"

"You could say that."

Detective Smith put a sheet of paper in front of her. The paper was a rental agreement from the marina.

Vivianna Marston. 13 Dolphin Street.

"Hey, that's not my handwriting."

The detective shook his head. "No, this is the clerk's who took the call."

"I didn't make a call to the marina. Why would I rent a boat?"

"To get rid of the weapon when the heat is on. Take it out in the Gulf and drop it to the bottom where it no one will ever find it again. I'm wondering how you got it on board without being seen by the dock cameras."

Vivianna startled. "Are you being serious right now? Are you trolling me or what?"

"Is there another reason you would hide a backpack in a boat?"

"I don't have a backpack."

"We believe it belonged to the victim."

"I never saw a backpack in the park. It certainly wasn't near the anchor."

"You sure about that?"

"I am sure," Viv said. "Are you arresting me?"

"Not yet," he said.

He pulled the *Citrus Times* from a file folder and set it in front of her. The paper was turned to her Snooty Foodie review of Lokol Made. The detective tapped the section of the photo where the victim stood. "See? He's wearing a backpack. Clear as day."

Viv shook her head. "I did not see a backpack in the park."

"What about this?" He replaced the paper with an evidence bag. It was another clipping from the newspaper, a grainy color photo with three people smiling. One of them had his foot on a wooden case that looked old and covered in barnacles.

She leaned in. "I think that's Aunt Viv," she said. "And that looks just like the guy in the park. When he was about the same age. I don't know who the other guy is." She looked up and shrugged.

"That's Captain Frederick Becker," the detective said. "Have you ever seen this photo?"

"No, never. Where did you find it?"

"It was in the backpack."

"The one on the boat with the murder weapon?"

The detective nodded. "You don't look anything like your aunt, by the way. Except for the way you wear your hair. She wore her hair on top of her head like that."

Viv touched the knot in place on her head self-consciously.

"What can you tell me about this?" He put another evidence bag in front of her. It was a piece of white paper torn along one side. Viv read it aloud. *Viv Marston knows everything.*

"What?"

"Yeah," he said. "That was my reaction. What *do* you know, Viv Marston? And why is your name on a message in the victim's backpack?"

Viv sat back against the hard metal chair. She was silent for a while, her thoughts racing.

"Let's hit the highlights," he said. "You inherit your aunt's house. You come to town and take up residence. A guy comes to town a few weeks later. You catch him accidentally in a photo.

Within hours this guy you claim you don't know winds up dead in a public place. His belongings wind up on a rental boat rented in your name in the marina. The only clue is you. *Viv Marston knows everything.*"

"No!" Viv screeched. "I don't know anything!"

"That's a little hard to believe."

Her shock turned to anger. "So, you think I called the marina to rent a boat to stash a backpack with a murder weapon … all while mysteriously avoiding dock cameras that would catch me in the act? Is that your take?" Viv demanded.

"No, wait. First, I'm going to fill the backpack with everything that can incriminate me, including my name!" Her voice rose with her temper. "But even before that, I have to get out my trusty old speargun because who doesn't have one in their garage... so I can harpoon someone I don't even know… and then wait patiently until morning to call 911 to report it! Oh yes, that all makes so much sense!

"If that's how it happened, why would I tell you about the napkin in the trash and that wishbone thing? Or show you that rubber piece? Wouldn't I just keep that to myself? My DNA is all over them!

"But you know what?" she continued, her emotion spent. "You won't find my DNA on that dude in the orange shirt. Or the backpack. Or that harpoon, either!

"Because why would I—"

"Precisely," he said, interrupting her rant. "Why would you do that? That's what we're here to find out."

"This is crazy thinking," Viv said. "I am an innocent bystander, and you know it. Someone is trying to frame me, and you know that."

A knock sounded on the door, and he rose, stepped out into the hall and closed the door behind him.

Viv felt the silence. She argued with herself about digging into the bites on her ankle, which felt like little fires. She was thirsty, and the water bottle was empty. She was hungry, but she had already eaten the stale peanut butter crackers he gave her. Was she really a suspect in the murder in Anchor Park? Or was the hex adding heated tension to her life?

"Somebody knocked the head off one of your statues," Detective Smith said as he settled back to the table.

"What?"

"That's the shoveling you heard last night. Your King Neptune is missing his head. I had a deputy run over and check the situation."

Viv put her hand over her eyes.

"Look," he said after a moment. "I told you that you were in danger. If someone is trying to frame you for this murder, they are doing a damn good job. Everything points to you. If that person is also the one who took the head off the statue, they're getting close to the bone."

"I don't get it," Viv said after a moment of reflection. "I haven't lived here long enough to make enemies. Why would someone frame me?"

"Because you know something about the crime. Or at least they think you do. Here it is in black and white." He tapped the torn paper fragment. "You've been spreading that news around loud enough that someone is feeling threatened. Very threatened."

"I'm not really a suspect?"

"Everyone is a suspect."

"Everyone? Everyone but the victim," Viv said, her tone edgy. "You had no right to bring me here under false pretenses."

"There's nothing false about it," he said stubbornly.

Viv gave him a hard look.

"Okay, okay," he said, holding his hands palm up. "I wanted you to see how dangerous this murder business is. How quickly things can slide sideways. I felt I owed your aunt a little grace or something. She was so good to my wife. And you don't need to be nosing around in homicide business that's none of yours. Criminals are dangerous."

Viv leaned forward in her chair. "I can think of ninety-nine ways this could have gone down differently."

Detective Smith grinned and nodded. "Well, you got the message, didn't you?"

"I understand the assignment," Viv muttered.

"How are your ant bites?"

"They sting like fire." She folded her arms across her chest.

CHAPTER FIFTEEN

"I didn't expect to have to bail you out of jail before taking you on a date." Jake opened the door of his truck and motioned for her to climb in. The truck was at least four feet off the ground. She was standing outside the police department still confused and fuming.

"You didn't bail me out," she snapped. "They didn't charge me with anything."

"Lucky you," he said. She could tell he was amused and teasing. "It's a good thing we're not going anyplace fancy," he added.

Viv glanced at her reflection in the visor mirror. Her hair was a tumbled mess, and she was wearing cut-off jeans and an oversized boyfriend shirt. Her mascara was smudged under her bottom lashes. She hadn't showered since her incident in the yard with the ants and the garden hose. To be honest, she was afraid to shower. She didn't want to wake the bites.

She pulled her hair free, ran her fingers through it and drew it back into a bun on top. The kind of bun Aunt Clara said looked like a Choux pastry coming out of the oven and Captain Fred said looked like a tidal wave ready to crash the shore. Everyone seemed to have an opinion about how she wore her hair, and frankly she was over it.

"I think you look cute," Jake said.

"No woman wants to look cute," she barked. "I need to go home and freshen up. And it's way too early for dinner. I called you because I didn't have anyone else to call."

"I'm glad you called me," he said. "Do you want to talk about it?"

"No."

"I brought you a burger," he added and motioned to the brown paper bag on the seat beside him.

"Dude," she said and brightened. "The way to my heart is food."

He grinned and Viv thought he blushed too. He wanted to walk her to the door, but she insisted he stay put when they rolled into her driveway a few minutes later. She slid out of his truck and shut the door. "I'll see you at six," she said and waved sheepishly, still bewildered over the past few hours of her morning.

Viv waited until Jake's truck was out of sight and then she detoured to the statue. It was one of a dozen that adorned the lawn. A gaudy flashback to the Florida trends of the 1970s when concrete was having a moment.

King Neptune's head lay on the ground next to his body. Someone had righted it, and he looked like a victim of the mythological hero, Perseus, who lopped off Medusa's head when she wasn't looking.

She picked it up, surprised by the weight, and carried it into the house. She put Neptune's head in the center of the kitchen table and opened the fridge.

"Your mother would not approve," Aunt Clara said sternly from a can of Blue Sky cola on the top shelf.

"No, Charlotte would not approve," Viv agreed with a grumpy huff.

"No one in our family has ever been arrested," Earlene said. She and Floyd were nesting in a carton of eggs that would probably never get used. "Floyd came close once, but they took pity."

Viv noticed Floyd didn't defend himself.

She pulled the Blue Sky out of the fridge and sat down to eat her burger, she and Neptune not quite eye to eye.

"I wasn't arrested and if you start ragging on me, I'm throwing every edible item in this kitchen out the back door and you won't have any place to manifest," she said, suddenly feeling hangry. "I don't want to talk about it. I don't want to hear about it. I want to be left alone."

It was as if she were talking to no one then because the minute she made her needs known, the gourmet ancestors disappeared without a further word. She sighed. She didn't mean to be cross, but she needed space; she needed quiet and alone time.

Viv finished her burger and pulled Neptune's head toward her. He had a rather annoyed look about him. As if he had been caught off guard with they poured the cement and inconvenienced by his beheading. His concrete eyes were cast slightly upward, the crown of his concrete hair curling around his head in deep mildew encrusted waves. She tilted the head and peered inside. It was hollow. A deep, empty cavern for brains.

The thought made her smile.

Why would someone knock his head off?

If she hadn't noticed the lone culprit in the middle of the night, she would have put this down as vandalism or a prank by neighborhood kids out for mischief. But there had only been one person in the gray lamplight, and it was no kid. Was it Zoe as she thought? And why did she think so? That had been her instant assumption. Dark hair. A full figure. A gait that was familiar. Were they wearing a hat? She tried to picture it. Really, it could have been anyone out there in the dark.

She hadn't shared her thoughts about Zoe with Detective Smith. Now, she wondered if that had been wise. He could put someone on Zoe's doorstep to watch for odd behavior. She couldn't picture Zoe as the killer, but stranger facts existed. What she could picture was this guy—whose name she still didn't know— —catching up with Zoe Diamante long enough to deliver his message and finish unfinished business. Did that have something to do with Neptune? The statue in her yard? It seemed a bit crazy, but she couldn't shake the idea.

Had the victim's unfinished business done him in? She couldn't shake that idea either.

How did this all fit together? She was sorting the pieces, as she had told Jake. They still didn't feel very sorted.

Why would someone frame her by planting the weapon on a rental boat in the marina? Why not drop it in the bushes outside her home? And come to think of it, how did they know her address? 13 Dolphin Street. Who else knew where she lived?

She made a mental list of the possibilities. Jake knew. He'd put out a kitchen fire more than once, and he just dropped her off at her driveway. The editor of the newspaper knew because Viv had filled out employment paperwork. Martie Grim probably knew because she listened to the scanner, and even though Viv's name wasn't broadcast, it wouldn't take much to figure it out. Amelia might know, too. Amelia seemed to know more than she let on. Katarina knew. The thought dawned on her. Everyone she had introduced herself to in the last few days knew she had inherited her Aunt Viv's house. And probably everyone knew where her Aunt Viv lived.

"And what about you, Your Highness?" she said to the statue. She stuck her hand in the hollow spot and raised the head. It was too heavy to make a one-handed puppet. "If only you could speak," she said and put the hollow part toward her ear like a seashell. A *whoosh* filled her ears.

~~~~~

Now nourished and overwhelmingly sleepy, Viv headed to the couch for a nap. She had enough time to nap, shower, and get dressed before Jake picked her up for dinner. All of that seemed absolutely necessary … and in that order.

She grabbed Captain Fred's book of treasure hunting adventures and propped herself up in bed to read. Even though she had only met Captain Fred once, she could hear his sand-gravel voice behind the stories as she read the prologue. She scanned the table of contents, and a chapter caught her eye.

The Jewel Thief.

Martie Grim had mentioned this tale.

Viv turned to that chapter and began to read.

She guessed she had been asleep for a few minutes when her eyes flew open. Something ticked in her dream state, and she remembered the leftover stationery in the desk drawer. The room, which most would consider a guest room, was likely Aunt Viv's bookkeeping office. A large, ancient-looking desk, a green glass banker's lamp, a file cabinet—which was locked—and an old leather swivel desk chair made up the furnishings. A corkboard hung on the wall, empty except for a few thumbtacks.

She had thumbed through the stationery earlier, intending to
~~~~~

send a note to Professor Mojo thanking him for his help in landing the job with the *Citrus Times*. She had noticed then that there was a bundle of postcards at the bottom. The rubber band holding them together was as old as everything else in the house. She pulled the box from the drawer now.

Like the vintage stationery, the postcards were illustrated on one side and blank on the other. She shuffled through them wondering if *Greetings from Florida* and *Visit Weeki Wachi* circa 1970 had any value on the vintage market. Maybe Martie at Tropical Tomes would know.

She almost missed it. It was smaller than the others, caught inside the *See Bok Tower* postcard and envelope. The illustration was of a boat on a blue sea, hugging an island with palm trees. The writing had faded and was terribly penned to start, but it was clear enough to read. The postmark stamp was Nassau, Bahamas. September 19, 1979.

Viv, hit a snag. Stuck at port. Crew laid low by crud, bad rum & poker. Port has my passport till the fine's paid. Wire 5K Nassau Port, c/o harbor master. Miss your arms, your laugh, your everything. Pray the gulls don't eat me alive. Tell K the usual.

Your favorite scoundrel, Fred

Viv rocked back in the chair. Viv and Fred. Aunt Viv didn't just keep Captain Fred's books. She kept him company. No wonder he mentioned her in the preface of his book.

She shuffled through the rest of the postcards, and another fell loose.

Viv, Anchor's a-weigh and making headway for home. Project is rudderless. Two divers down & need to regroup. See you by Christmas. Tell K the Captain has gifts.

Your naughty Santa, Fred

K had to be Katarina, and she would have been very young in 1979. Where was her mother? Who was tending her care while the captain was at sea? Aunt Viv?

Viv dug through the pile more carefully, looking for a stray message she might have missed. There weren't any, but this was an interesting development. Fred and Viv and Katarina had history. No one had shared that tidbit with her.

The file cabinet was locked, but after snooping through the debris in the desk drawer, she found keys on a paper ring. One fit, and the lock clicked, and the drawer opened.

Inside the drawer were two items—a small wooden box and a hardbound ledger, the kind a bookkeeper would use. Viv tried the keys on the locked box, but none was a match. She set the box aside and grabbed the ledger.

The lines were tiny and the writing even smaller, and Viv's eyes nearly crossed trying to focus on the entries. Pretty boring stuff. Utilities, supplies, payouts, payroll, anchors, ropes, and boat repair. She ran her finger down the page.

Statuary, the entry read. *Gift. (Triton) $75*

Curious, Viv thought. Was this the beginning of Aunt Viv's obsession with statuary? Was it a gift from Captain Fred?

She ran a finger further down the page.

Statuary, another entry read a few pages later. *Gift. (Mermaid) $65*

She scanned the pages. There were four more statuary listed.

So, Captain Fred Becker gifted his lover a piece of statuary every Christmas. No wonder Aunt Viv had so many. What a strange gift, she thought, peeking out the window at the headless Neptune on the lawn.

She jumped up from the chair, leaving it squeaking as it spun, and ran to her hamper. Digging out the pants she wore that day in Anchor Park, she shoved her fingers in the pocket.

"Yes!" she said aloud.

It was a scrap of paper like the one Detective Smith showed her in the evidence bag. This scrap had two torn edges. The message was in the center. The handwriting looked the same.

Find the statue and you find…

Dew and bird pecks blurred the last words.

She rushed back to the desk, pulling out a magnifying glass she had noticed earlier.

Find the statue and you find…

She brought the magnifying glass closer.

treasure

Find the statue and you find the treasure

"Yes!" she said aloud. "This is about treasure!"

She looked at the torn edges. If she was right, the message in Detective Smith's possession was the bottom part of the page. The last line of the message. It had one straight edge and one torn edge. This message, with its two torn edges, must be the middle line in the riddle. And that meant there was one more: the beginning of the message.

Something something unknown
Find the statue and you find the treasure
Viv Marston knows everything

Where was the other fragment? Who had the other fragment?

She retraced her steps in her mind, remembering the paper on the ground and the bird giving it a royal pecking. She had picked it up because it was litter and put it in her pocket.

If the last fragment of the message was in the backpack, maybe this one was shaken loose when the culprit rummaged through it. Maybe it had fallen to the ground undetected. If the killer was rummaging through the backpack while the poor guy in the orange Hawaiian shirt was dying across the anchor, then the killer didn't know about this message. Did they know about the other?

Of course they did, Viv thought.

That's why she was being framed.

Viv Marston knows everything…

Was it some kind of code?

Viv turned the paper over, raised it and gave it a whiff as if detecting ingredients in a culinary dish. Much like sniffing dish for the nuances of herbs and spices and broths, she was after its history. Paper. Canvas. Cigarette smoke. Something minty like peppermint. But not perfume. Minty. Sort of. And spicy. Like geranium But not like Mimi's rose geranium pound cake. She wished now that she could have sniffed the backpack itself.

She really should let Detective Smith know about this message fragment, she thought. She stuffed it into the desk and closed the drawer.

CHAPTER SIXTEEN

"Have you recovered from your tangle with the law?" Jake's eyes gleamed with amusement over the citronella candle in the center of the table. They had already ordered the special. A dozen each of boiled shrimp and blue crab. The tablecloth was red gingham plastic, and the placemat was a huge stretch of butcher paper. Easy cleanup for the waitstaff.

Viv ignored the gest. The waiter appeared, holding a metal tub with a pair of tongs hanging out of the top.

"Best in the state," Jake said. "Local shrimp. Local crab. They probably came out of the water this morning."

The two of them dug in. Jake showed her how to remove the legs and claws. Then how to crack the crab, leveraging the shell and around the lungs to get at the tender meat inside. It was work, but it was finger-licking delicious work, and the hot seasoning on the outside made their beer taste even better. The waiter appeared again with a basket of hush puppies still steaming from the fryer.

"What did the police want?" Jake pushed. "Why were you detained?"

"A misunderstanding," she said, knowing she was being evasive. Earlene's comment that Jake might have something to hide was fueling her guardedness. She wasn't a clam, but she wouldn't spout everything if she could help herself.

"Did it have to do with the murder in Anchor Park?"

"Yes." She shoved a hush puppy into her mouth.

"Are they any closer to the truth?"

"I think so."

He grew quiet and focused on the food in front of him. She did the same. The silence felt awkward, as first dates often do, but she had not expected this first date being awkward. So far, every time they saw each other—which, admittedly, hadn't been that often—but every time they had an easy rapport she rarely felt with others. She didn't want things to get awkward. She wanted light-hearted and fun. Why had she pulled back? Why had she shoved her mouth full of food rather than tell him the details of her visit with Detective Smith?

"Tell me about your business," she said cheerfully. "How long have you been doing your ceviche business?"

"This is my second year," he said, beaming. "Zoe Diamante talked me into it. I used to crew for her when she had a fishing boat."

"I didn't know you were friends with Zoe."

He nodded.

What a dumb thing to say, she thought, and put her head down to survey the pile of shrimp shells. She was the newcomer in town. Not everyone else was. Why wouldn't he and Zoe be friends? Or at least acquaintances.

"And you like it?"

"Love it," Jake said. "I'm waiting for a paid post on the fire squad to open, but right now the positions are all volunteer. Until then, I need to make a living. I have a hobby farm. Mostly I grow what I use for ceviche. Tomatoes, peppers, onions, and cilantro. Stuff like that."

"And tangerines." Viv grinned.

"I get them from Aunt Gerry's. Her yard is loaded with sour tangerines. Did you know that Ponce de Leon planted the first orange tree in Florida back in fifteen-something-something? Oranges weren't native."

"Really?"

"And the tangerine is a hybrid orange grapefruit. A tangy orange. Florida tangerines are not the sweet mandarins you buy at the grocery store."

"Really?" She felt like a parrot.

He looked up. "I'm boring you."

"No! I think it's fascinating. I love food origin stories."

"So, what about you? How did you get into writing food columns? "

Viv hesitated. "I graduated from culinary school in Orlando a few months ago, but I haven't found the right kitchen position. My dream was to be a chef, but, well—things are not working out the way I thought they would. I like to write, and I like to write about food, so I kind of fell into the food column thing. I like it." She felt satisfied with her explanation. No need to walk that bridge just yet.

"You're good at it," Jake said. "Are you going to include recipes? The Snooty Foodie might help up my game in the kitchen." He shoved a peeled shrimp dripping with butter into his mouth. "I'm going to make marinara," he added. "I always have more tomatoes than I can use in the summer."

Viv beamed. This was cause and effect she hadn't expected.

"But you really need to get a fire extinguisher in your kitchen," he added and grinned. She could tell he was serious. "Dolphin Street has been on the scanner too many times. I can help you install a fire extinguisher, if you want."

Dolphin Street. He said it with as much familiarity as he said the word tangerine. "Sure, that would be great," she said. Then added quickly, "Did you know my Aunt Viv?"

He shook his head. "Not really. I know she was the bookkeeper for a lot of local businesses."

"Aunt Viv was mentioned in Captain Frederick's treasure hunt book," Viv said. "He claimed she was his right hand on the books. I got the impression he meant like a right hand on the Bible. I guess she handled the company's bookkeeping. I think she handled the captain, too." Viv grinned. "It sounded like he was fond of her. More than just a business relationship."

Jake shrugged. "I doubt if Katarina would let that happen. She has always guarded her dad the way a dog guards a bone."

"When I introduced myself at the museum he perked up. He thought I was Aunt Viv. He looked disappointed when I wasn't."

"It's cool that you have the same name. It's an old-fashioned name. I like Vivianna. And I like Viv." He smiled seductively and Viv's heart raced. Now was not the time to get all twitterpated like some bird. The idea made her think of Anchor Park, and she circled back to something she had been wanting to ask since Jake had picked her up in her driveway.

"You said you were running late last Saturday morning the day we met at the Farmer's Market. You never said why you were running late. Nothing bad, I hope?"

His expression changed and he knew it. He covered it by raising his beer mug, but Viv saw through it. Either he was uncomfortable with the question, or he wasn't comfortable with her asking.

"I had to help a friend," he said, his blue eyes dark in the candlelight. "She needed a favor, and I had one to return."

"Oh? Anybody I know?"

He narrowed his eyes at her, and she knew she had stepped one step too far. Maybe three. Maybe three and a half. "Sorry," she said and meant it. "I guess I'm still trying to sort out all these pieces."

"You mean about the guy in Anchor Park?"

"Yeah."

"I had nothing to do with that scene. I was nowhere near the park."

Her sigh was visible, and he cocked his head and looked at her. "You were thinking I had something to do with that? That I was late to the market because I bumped off some dude in the park and took his wallet?"

"Nobody took his wallet," Viv said, her tone short. "That's how they identified him. Although he has not been identified to me. I still don't know his name or who he was."

"I know who he was," Jake said quietly. "I know why he was here. But I don't know who killed him."

Viv realized she was gripping the handle of her mug like the doorknob to a haunted house. Her hand was frozen mid-air. She couldn't let go.

"You know?"

"He was here to talk to Zoe."

Viv gasped. She knew Zoe knew more than she was letting on!

"Zoe and his father were tight back in the day. His father's last request was to find Zoe and deliver a message."

"What was the message?"

"Dude, that's a bit extra. I didn't even ask her myself, and we're tight!"

"Then how do you know she's not involved in his ... uh, in his death?"

"Because I know Zoe." His tone was exacting. He picked up his mug, but there was nothing in it. He set the mug down and then drained his water glass.

Viv felt terrible. She was trying to keep things light, and now she had just accused his friend of murder. She really was a bit extra.

"I like Zoe," she said. "And I don't think of her in that way. But someone tried to frame me for that murder by planting the weapon on a rental boat at the marina. I didn't hire that boat. I didn't hide the spear. Someone is trying to pin this murder on me. Zoe told me she didn't know who the guy was. That wasn't true. Why would she lie? What else is she lying about?"

Jake looked at her as if she were a stranger he had never met. "I don't know," he said finally, as if considering the implication. "But there's no way she's involved. And, for the record, I was late Saturday morning because I was helping her bust up a statue in her yard."

Viv's eyes widened. "A statue? Why?"

"Because she said it was too heavy to move in one piece."

CHAPTER SEVENTEEN

The mood was moody. Maybe the worst first date ever. It was all her fault. Jake had turned silent and turned up the radio for the ride home. She didn't know what to say to smooth things over. Maybe there wasn't anything she could say. She really had put her foot in it.

The scanner barked with static and Jake automatically turned down the radio from the controls on the steering wheel.

"10-17 museum. 10-52 one-one-twelve Old Main. 70-year-old male. Possible injury. 10-80 reported. No smoke visible. Possible 10-62 in progress."

The words went by fast and full of static. Viv glanced at Jake for clarity.

"Somebody's broken into the Sunken Treasure Museum," he said, and floored the truck. "The fire alarm went off but there's no visible smoke. Looks like Captain Fred might need an ambulance. I don't know if I have time to drop you home first. I have to respond. I want to respond," he corrected.

"It's okay. I can either wait or walk home," Viv said, although she knew walking home wasn't an option. She was too curious not to be an eyewitness.

~~~~~~

They pulled up to the curb half a block from the museum and joined the flashing vehicles in the road.
~~~~~~

"I hope everybody's okay," she called as Jake hurried into action, leaving her standing by the truck. She glanced across the street in time to see Martie Grim walking around the corner of the building. Viv crossed the street to greet her.

"You heard it too?"

Martie nodded. "On my scanner. I hope the old man's okay. A break-in. Somebody's injured and the ambulance is on the way," she said.

An EMT walked by on his way to one of the vehicles. "You know what happened?" Martie asked.

"Someone broke in and smashed one of the display cases," he said. "Triggered the alarm. Fred Becker caught them in action, and they whacked him good. Hit him on the head. But he's okay, that old coot. He's seen worse, that's for sure." He smiled at Martie. "Are you doing okay these days, Martie?"

"Right as rain," she said.

"Good to hear," he said and went on.

They stood in the dark with the lights flashing around them, neither willing to move away, nor having reason to get closer.

"If they're looking for the statue, they won't find it in there," Martie said. "Goodness. That's a given."

"What statue are you talking about?" Viv said, her ears perking up at the mention. "Why would somebody be looking for a statue in the museum?"

"Oh, it's just something I heard on the scanner," Martie said and waved her hand, as if waiving away the importance of her words. "It's easy to get caught up in that chatter. Sometimes you have to piece it all together with your imagination to figure out what they're talking about. Code and more code and a lot of static. I heard that somebody broke into the museum a few days ago. I didn't hear if they got away with anything, but I'm sure the officer made a report. Kids. They're always up to something. I know mine are. Nothing illegal," she added, seeing Viv's concern. "Just kids being kids."

"You told me that Anchor Park was donated by Fred Becker," Viv started. "Is that accurate?"

"Oh, yeah. That spit of land was given to the city. To be honest, I think the taxes were higher than its value as property. It floods in a hurricane. Not good for a house or a business, but it works perfectly as a park."

"And then he donated the anchor in the center," Viv said. "That's why it's called Anchor Park? Is it a special anchor or something?"

"It's not from the Nina, Pinta or Santa Maria," Martie joked, "if that's what you are getting at. I believe it was a Spanish galleon ship that sank somewhere off the coast of Florida around the 1600s. Full of all kinds of cargo headed back to Spain. Another one bites the dust." Martie laughed. "I guess that's not so funny if you were on a sinking ship. Florida hurricanes and uncharted reefs were a disaster waiting to happen in those days."

They were still standing in the same spot when the ambulance gurney came out of the building. It was empty. In a few minutes, Captain Fredrick appeared, his daughter Katarina at the helm of his wheelchair.

"That's a good sign," Martie said. "I couldn't picture him getting in the ambulance anyway. Tough as leather, that old salt."

They watched Katarina wheel her dad down the street toward them. The pair of bystanders did not appear to be Katarina's destination, but they were in the path. Martie stepped forward and put a gentle hand on Fred's arm. "You're okay?"

"No! It's horrible!" Katarina bellowed. "He could have been killed!"

"No such luck," he muttered. "Damn thieves. I am always on the lookout for thieves."

"He won't get in the ambulance," Katarina whined. "I'm driving him to the hospital. He's got a gash on his head."

Martie *tsk tsked*. "What happened?"

The old man's gravelly voice sounded tentative at first. "I was moving toward the back room getting ready to leave when I heard a crash. I went in to see what was going on, and somebody was trying to steal my Bella Dona jewels. I yelled, *thief!* Wheeled around to turn on the light and then he whacked me." He put his hand on the back of his head and grimaced.

"Just a few days ago, somebody stole an artifact right off the wall," Katarina said. "I reported it to the police. It was a vintage speargun." She looked at Viv pointedly. All the sweet, new friend, new town flattery seemed to dissolve in the dark.

"I was going to ask you about the harpoon missing from the wall," Viv said, meeting Katarina's gaze.

"Maybe you should ask your friend Zoe Diamante," Katarina said, her words exacting and ice cold. "I saw her running out the back of the museum right before the alarm went off. Why don't you ask her what happened to our artifact?"

Viv felt like she was being accused right along with Zoe.

"You caught everything on camera, didn't you?" Martie asked.

Katarina scoffed. "If we lived in the modern day, we might have. But we still live as if it's 1980. There's an ancient camera attached to a VCR tape so thin you can hear it whine."

"Works like a charm," Fred barked.

"Not if you need to record something other than black and white snow."

Fred grumbled something unintelligible. "Get me home, Kat."

"We're going to the emergency room," she replied.

"Over my dead body," he muttered.

"That can be arranged," Katarina spat and wheeled him away.

"I wouldn't want to get in the middle of that," Viv said when the Beckers were out of earshot.

"Oh, you don't know the half of it," Martie said and shook her head. "Sometimes it sounds like they drag out the cannons."

~~~~~

"I'd invite you in for coffee and a nightcap, but I don't have either," Viv said. They were still sitting in Jake's truck in the driveway. "You probably wouldn't accept. I wasn't on my best behavior tonight."

Jake shook his head. "Me either. I should never have left you sitting in the truck like some loyal dog."

"I'm going to pretend you didn't just call me a dog," Viv said and laughed lightly. "Although some dogs might be a better dinner date than I was."
~~~~~

"You did *wolf* down those shrimp," he said, and laughed at his pun. The tension slipped away.

"So, what do you make of what happened at the museum?" Viv asked.

"I think Fred was lucky. He could have gotten killed with a blow to his head. No jewels are worth risking your life for."

"I think Captain Fred would disagree," Viv said. "He's risked his life many times for less. I've been reading his book. He's an adrenaline junkie. He may be older now than he thinks he is, but he likes a risky adventure."

Jake nodded. Viv reached for the door handle.

"I'm not going to ask you for a second date just yet," he said. "I don't want you to say no."

"I'm not going to say no," Viv said. "And I would definitely go back to 'not fancy but good'. Now that I have that crab-cracking thing down, I could put some crab away in much better time."

"Look, I know you have questions about Zoe and what happened to that guy," he said. His voice was almost tender. "It's not what you think."

"I'm not sure what I think," Viv replied. She glanced at the headless statue in the yard. Jake's eyes followed.

"What happened there?"

"Zoe happened," Viv said. "And I don't think it's because the statue was too heavy to move in one piece.

Focaccia Lightens the Load

By Vivianna Marston, The Snooty Foodie

"Cook with passion and you feed the world." That's what Mimi always said. When I was little, I literally envisioned the whole world sitting at her table. "There won't be enough!" I would say, and she would laugh.

She wasn't wrong. When we cook with love, we touch with heart. The expression, breaking bread, is not a cliched expression. It's a prime example of how food brings people together. You can't be hangry when you have bread and a table full of guests.

While baking bread feels daunting for some, even non-bread bakers can make a pan of focaccia and feel super-cheffy when everybody bites into this crispy, tender, flavorful bread.

Focaccia, pronounced foh-KAH-chya, is a flatbread made famous by the Italians. The word itself comes from the Latin word "focus" which doesn't mean you have to focus your attention on making the bread to make it great. The focus is all about the fire. The oven. The hearth at the heart of the home.

Focaccia needs time to rise, so plan ahead. A quality flour, spring water, yeast, olive oil, salt and something to feed the yeast is all you need. Mimi often steeped fresh rosemary in hot water before straining and adding it to the yeast and honey. I have discovered that lemon thyme and pink peppercorns are delicious. Be sure to check the water temperature, or you will kill the yeast if the water is too hot. The dough won't rise if the water is cold. This is the only Goldilocks rule of working with yeast. Not too hot. Not too cold.

In Mimi's kitchen we said prayers of gratitude into the dough as we were kneading. It's not necessary for success, but what a great way to remember we have so much to be thankful for.

Now it's time to set your focaccia to rise. Cover it with a fresh dishcloth in a warm spot and wait. Once doubled in size, you can knead a few more words of gratitude into the dough before spreading it onto a stone bar pan or pizza stone to let it rise again.

Dimple it with your fingers to hold a drizzle of good olive oil, flaked salt, and maybe a sprinkle of fresh rosemary. If you want to get fancy, add caramelized onions, walnuts and brie cheese; grated parmesan or pecorino cheese; or sliced tomatoes and salt-cured olives.

It's best eaten warm, but focaccia makes a great sandwich bread for later. Serve it with soup, salad, your home-made marinara, or on its own. The workhorse of the breadbasket, focaccia elevates an everyday meal into something quite special.

Go ahead. Lighten your load with a slice. You'll be grateful you did!

CHAPTER EIGHTEEN

The house on Dolphin Street felt empty. She felt empty.

There was no popping sound as she entered the kitchen. The basket of fruit didn't dance with their witty banter. She opened the fridge. Nothing smiled back.

For a moment she panicked. What if her gourmet ancestors had found the remedy for the hex? What if they happened upon the remedy and then popped off this realm? On. Off. Just like Uncle Floyd had said. Here. Gone. Her heart ached at the thought. The house seemed to weigh on her like cold stone.

Neptune stared off into space from his place at the center of the table. Cold stone. Hollow stone. Staring into the abyss with eyes wide open and seeing nothing.

What was Zoe after? She wasn't trying to move heavy statues. Even if that's what she told Jake. Zoe has been destroying the statue. But why? And why had Zoe moved from the statue in her yard to the one in Viv's? What was she after?

Find the statue and you find the treasure.

That was only part of the message, but Viv wondered if the son had delivered the complete message to Zoe. She denied it, but it seemed more likely that he did and that the message had to do with a statue. And probably a treasure. And also, Viv Marston. Not herself. Her late aunt.

Viv glanced at Neptune, King of the Sea, hoping for answers, but he was as silent as ever.

"Who killed that guy in Anchor Park?" she asked out loud.

"And why? What did he know that we don't? And how is that connected to me, the hex, and you?"

The King of the Sea stared, his blank eyes turned eternally upward. His cold stone mouth was stone-cold silent.

"I give up," she said to no one. "Detective Smith better solve this case before he retires or we're in trouble."

There was a tiny pop, and her heart leapt.

She threw open the fridge and there they were!

Three grapes blinked from a cluster on the plate.

"You're back!"

"Back?" Floyd said.

"I was scared you had dissipated," Viv said. "You know, like disappeared with the hex."

"Oh," Earlene said. "What a sweet thought, Viv. But no, we're still here."

"Even specters have to sleep, my dear," Clara said.

She closed the refrigerator door and the room grew silent.

Viv ran through the day in her mind in the quiet of her kitchen.

She couldn't get Captain Fred out of her thoughts. He was startled when she showed up at the museum and introduced herself. She imagined how it might feel when a ghost from your past reappears. Especially one you loved. Yes, even wind-swept Captain Fred was capable of love. She wondered if her Aunt Viv felt the same way about him. She recalled the old newspaper photograph the detective had shown her. The photo only told part of the story about Captain Fred, Viv Marston, and whoever Zoe's old flame was—she hadn't caught his name in the caption and Zoe had never said. The three of them were a team of sunken treasure hunters. One by land, two by sea. A bookkeeper and two divers. Were they caught in a jealous love triangle? Had the odd man lost out?

Is that why Zoe's ex was blamed for the theft? Or had the theft ever even happened?

The diver and his son.

The son who came to deliver a message. And it got him killed. But why?

In all her explanations about their visit to watch the fish at the shore, stolen artifacts, and a harmless, grumpy old man, Katarina's excuses felt like excuses. Like a cover-up for something undoable.

The young man had troubled Captain Fred when he went into the museum. Katarina had shared a little of what had happened, but it didn't matter what was said to offend him, he looked so much like his father that his sudden appearance would stir anger in the old man. Between Viv and the son, the Captain's past was back on his doorstep. Back in the spotlight. No longer confined to the dark theater of his museum.

Wheelchair tracks in the sand.

A missing harpoon.

An airline ticket stuck to a dedication placard.

She remembered Katarina's comment.

Veni, Vidi, Vici.

I came. I saw. I conquered.

Katarina wanted to protect her father. No, Viv decided, she *needed* to protect him. No matter the unspeakable. He was hers. And yet, he was never hers. She was the daughter who wanted one thing: her father's devotion. And that was never hers to own.

Viv sighed with an ache in her heart. She thought of her own father who loved his family as much as any man could. Luck of the draw? Who's to say?

Life seemed so hard at times.

CHAPTER NINETEEN

The air was thick with patchouli and Nag Champa incense. Viv glanced at the hodgepodge decor in the store, an old house with clapboard siding and a tin roof. The room was full of tie-dye saris and djembe drums, candles and incense, crystals and rocks. An entire sideboard of teas held glass jars with strange names written across the labels. Mud Water Moon. Winter Wise. Ancient Love.

"Tell me what's really going on with you," Amelia said, peering through her bangs, the familiar impish smile on her red lips. They were seated at a little round table draped in a tie-dye scarf. Viv thought the only thing missing from the kitsch was a crystal ball in the center.

"You look like someone stole your boyfriend," Amelia said.

"I don't have a boyfriend," Viv replied.

"Is that the problem? Is that why you're here?"

"No."

Viv looked over Amelia's shoulder at the jars of tea. Heartspell Brew. Unbreakable Charm. Potion Number 9. Evidently, finding love was common ground in a guru shop like this. "Do people actually use teas and stuff like that to find love?"

"Teas and a whole lot weirder," Amelia said and laughed lightly. "You would be horrified at what people will do for love. But that's not what you're looking for, is it?"

Viv shook her head. "Have you ever put a spell on anybody?" she asked.

"Me?" Curiosity glistened in Amelia's eyes.

"What about a hex?"

Amelia laughed and cocked her head. "That's black magic stuff."

"Like *Tears Yet Cried*," Viv read from the jar. "Is that black magic? What does that come from? How do you get tears before they're shed?"

"You don't want to know," Amelia said coyly. "And no, that's not black magic. But it is pretty strong spell stuff. Mothers used it for protection spells when their sons went to war. Now I guess you'd use it so you don't crash your new Mercedes."

Viv chuckled. She really was out of her element. Before the ancestors had arrived in her crème brûlée, magic was fiction. Now open to a reality she never considered, she felt lost in a world with no tether. She would have felt better if the gourmet ancestors came along and she wondered what they would think about all this spell stuff in jars. She didn't think they were present at the shop. If she had thought about it, she would have slipped an apple in her pocket and brought them along.

"How come you're not baking?" Viv asked, knowing her question was coming from outer space. "You were so pumped about starting a bakery. What happened?"

"What happened?" Amelia echoed. "Money. Rent. Debt. Unexpected twists. Dreams that went up in smoke before they ever got in the oven."

The words caught Viv's attention. "You mean, literally went up in smoke?"

"No, but the closest I've been to a pan of croissants in six months is the bakery aisle at Publix. They taste like buttered cardboard. Trust me. They do."

Viv grinned. "I haven't put a pan on the burner in weeks. The last time it went up in smoke. Literally."

Amelia laughed. "Literally."

"No, I mean… literally. The pan caught fire. The alarm went off. The firetruck came. I haven't cooked since."

"No way."

She glanced at Amelia, wondering if her admission would lead to a confession, should the gourmet ancestors be right about the source of the hex. Uncle Floyd seemed convinced Amelia was behind it because he had a twist in his tale about the *Book of Nines*. He was confident Amelia was one of the nine. The *Nèf Sentes*. The Nine Saints.

That was the real reason she was sitting here nearly choking on incense smoke.

Viv shrugged. "I'm getting used to eating cold food."

"Bummer," Amelia said. "That's gross."

"Yeah," Viv said. "I dream of soufflés and homemade pasta with sauces that would make your head spin. I'm eating charcuterie and crackers."

Amelia chuckled. "What a disaster. We're both nothing but almost chefs. Wanna-bes with culinary degrees. Pedigrees of a sort. Pedigrees and Petit Fours," she muttered as an afterthought. "That sounds like it belongs on a jar of tea." She motioned to the shelf behind her with a quick nod.

Amelia picked up the deck of cards in the center of the table and shuffled them absently. "Like the stove really caught on fire, fire? Like it did that time at school?"

Viv nodded.

"Bummer," Amelia repeated. "That sucks."

Amelia shuffled the deck again and placed it in front of Viv. "Are you sure you still want a reading?"

"Sort of," Viv said. "I'm a little freaked, but I'm here."

A circle, the gourmet ancestors had said. Magic that made a loop. She was determined to follow this loop wherever it led. There were certain facts that made Floyd's assumption solid. Amelia was the only person she knew at culinary school who also now lived in Crystal Bay. Proximity being something Earlene had suggested was an ingredient for the hex. Amelia had been openly competitive in the classroom, almost hostile toward anyone whose dish turned out better. That put Viv on the spot a few times and she had sensed Amelia's jealousy more than once. The feeling had passed quickly and without incident. Now she wondered if the salt and sugar mix-up during the chocolate bake-off had been revenge. It seemed so childish, and yet, she knew people did worse for less.

Added to this new fact that Amelia was involved in the world of magic—or at least her family was—she was beginning to side with Uncle Floyd. Viv thought Amelia's sometimes surly behavior was covering up for insecurities. But what if those issues went deeper? Went darker? She couldn't deny what she had recently learned. Amelia had lost her bakery dream too.

The hex magic wasn't linear, the ancestors had said, and it came with a price. Amelia was as thwarted in her dream career as Viv was in hers. With Floyd's ethereal sleuthing leading her here to this strange little shop of spells, there was no turning back. Maybe there was no turning back for either of them. She couldn't name a reason Amelia would put a hex on her, but that didn't mean there wasn't one. Maybe Amelia hadn't realized one bad turn earned another. Tit for tat. An eye for eye. Woe for woe.

"Well, do you want to do this thing or not?" Amelia asked, shuffling the cards again.

Viv nodded slowly.

"Then focus on the question you want answered. The one question above all else."

Viv nodded again. She was clear the question she would focus on.

"Now separate the cards into three piles. Do that with your left hand."

She did as she was told.

"Close your eyes. Is the question clear in your mind? You don't have to tell me what it is, but you can, if you want."

Viv nodded again. Amelia closed her eyes and was silent. When she opened them, she laid the first card on the table.

"This card represents you. The place where you are now." Amelia looked up with dark eyes. "The Tower."

Viv looked at the card and silently drew in a breath. It was a picture of a tower, the kind fairytale Rapunzel would have lived in. Except this tower was on fire and Rapunzel was fleeing from the only open window, falling headfirst to the ground. Their eyes met again as Amelia laid the second card crosswise against the first. Viv heard Amelia take a quick breath.

Death. The card gave Viv the creeps. It was a black knight on a white horse. The guard to his helmet was open, and his face was nothing but bare bones, a skeleton riding a pale horse. She thought of Captain Frederick. Of how he had talked about his long-awaited date with the same lone rider. Death on a pale horse. He said he wasn't afraid of death. Viv couldn't say the same.

"This represents the challenges you are facing."

Viv wrinkled her nose. "I don't know if this is such a great idea."

Amelia glanced up. "You're not going to freak out, are you? This card doesn't mean it's your death on the table. It's just a symbol."

Amelia built the spread slowly, her eyes moving between the stack of cards in her hand, the spread before her, and Viv.

"Bonkers," Amelia said when the cards were laid in order. "This is not a simple spread. You have several Major Arcana cards showing here. That means you are at the mercy of some big and powerful influences."

"Tell me about it," Viv said and clasped her hands in her lap.

"Wow. Your life is in upheaval," Amelia stated simply.

Viv nodded slowly. "For real."

"I can see it. Things are happening around you and to you that seem totally out of your control. And the more you try to change it, the more chaotic it gets."

Viv eyed her with curiosity. She couldn't tell if this information was something Amelia already knew or if it truly was coming from the cards in front of her.

"So," Amelia said, now sounding somber. "This card represents the challenges you face. The good thing about current situations is that they are usually temporary. So, there's that." She smiled briefly and then exhaled deeply. When she spoke again, Viv was struck by how she no longer sounded like the young Amelia she had overheard arguing about the temperature of butter and the protein content of flour. Her voice sounded deeper, even older. How was that even possible? Was that a trick? Or had she tapped into some kind of magic of her own?

"I want to repeat that," Amelia said quietly, breaking into Viv's thoughts. "Current does not mean forever. This card says you are simply clearing space for something new. Maybe something better."

"Okay," Viv said, feeling a teeny bit better.

Months ago, before the gourmet ancestors appeared, Viv would have considered this fortune reading business nothing but a parlor trick. A fun thing to do on vacation. No more than a game of colorful cards with a lot of woo and over the top delivery. Now, she knew there was more to the day-to-day universe than she ever thought possible. Magic existed. Magic of some sort, anyway. The gourmet ancestors popping in and out was proof. The hex was proof. She wasn't accidentally setting things on fire.

"In the Phoenix Rising spread, this card represents your career," Amelia said and tapped the card with a long, red fingernail. "Remember, it's just a symbol. It's a cycle. Like maybe the way you saw yourself in a career has faded." Amelia looked up quickly. "Boy, this is trippy, isn't it? Career ashes. Just like you said. Your old identity as a chef literally went up in flames."

Viv rolled her eyes in agreement.

"But look, you have powerful support." Amelia tapped the next card. "You have help if you accept it. You are not facing your struggle alone."

Viv peered at the card on the table in disbelief. "It says all that?"

The card showed an angel with wings, a trumpet, and a Red Cross flag. Maybe this card was about the gourmet ancestors, her kitchen helper folk, who popped into her ramekins right before the stove caught on fire the first time. Red Cross. Rescue. That fit. She really was a rescue mission, wasn't she? Clara, Earlene, and Floyd had appeared as if on cue, manifesting in a shower of sparks, eager to lend emergency assistance, disaster relief, and humanitarian support. Even their funny sibling banter eased her scramble to cope.

Viv leaned in to look at the next card. A lone figure stood looking at the horizon before him, but she couldn't tell if he was looking forward to where he was going or looking back from where he had been.

"This is the Dangerous Waters position in the spread," Amelia said. "This card says somebody doesn't want you to reach your goals. Somebody doesn't want you to step off into the unknown. They worry about your vulnerability. Afraid you will make a mistake that will cost you everything. You should be very careful around them."

"Who is it?" Viv asked.

"Can't see that," Amelia answered. "Can you think of anyone

who doesn't share your point of view?"

Viv laughed.

Amelia looked up and frowned. "Are you laughing at me? I can stop."

Viv shook her head. "No, I'm laughing because that sounds like Charlotte."

"Who's Charlotte?"

"My mother."

"You call her Charlotte?"

"She insists."

"That's weird."

Viv nodded. "Charlotte's weird."

She started to retract that, then decided against it. Charlotte was a little weird. Not unpleasantly weird or unhinged or any-thing—just very set in her narrow-thinking ways about how things had to look right to be proper and keep up appearances. When Viv announced she wanted to go to culinary school, Charlotte had been dead set against it. It wasn't a suitable career. Not a practical one. Not good enough to make a proper lifestyle. Charlotte was afraid Viv would ruin her life if she worked in a kitchen.

How would that look to everyone we know? I absolutely will not allow it!

Viv remembered how upset Charlotte was. How angry Mimi was at Charlotte when Viv went running to her for comfort. A battle of wills. Oil and water. Two against one. It was always two against one. Even with two sisters, one Viv.

Cheffing was a noble career, Mimi had scolded Charlotte. Who didn't want to feed souls through their bellies?

Viv knew she was losing the battle against Charlotte's wishes, but when Mimi died unexpectedly, Viv found the courage to fight back. She used part of the money Mimi willed to her to fund culi-nary school. Defying Charlotte like she had never done before, she enrolled and moved to a tiny apartment near the school.

And now look.

Viv touched the next card that showed yet another angel. "What is this card about?"

"This card says you have another ally, but this one is totally different from the other. This relationship is not as simple as it seems on the surface. Everything must be in balance, you see. A circle. If you take, you must give. If you change one reality, you must give up another."

Amelia's words struck her as familiar; goosebumps covered her arms. Hadn't Floyd and Earlene said much the same thing? A life for a life. Change one reality, and you must give up another.

"This angel is all about guiding harmony and balance, but the card is reversed, which something has disturbed the balance. It has been turned on its head. Everything is upside down," Amelia added and then frowned.

"What?" Viv said. "What do you see?"

"Uhm, well, this person, this ally, they are … well, something unexpected happened and they were unable to right a wrong. See?" Amelia tapped the card. "Did someone you love pass unexpectantly?"

Viv felt the air escape her lungs.

"My, my grandmother," she said finally, stumbling over the words. "She had a stroke." Tears pooled in Viv's eyes. "I was supposed to be with her, and I wasn't. It's all my fault."

"I'm sorry to hear that. But you know, the veil is thin at times. Like now. Like this card in your spread. Don't assume she is lost to you forever. Love like that is powerful magic."

"But she wasn't magic," Viv said. "She was just Mimi."

Amelia raised a brow beneath her dark bangs. "Right," she said. "Not magic. That's just a figure of speech, anyway." Amelia returned her gaze to the cards on the table. "I told you this reading wasn't a simple spread," she added. "It's complicated. I wasn't kidding. Your life is a mess."

Viv nodded and closed her eyes. Something out of balance? Powerful magic? Mimi?

"Oh, and look," Amelia said, interrupting Viv's thoughts again. "There is a new person standing at the Lover's Crossroads. A guy. A new connection. Although it's not quite clear if he is a good thing. He might be a good thing. He could be a distraction. Or a test." Amelia laughed lightly and the flame in the candle on the table flickered. "I think all boyfriends are a test."

"I did meet a guy I like," Viv said, picturing Jake's funny little smile. "I hope he's not a test." Viv looked down at the table. Three more cards to go. She was no closer to knowing who the hex culprit was than when she sat down. No closer to proving Amelia was behind it, either. She had focused her mind on the question: Who put this hex on me? Who would do this to me? Why would they do this to me?

Maybe that was the problem, she thought. That was actually three questions, not one.

She looked across the table and saw her former classmate sitting across from her. Since their chance meeting on the sidewalk, Viv had been remembering little tidbits of her time spent around Amelia. She had been so focused on her own performance at school that she let many things slide from her awareness. Now, little skips of memory were surfacing after the mention of Chef Flame Thrower. The name had stuck in her mind.

Tidbits were popping up and landing like the taste of rotten food. She could picture Amelia in her sauce-stained chef's apron, with a smug and satisfied look at having finessed the velouté when most everyone else had failed their first few tries.

She could picture Amelia steaming with anger when another student received *best in class* for the seasonal tart assignment. And then again, literally stomping with anger when Amelia's *mille-feuille* Napolean oozed its layers onto the plate.

She had not thought much about it when a classmate's sponge cake turned into a brick, and Chef Mojo had pointed to the cornstarch on their station. There was not a flour bin in sight. Now she wondered—where was Amelia when these things happened? They had so easily marked the mishaps as learning curves, but were they?

Pranks were one thing. Sabotage another. But why would Amelia put a hex on her? A fire hex, no less.

She looked up as Amelia flipped her bangs out of her eyes. "Rivalry," she said, and Viv's eyes widened, wondering if she was reading her thoughts, but Amelia focused on the card on the table. "There's rivalry, competition, and jealousy," she said, tapping the card. "There is someone in your life who doesn't want you to win. Or at least they want you to surrender. I think they're hiding something. They're hoping you won't look too closely at what they have hidden from view. Once you see it, the secret is out of the bag. No, it's not a bag. I want to say—out of the book." Amelia looked away, as if listening. "Yes," she said. "A book. It's definitely a secret book. Someone is hiding a secret book."

The only rival she could think of who seemed to fit the jealous type was sitting right in front of her reading into her soul like a mind-meld with Mr. Spock. Viv sat back in the chair. She hadn't realized how tense she held her body. Her hands were still clasped in her lap, but her fingernails had dug little crescent moons into her flesh. She flexed her fingers, shifted her shoulders.

"And here is the Queen of Wands standing watch. She's not likely to surrender," Amelia said and laughed lightly. "She's energetic and confident, passionate and independent. Just like you." She looked up briefly. "This is you, Viv, facing your struggle head on," Amelia said. "And while you are being all of that, confident and independent—don't forget to give thanks."

Viv's eye widened. Give thanks. Like kneading gratitude into bread. Something she and Mimi did when they baked. With every punch and pull, she and Mimi threaded good thoughts and gratitude into the dough so everyone who ate a slice would feel loved. Viv felt overcome with emotion. Maybe Mimi really was closer than she thought.

"And look at this!" Amelia said. "The Shining Star. There is no brighter future than that! It's the best possible outcome for your situation."

Viv looked at the last card in the spread. A woman was pouring water from a pitcher into a pool of water. Above her were stars. One star was as big and bright as the sun. It was a feel-good card. A feel-good ending, even if she had no more information about the hex than when she had walked in the door.

Amelia looked down at the cards spread on the table, and Viv thought she saw tears rimming her eyelashes. "This is powerful stuff," she said and sniffled. "Your ordinary world has been ripped apart and burned to ashes, making you doubt yourself and your decisions. Other people doubt you. They may even seem to betray you. But here's the deal—the phoenix rises, and the star is born. The sun is out."

Amelia looked up and into Viv's blue eyes with her dark brown ones, a look as intense as a hawk on its prey. "I just want to say I'm sorry you can't cook right now," Amelia said. "With that fire thing and all. It's a shame because you really are a talented chef. For real. And, you know… I mean, I just," she stumbled and paused, and Viv leaned forward, hopeful. "Well, I'm just sorry that's all. And I hope everything turns out for the better."

Viv blew out the breath she didn't know she was holding.

Amelia's dark eyes flashed. "You just have to ask yourself, who do you want to be?" Her voice dropped to a breathless whisper. "Who is it that controls your destiny? You? Or someone else? And what are you going to do about it?"

Amelia closed her eyes and exhaled and then shivered her shoulders slightly, as if the power of the seer behind the cards was releasing her from its grasp.

Viv didn't know whether to applaud or say the Rosary.

"Wow," she said finally. "Where did you learn to do that?"

Amelia grinned and then shrugged. "I grew up around tarot readers," she said. "All the women in my family read cards. And palms. And tea leaves. And other stuff I don't need to go into." She motioned to the shelf with a nod. "There are many ways to see. But really, I did nothing but share what I saw in the symbols of the cards. You did the work. You picked the cards."

She smiled at Viv.

"Or maybe they picked you."

CHAPTER TWENTY

Viv set the bag on the kitchen table and began unpacking its contents. The concrete head of Neptune was still staring off into space from the table.

"That's quite the haul, young lady," Aunt Clara said.

"She wouldn't let me pay for the tarot reading," Viv said, looking around for a familiar face. "So, I bought a few things. I thought we could use them to dispel the hex."

"Excellent," Floyd said. Viv still didn't see where they were manifesting. They weren't in the wire fruit basket.

"How did it go?" Earlene asked. "Did you get a sense that she is the culprit?"

"I'm not sure. I couldn't figure out what her motive would be, but she has the skills, I think. That was the trippiest tarot reading," she replied, before adding, "Where are you?"

"Up here," Floyd said and whistled. An empty tin of Christmas popcorn on top of the fridge seemed an unlikely place to manifest, but the gourmet ancestors were unpredictable in that way. If there was any popcorn left inside, it would be stale, but the tin had inadvertently become part of her kitchen decor. Today they were manifesting in the three Campbell Soup kids in chef hats dancing on the front of the tin. She reached up and pulled the tin to the table.

"A black candle, a bottle of Florida Water, and a bag of rocks," Earlene said, as Viv unwrapped the items.

"It's not a bag of rocks," Viv protested. "There's black tourmaline, obsidian, hematite, and amethyst. I asked Amelia which stones helped against unwanted forces, and this is what I got."

"I haven't seen Florida Water since we were in high school," Floyd said. "I loved wearing that as cologne."

"We know," Clara said. "You reeked of sweet orange and clove."

"I smelled great," Floyd replied. "Reminds me of the barbershop, or at least the old men in the barbershop."

"That figures," Earlene said. "You loved hanging out with those old guys."

"I loved their old tales. Probably none of the stories were true, but as a kid with no daddy, I was all ears. I swept the floors every Saturday for a free haircut. But the company was what I craved."

"Did you get what we told you to get?" Earlene asked.

Viv pulled out her phone. "I couldn't get hair, a fingernail or shoe dust," she said and laughed. "But I got a selfie. I hope that will work. Her hair and fingernails are in the photo. And so are her shoes. If there's shoe dust on them, it's sort of in the picture." She put the phone on the table in front of the tin. She and Amelia were smiling into the camera, with the jars on the shelf right behind them. The labels were blurry, but Viv knew what they said. Heartspell. Ancient Love. Tears Yet Cried.

"Did any of that stuff come with instructions?" Clara asked.

"I thought you three were hunting the hex removal instructions," Viv answered. She was getting hungry and thinking about a dinner she couldn't cook. "I wonder if I could grill a steak outside," she said dreamily, knowing she didn't have a steak to grill. A trip to the grocery store seemed too much trouble for the off chance she would succeed. She got up and grabbed an apple from the basket and took an enormous, crunchy bite.

"I also bought some bath salts." Viv said with a full mouth. She lifted the lid to sniff. "It's called Dream Away. Smells like rosemary and lemon."

"Are you ready to get rid of this hex?" Clara asked.

Viv nodded. "I'm ready to get rid of the hex, but not so ready to lose you."

"Aww, sugar," Earlene said. "We feel the same way, but you've got a life to live, and you can't be a chef if you can't turn on the flame without it going wild. Besides, we don't know what's going to happen to us. We may just go back to where we came from."

"Wherever that is," Uncle Floyd interjected.

"And we may go nowhere," Clara added. "This is new ground for us, too."

Viv felt tears welling up. "I feel like Dorothy in the *Wizard of Oz*," she sniffed. "Goodbyes are hard. And we can't even hug."

"Aw, sugar," Earlene repeated. "Don't get soggy. We've got a job to do. Ready?"

Viv sniffed and nodded.

"Then there's no time like the present," Clara said. "Floyd is 99 percent confident that Amelia is the problem. We might as well try a remedy and see what happens. You're wasting away before our very eyes, Viv, living on leftovers and cold cuts."

Viv thought she was looking better than she ever had.

"Arrange the stones in a circle around the candle," Floyd commanded, stepping up to the task. "Light the candle and then write Amelia's name on a piece of paper. We'll burn the paper and sing a chant while looking at her photo. The magic of the *Book of Nines* is always sung into being."

Viv did as Floyd requested, a flash of fear hitting her mid-chest when she flicked the match and touched the wick of the candle. There was no predicting how a match flame would respond in her kitchen. The flame sparked and sputtered as the wick flickered into flame, but nothing else happened, except a whiff of scent that rose from the jar.

"Take three deep breaths and repeat after me," Floyd said. "As I will, so mote it be…"

Viv exhaled and repeated the words.

"What was sent now returns to thee."

Viv echoed the command.

"Maybe we should repeat it nine times," Earlene suggested.

"How about three?" Clara said. "That should be enough."

"As I will, so mote it be—what was sent now returns to thee," Viv said and then repeated it once again.

"Burn the paper," Floyd directed. "It's time!"

The paper caught and flared instantly, with little shreds of ash dancing up from the candle before settling back down on the table.

Viv pressed them with her fingertip to make sure they were not live embers.

"What shall we sing?" Earlene asked. "I don't know any chants."

"How about '*A Mighty Fortress is Our God*,'" Clara suggested and started humming. Her voice took up the chorus. "*A mighty fortress is our God, A bulwark never failing; Our helper He, amid the flood / Of mortal ills prevailing.*"

For Viv, the kitchen resounded with the hymn and three powerful voices, although they were all in her head. The final time they sang the chorus, Viv found herself singing along, a lone voice in the kitchen, probably way off key, but no less joyful. And then the room grew silent, save for the sputtering of the candle on the table.

She glanced at the popcorn tin. "Are you still here?" she whispered.

"Still here," Uncle Floyd said. "But I don't think it works that fast."

"Now, you go take a bath with your Dream Away bath salts," Clara said. "It will cleanse you of any magical residue left behind."

"When you wake up tomorrow," Uncle Floyd added, "the hex will be gone."

"Sweet dreams," Aunt Earlene said, and the three of them disappeared from the tin.

CHAPTER TWENTY-ONE

She opened her eyes when the sound came again. Still groggy from a night of restless dreaming, she realized someone was knocking at her door.

"Zoe!" Viv exclaimed when she finally made it to the door and swung it open. "What are you doing here?"

Zoe held out a Lokol Made bakery bag. "Peace offering," she said and smiled. "Jake shared your comments with me."

"Oh, shoot," she said, accepting the bag of goodies. "I wish he hadn't done that."

"No, it's a good thing," Zoe said. "I don't want to be the thorn between you two. And I need to clear the air. You were right to question my motives. I lied to you. I knocked the head off your statue. And if you don't want to invite me in, I understand, but I have things I need to get off my chest."

Viv eyed Zoe and then glanced over Zoe's shoulder. She could see no one else outside. Stepping aside, she motioned for the woman to enter and then directed her to the ancient couch.

"I'll take a cup of coffee if you're offering," Zoe said.

"Yeah, about that…" Viv started, then wondered if this morning would be the morning she could make coffee without setting her kitchen on fire.

"I have orange juice. Fresh squeezed."

Zoe shook her head. "Never mind. I'm just trying to calm my nerves."

"I'm not following," Viv said.

"I lied to you," Zoe started on an exhale of breath. "I looked you straight in the eye and told you I didn't know who that guy was. Well, I didn't. Not at first. But then he told me a strange tale. And then, well, you know what happened next. I was too frightened to say anything. No one wants to get dragged into something that horrible."

Viv felt the same way. An innocent bystander. A 10-107, dragged in like seaweed. As she listened to Zoe, she thought if there was anything in the world she could wish for and receive, it would be a piping hot cup of fresh brewed coffee.

"He looked familiar to me because he looks just like his father, who I was crazy about. He was a diver. I think I told you that. I didn't know him when he worked for Captain Fred. I didn't even know he did. I didn't come into the picture until after he left treasure hunting. His son said he had passed away a few months ago."

"I'm sorry to hear that," Viv replied.

Zoe nodded. "His last request was for his son to find me and deliver a message. At first, I didn't understand what he was talking about because I didn't know that part of his history. But then…"

"I'm going to make a pot of coffee," Viv said finally, defiantly. "Come back to the kitchen with me."

"Oh," Zoe said when she caught sight of the statue head in the middle of the table. "Sorry about that," she said. "I hope he wasn't one of your favorites."

Viv pulled out the old percolator she had discovered in the back of Aunt Viv's cupboard. The drip coffee maker had long since died a treacherous death.

"No. I haven't settled on a favorite yet," she said, grinning. "I may never. There are so many to choose from."

Zoe made a noise in her throat that wasn't a laugh and wasn't a harrumph but close to both. "I need to explain how and why that came about," she said, pointing to the head still on the table. She pulled out a chair and settled herself. "It's not something I would normally do."

Viv laughed. "You mean you don't normally knock the heads off statues in the middle of the night?" She washed the coffeepot, filled it with water and coffee grounds from the can in the fridge. "Here goes nothing," she muttered, electric cord in hand. She plugged it in and waited.

"I was hoping you'd think somebody ran into your yard with their car and hit that thing accidentally," Zoe said. "And, well… I was looking for something."

"Hidden treasure?"

Zoe sat up straight in the chair. "What do you know about that?"

Viv shrugged. "I was being sarcastic."

"But it was about hidden treasure! A necklace that went missing from one of Captain Fred's treasure dives decades ago. My old diver boyfriend was blamed for stealing it, even though he swore he hadn't but that didn't matter to Captain Fred."

Zoe paused momentarily. *"The treasure sleeps with Triton. Find the statue and you find the treasure. Viv Marston knows everything."*

"He gave you the entire message!" Viv yelped. "I knew you had all three parts!"

Zoe looked up with a furrowed brow. "How did you know? How did you know there were three parts? Oh well, it doesn't matter anyway," Zoe said, scratching her head. "There was no treasure in this one. Not in the one in my yard, either. We could spend a lifetime trying to find the right statue!"

POP!

Viv wondered if the popping noise was the gourmet ancestors about to make themselves known. Or maybe the popping sound was the Florida limestone-ridden water heating in the percolator. She looked at Zoe and crossed her fingers behind her back.

POP! POP!

"Oh, no!" Zoe said and pointed. "It's on fire! Your coffee pot's on fire!" She jumped up from her chair. "Where's your fire extinguisher?"

"I don't have one!" Viv wailed, more disappointed than ever.

"You can't pull the plug. It's on fire!"

The lid of the pot rattled. The clear knob on the top gurgled and gushed with an amber glow. A ring of orange fire danced beneath the pot and then spiraled upward. The lid blew open. Coffee grounds, still dry and untouched by water, flew out of the pot like sand in a storm.

Viv grabbed a glass from the counter that still held the dregs of tea.

"No! Don't!" Zoe yelled just as Viv tossed the tea at the fire, now marching toward the curtains above the sink. As the tea hit the live coffee pot, sparks sputtered, and an arc flashed across the counter like a rainbow unleashed from a cloud.

"Get back!" Zoe yelled. "Don't touch it! You'll get electrocuted!"

Viv jumped back just as the kitchen lights went out and a siren wailed in the distance.

CHAPTER TWENTY-TWO

"I see you're at it again," Jake said. He released the strap of his helmet so that it hung below his chin. "Another fire on Dolphin Street," he said, his tone dry and full of reproach. Viv noticed it said Palmer on the back of his jacket and his helmet, both in reflective tape. She probably wouldn't have recognized him otherwise. He was wearing full turnout gear.

"All she did was plug in her coffee pot," Zoe said. "I was right there when it happened."

"Thank goodness it tripped the main circuit breaker and killed the power to the house. Your neighbor heard popping sounds coming from the house and smelled smoke. I guess she's getting used to your mishaps."

Viv felt her cheeks get hot. "It happened so fast."

Zoe nodded, and Viv glanced at her with a warning look. Jake didn't need to know that she still didn't have a fire extinguisher, or that she had thrown tea at the spark.

He looked at the two of them and smiled. "Did you get your stories sorted? I sure hate for my two best girls to be at odds with each other."

"Best girls?" Viv said sardonically and then could have bitten off her tongue.

"We were just getting down to the crux of it when the fire started," Zoe offered. "We were needing coffee."

"Still needing coffee," Viv declared. "And breakfast. I think your pastries got in the way of my *mishap*." She emphasized the word.

"We could go down to Lokol Made," Zoe said.

"Or we could walk to Denny's," Viv countered.

"Denny's," Zoe said with a smile. "I haven't been there in eons."

"It's three blocks," Viv offered. "You up for that?"

"I'm up for that," Zoe said. "Can you join us, Jake?"

"I need to decontaminate my gear, but I could be there in about forty minutes."

"We'll save you a pancake," Viv said.

~~~~~

Viv waved to Bree, the cashier, who waved them to a table in the window. It was Viv's favorite spot.

"I haven't seen you lately," Bree said.

"Trying to save money. How are things going with you?" Viv asked with a knowing look.

Bree exhaled. "I guess I'll keep him," she said. "He promises there's no one but me. I'm just too overwhelmed with motherhood to see it. Honestly, he's about as good as the next one in line. So, there's that."

Viv grinned and nodded.

"Your usual?" The waitress asked, smiling at Viv.

"I need a menu, please," Zoe said. "What's your usual, Viv?"

"Three eggs over noisy, extra crispy hash browns and a waffle on the side," Viv said.

"Eggs over noisy?"

Viv shrugged. "Yeah. My eggs are usually noisy."

She didn't plan on explaining, and she wouldn't have to because the gourmet ancestors were absent. Not that Zoe would ever know they were present at all. The hex removal had failed. Failed horribly. And she guessed that neither Clara nor Earlene nor Floyd was eager to accept defeat face to face.

She looked around the table. At the salt and pepper. In the sugar dispenser. Around the bottles of condiments and syrup. No suspicious specters looking out.
~~~~~

"I'm sorry about your kitchen," Zoe said. "I don't think it's as bad as it seemed at first. I've never seen a fire behave that way, but I can't say I have a lot of experience. I got lucky that way. I never had a big fire in my food truck. You will need to replace some wiring and get a new coffeepot. That thing was ancient."

Viv nodded, uncommitted to any of it. She felt she would never be free of this hex in the kitchen. That she was destined to eat cold, raw food for the rest of her life. To write stories about other people making food while also making a name for themselves. Earlene said if they found a remedy and the hex disappeared, they might disappear as well. She didn't want that to happen either. It was all so frustrating and bittersweet. Aggravating and mind-boggling. A hex. A chef hex. She had to be the only one in the world with a problem like this.

Zoe was watching her closely. "You're really troubled about this, aren't you?"

"If you only knew," she answered, and then heaped sugar and cream into her coffee.

<div align="center">~~~~~</div>

"I'm ready to go over all that again," Viv said, when their second cup of coffee was poured. "You said your ex was blamed for stealing a necklace that he didn't steal. He knew who did, but he couldn't say who did and that caused friction between him and Captain Fred."

Zoe nodded. "That was before I knew either one of them, but evidently, the theft was never solved, and the friction never got settled. The antiquity authorities thought Captain Fred had the necklace and was trying to scam them, and they put him in jail. No one could find the necklace. No one could prove it was missing. No one could even prove it came up from the sea. They had to let him go. That's the gist of what his son said when he delivered the message."

"Must be some necklace," Viv said.

"Worth millions," Zoe agreed. "I saw the greed in that young man's eyes, and I knew he was headed for trouble. I didn't know what to do."

"How did one message become three?"

"He ripped it. Right there at Lokol Made. He gave me one piece. He put the other two in his backpack. He said no one could find the treasure without all three pieces. I guess he trusted me because his father did."

"You thought the last one was about me, didn't you? *Viv Marston knows everything.*"

"I did," Zoe agreed. "I thought you were involved. That's why I couldn't tell you about any of it. I didn't know whether you were pro or con."

"Gee, thanks," Viv said.

"Well, now I know better."

"My Aunt Viv was Captain Fred's bookkeeper," Viv said. "But I think there was something romantic going on. She kept the postcards he sent, and while they weren't risqué they did have an undertow if you catch my drift."

Zoe grinned. "This is making sense. It's possible my ex and Viv were romantically involved and that became part of the problem."

"I wondered the same thing," Viv said. "The police have a news story photo of the three of them together."

"That fits him," Zoe said. "He was a good-looking, smooth-talking ladies' man. I knew there had to be a reason he left Florida and never looked back. I didn't want to know. Not back then. I was young and foolish and head over heels. Not much younger than you are."

"So, what now? We have a crazy little riddle from the past that fits a piece of the picture in the present," Viv said through bites of her waffle, dripping with syrup. "How did he know where the treasure was if he didn't steal it? And is the treasure actually in the statue? Or does is lead to another clue? Like a pirate map where the X marks the spot? We can't ask Aunt Viv, and we can't ask your ex.

"The police have the message, the backpack that belonged to the victim, the murder weapon, and an old newspaper photo. All of that was in the backpack. I think whoever killed that guy, saw the message and the photo and tried to frame me, thinking I was the Viv Marston who knew everything. Detective Smith is smart. He figured that out and let me go with a warning to watch my back."

Zoe leaned forward. "How did you know about the messages, anyway? How did you know there were three?"

Viv eyed Zoe for a moment. Could she trust her? Seemed like Zoe was trusting *her*. Did it really matter now, pro or con?

"Tell me why you broke into the museum the other night," Viv asked, her eyes steady on Zoe's. "Why did you have to knock Captain Fred in the head? What were you after?"

Zoe sputtered into her coffee. "Who told you that?"

"Katarina told me that. Let me think. She said, *ask your friend Zoe Diamante. Ask her what happened to the artifact.*"

"What artifact?"

"The harpoon is missing from the wall. She saw you running out of the back of the museum just before the alarm went off."

Zoe exhaled. "Well," she snapped. "That's not true. I never stepped two feet inside the back door. Which was open by the way. I heard someone, panicked, and ran. I never hit Fred. I never even saw him. Honest. Honest to Pete."

"What were you looking for?"

"I have a key," Zoe said and reached into her pocket. She pulled out the heart-shaped keychain Viv had noticed her clasping a few days prior. Viv had watched Zoe's knuckles go white when they talked about the murder. She saw the small key that hung from the loop. "He sent it with his son, but I have no idea what this key fits. The keychain is from a Heart concert we went to a thousand years ago. I bought it for him. I called him Barracuda. I was his Little Queen." Zoe sighed and lowered her eyes. "He kept it all this time. I thought maybe…"

"You thought what, Zoe?" Viv pushed gently. "That it fit a box of treasure at the museum? That you could walk in with a key and out with a fortune? A treasure that doesn't belong to you, I might add. And probably didn't belong to your ex, either."

"Oh, now that sounds so foolishly dumb," Zoe said and put her head in her hands. "I don't know what I was thinking. I can understand why he kept the keychain all these years. I can even understand why he sent it back to me. The heart was sentimental. He wanted me to know how he felt. But what does the key fit? I thought, I thought … well, I don't know what I thought. I really did love him. I did."

Viv felt her heart thud for a couple of achy beats. Was she satisfied with Zoe's explanation? Could she be? How would she know? Everyone was lying about something. Everybody lied about some truth they wanted to hide from view. She sure was.

"I found one of the messages at the park that morning," Viv answered finally. "I'm guessing it was accidentally dropped out of the backpack. The birds were pecking at it, so I picked it up, but I didn't even look at it then. The police found the other one *in* the backpack, which is now in their possession."

"So, the police have those two pieces of the riddle?"

Viv shook her head. "Just the one."

"What? You didn't give them the one you found?"

"You didn't hand over the one you have."

"Well, I will," Zoe said, glaring defiantly at Viv.

"Well, I will too," Viv said, glaring back.

A moment passed before they both giggled.

"It's a million-dollar necklace," Zoe whispered. "I mean, really. What a girl couldn't do with a million bucks."

"It's not worth dying over," Viv said.

"No, it is not, young lady," Aunt Clara barked. Viv looked down at her plate. The three decorative maraschino cherries she had pushed off her waffle were glaring back—the three rosy-red faces of Clara, Earlene, and Floyd. "It is absolutely not worth dying over," Clara repeated. "If you don't stop these dangerous shenanigans right now, we're going to manifest in Charlotte's raisin toast and tell her exactly what's going on."

"You can't do that! Your magic only works with me!" She squeezed her eyes shut, regretting her outburst.

"My magic? What are you talking about?" Zoe asked. "I'm not saying we find the necklace and keep the money, I'm saying … well, I guess I was saying that. But I was only rehearsing the thought in my mind."

"I wonder if there is any INSIDER information we might have access to," Viv said loudly. "Like information from ANOTHER source."

Zoe raised a brow.

"We are dead but not deaf," Floyd said.

"Speak for yourself," Earlene countered. "Your hearing wasn't good when you were Viv's age. It hasn't gotten better."

"I only pretended not to hear *you*," Floyd said, his nasal-whine higher than usual. "I prefer to listen to people who have something to say."

"You prefer to listen to people who have something to say about *you*, and only if it strokes your ego!"

Viv thought the cherries shook in the plate.

"Stop bickering, you two! We have a pickle in a poke on our hands. Our Viv has caught the eye of a ruthless killer, and we cannot help her solve both hex and murder if we're arguing about who is the vainest of you two. If Mama were here, she'd cut a switch and tan your hides!"

Viv blinked. She had to remind herself they were from a different era.

"Just because your Aunt Viv couldn't keep her men straight and in ship-shape order doesn't mean we're lost at sea," Clara continued. "You need to focus on that last message, Viv. What did your Aunt Viv know? Why did she know it? Something is fishy in this paradise."

"Right," Viv said.

"Right," Zoe echoed.

"What if she stole the necklace?" Viv asked.

"She who?" Zoe looked around the room. "Who are you talking to? Are you okay?"

"I'm talking about Aunt Viv. Could that be what your ex meant? Viv Marston knows everything. Did he know Viv had burgled the necklace? That would fit why your ex couldn't out her. A— because who would believe it? B— because she and the Captain were a thing. And C— because I think he and Viv were also a thing and you can't rat out your lover. Honor among thieves and all that."

"Interesting points," Zoe said. "The treasure sleeps with Triton."

Viv wrinkled her nose. "It's hard for me to go there."

"Point taken," Zoe said. "I have a similar feeling, especially since C is probably true."

"Now we're getting somewhere juicy," Earlene said, and Viv watched as a cherry rolled into the syrup pooled on her plate. A second cherry followed.

"I feel like Esther Williams in the *Million Dollar Mermaid*," Floyd said. "Remember her Cypress Gardens TV show? What was that called?"

"*Esther Williams at Cypress Gardens*," Clara said sharply.

"I especially liked the prince," Floyd said.

"*Meeee too*," Earlene purred. "Fernando Llamas. Dreamy."

Viv grinned at her plate.

"I found an old bookkeeping ledger in the office and probably the reason for Aunt Viv's obsession with statuary," Viv said, pushing her nearly empty plate to the side. She wasn't going to eat the cherries. "I think Captain Fred gifted a statue to Aunt Viv every year around Christmas. Or at least, the company gifted the statuary. I'm wondering if the two fit a timeline. The statue and the hidden treasure."

"Good guess," Zoe said.

"Excellent deduction," Clara added.

"Wait a minute," Viv added. "How old was Katarina when the jewel thief thing went down?"

"Gosh. She would have been in her very early teens, I guess."

"A teenager without a mom, who thought the sun rose and set on her father's shoulders but could never get enough of his attention."

"That sounds like our Katarina."

"Maybe someone put the necklace in the statuary shortly after the heist. If we can match a statuary purchase around the same time as the heist, we can figure out what statue your ex was talking about in the message. Obviously, finding the right one is not as easy as we think."

"I wonder how many statues from the 1990s are left?" Zoe asked. "We're down two. Mine and yours. Neither had treasure inside."

"Are we on the hunt for treasure? Or are we looking for a killer?" Viv asked.

"Don't forget the hexer," Floyd added. "We're still on the trail of the hex, Viv. You can't lose sight of that."

Viv grabbed her coffee cup in both hands and leaned her back against the chair. "I think the harpoon missing from the wall in the

Sunken Treasure Museum is what the police were looking for. Katarina noticed it was gone, and she reported the theft to the police. What if she staged the break-in so the Captain wouldn't get caught?"

"Caught for what, exactly?" Zoe asked.

"For the murder in Anchor Park," Viv said, feeling cold in the pit of her stomach. "The missing harpoon could be the weapon that killed our guy. Or it could be a red herring. I don't have evidence, but the police do." She exhaled sharply. "He's tough. He looks old and crippled, but I think he's acting half the time.

"Think about it," Viv continued. "Captain Fred sees this out-of-town guy and thinks it's the old diver. Just like you did. He thinks his old nemesis is back. It spurs him to uncontrollable anger. Fred demands to know where the necklace is hidden. He's eager to close that impasse after all these years. But this young guy doesn't know. He only has a weird riddle he's not going to share with Fred. They have heated words. Fred lures him to the anchor and *boom*, Fred lets the harpoon fly."

"What madness," Zoe said. "All this for a necklace?"

"Not just any necklace," Viv said. "Part of the Bella Dona jewels. One of the biggest sunken treasures in Caribbean history. Whoever returns this necklace to its rightful owner—which I am sure is not Captain Fred—goes down in history as a hero. A legend. A luminary in their field."

"A rock star," Zoe added. "Doesn't everybody want to be a rock star? But where is the statue? Where are we going to find Triton?"

Viv chuckled. "You must not know much about Greek mythology for all your Greek ancestry, Zoe Diamante. Poseidon was the Greek god of the sea. The Romans called him Neptune. And he had legs. Triton was his son, and he was the original merman. He had fins and fish scales. Most people think Neptune and Triton are interchangeable, but they're not. You've been looking for the jewels in the wrong place."

"A+!" Aunt Clara said in a singsong voice. "I knew you were paying attention in school. Now go get 'em."

Viv laughed, and she heard the little pop she was accustomed to hearing. Breakfast was over, and the gourmet ancestors had vanished.

"Hey ladies," Jake said, snaking his way through the tables and chairs. "That took me longer than I thought it would." He frowned at Viv's empty plate. "I missed breakfast."

"Oh, you missed more than that," Viv said and smiled.

"They serve all day," Zoe said. "Order up. We're headed back to Viv's house for a job left undone. You can catch up with us there."

CHAPTER TWENTY-THREE

Viv aimed for the statue of Triton. The statue was not far from the ant mound, and she was cautious of where her feet were placed. King Neptune, the one Zoe had attacked the other night, was several yards away. The shovel hit the concrete, bounced, and then the head of Triton rolled to the ground leaving his enormous tail still anchored to the ground. She peeked inside the hollow space.

"No, it can't be! No jewels!" she yelled. "I was certain that's where they would be!"

Zoe shrugged. "It was a good guess. At least you knew your mythology."

"Two down, ten to go," Viv said. "We might as well check all the statues on Aunt Viv's lawn. The treasure has to be in one of them!" She had felt tremendous satisfaction whacking the concrete with all her might. Take that, you hex! Take that, you hexer! Take that, you ugly concrete!

"You really think the necklace is in one of these?" Zoe motioned to the expanse of statuary dotting Viv's lawn.

She nodded. "I have two theories. One, if Captain Fred faked the heist to scam the authorities, he would have hidden them completely out of sight. Knowing what we know about Captain Fred, I'd say that is entirely possible. A safe deposit box would be out of the question as a hiding place. Too risky. And who would pay the rental? Buried treasure is cliché. Besides, land excavation is happening all the time. He wouldn't risk it being unearthed.

"I say he put it in a statue and then gifted it to Aunt Viv. No one the wiser for what it held. Not even Aunt Viv. Then he blamed your ex for stealing it. A perfect foil in his scam. No wonder your ex left town." Viv wiped the sweat off her forehead.

"I think it's possible Captain Fred came to believe that story even if it wasn't true. That your ex was guilty of stealing the necklace, I mean. Captain Fred told the story of the jewel thief from that angle day-in and day-out at the museum. He told the same story in his book. What if that became his reality? It happens, you know. People tell themselves a story so many times they come to believe it. One hundred percent. And so does everybody else. Why would they believe anything else?"

"And your other theory?" Zoe asked.

"Aunt Viv. Everything seems to come full circle back to Aunt Viv."

"But she never revealed the theft or where the necklace was hidden," Zoe said. "Why? If she knew. And if her time on earth was up, what did it matter?"

"Who knows? I didn't know her, so I can't say who she was on the inside. Maybe she thought the jewels were better left hidden. Maybe she thought lives would be ruined if the necklace ever came to light. Or perhaps she died without being able to reveal their location. It could be wrong she was unable to make right."

Viv leaned on the shovel and shifted her feet. Hadn't Amelia said something similar when they were drawing cards?

"Your ex had a very different story," Viv continued. "He either didn't tell his son, or his son didn't tell you. Either way, that page of the story is gone. He didn't know Aunt Viv had passed, I don't think, so he may have been cautious in case it implicated her. It sounds like he was hoping there would be a resolution. You know—
—to both the theft and the triangle friction. Otherwise, why did he send his son with that message? What did it matter after all this time? Why not let sleeping dogs lie? Or sleeping jewels, since we're talking about hidden treasure.

"It sounds complicated," Zoe said quietly. "Who knows why people make the final wishes they make."

Viv nodded, dragging the shovel to the next statue in her line of sight.

"I think the son started out with pretty good intentions to honor his father," Zoe said as they walked side-by-side. "Greed got a hold of him when he realized how valuable the necklace was. He even said he'd share the spoils with me. Fifty-fifty if I helped him find it."

"Nice guy," Viv muttered.

"No, I didn't get the impression he was such a nice guy," Zoe said. "I don't think he would share. He was a braggart. He seemed to be all about getting rich and being better than everyone else."

"He bragged about it to the wrong person," Viv added. "He bragged to Captain Fred. The one person who had more than a vested interest in finding the jewels. That was his fatal mistake. Don't kill the messenger. Especially before he gives up the goods," Viv added, and shuddered involuntarily.

"Wait a minute," Viv said after a moment's pause. "Do you still have that keychain with you? The heart with the key?"

Zoe nodded and reached into her pocket.

"I think I know what it fits," Viv said, reaching for the key. "I bet it fits the box in Aunt Viv's office. It's not a statue, but…" She held out her hand and watched Zoe's grip tighten against the key.

"Really?" Viv said. "Really, Zoe? We're in this deep and you still think I'm the bad guy?"

Zoe narrowed her eyes. "Greed makes people do weird things."

"Greed makes people nutty as a fruitcake," Viv snapped. "What is your problem? Do you want to solve this mystery with your ex or not?"

A movement caught her eye. Viv turned to see Martie Grim. "What are you two doing now?" Martie asked as she joined them in the yard. "So, this is your house, Viv?"

"If I can manage to keep from burning it down," Viv muttered. She glanced at Zoe, noticing the key was gone. Back in Zoe's pocket, she presumed.

"I heard on the scanner that Dolphin Street had caught fire again. You really have some bad luck that way, don't you?" She didn't wait for an answer, but Viv wasn't going to offer one. What business was it of anybody's?

"I had to come see for myself." Martie eyed the headless statue and waved to Zoe. "Why are you knocking down your statues?"

Viv looked at Zoe and back at Martie. She was out of explanations.

"You really have a way a showing up when something interesting is happening," Viv said, realizing the moment she said it that her tone was more accusatory than she intended. "I only meant that scanner of yours puts you in the middle of the action all over town, doesn't it? You're everywhere!"

"I like to know what's going on, that's all," Martie said defensively. "Sometimes you have to go see for yourself. You never know when they might need an extra hand. Emergencies can turn from bad to worse pretty fast."

Viv nodded. "I really didn't mean to sound rude or ungrateful. You're just Martie-in-the-Know."

"In the know," Martie repeated. "That's me. Martie-in-the-Know." She chuckled to herself as if the label felt right for a bookworm bookstore owner.

"Why are you knocking down the statues?" she repeated.

"Because they're too heavy to move in one piece," Viv said finally.

"Oh," Martie said, seemingly satisfied. "I can see that would be true. I could take them off your hands if you wanted me to. My brother has a little forklift."

"Thanks," Viv said, now unsure which way to take the conversation. "I'll think about it."

Martie wrinkled her brow. "You'll think about it? Are you okay, Viv? You might be in shock after the fire. There's no reason to ruin all these statues just because you can't move them with your bare hands. I think you need to get out of the sun and have a glass of water."

She reached for the shovel in Viv's hands. Viv froze. Their eyes locked. Panic rose up Viv's spine.

Why was Martie everywhere?

Did she know more than she let on? Martie-in-the-Know.

Viv tightened the grip on the shovel.

Martie had details about the crime in Anchor Park even before the police arrived. She thought Zoe had something to do with it.

Viv remembered Martie had suspected Zoe of having something to do with the victim. Of having secrets to hide. And Zoe did. How did Martie know? Did information come across the scanner that put Zoe in her mind? Or was there another reason?

Martie was in the parking lot when the museum got broken into and Captain Fred bashed on the head. She said something then that triggered Viv's curiosity.

If they're after the statue, they won't find what they're looking for in there.

Martie claimed she was repeating what she had heard on the scanner, but was that true?

And now she was here. Standing in Viv's yard with her hands on the shovel.

Did Martie know more than she should?

Martie knew history. She knew families. Martie knew places, people, and things. She was the town's institutional memory bank. Martie-in-the-Know.

What had she said about Anchor Park? Something about hurricanes and flooding and the Spanish anchor Captain Fred donated.

Another one bites the dust, she had said and laughed. *Disaster waiting to happen.*

"Viv?" Martie was tugging at the shovel handle. "You okay, Viv? I think you need to get out of the sun."

Martie smiled, and Viv's angst vanished. She was letting her imagination take over. She was letting stress and fear and angst make poor decisions. Just like Amelia said.

Viv relaxed her fingers. Martie Grim was just Martie-in-the-Know. Wasn't that all she was?

"Shade is not a bad idea," Viv said finally, and pushed the handle in Martie's outstretched hand. "Water sounds good, too."

She glanced behind her as she passed the mermaid on the sidewalk and then opened the door to the house. Both Zoe and Martie were following her, the shovel still clenched in Martie's hand.

It was definitely cooler inside. She poured three teas from the pitcher in the fridge. The electricity was still out, and the inside of the fridge was dark.

The kitchen smelled of electrical smoke and something else Viv couldn't identify. Charred coffee grounds, perhaps. The outlet where the coffeepot had sparked was black. Jake and his team had axed a hole in the wall beside it looking for flame behind the wall. The hem of the curtains above the sink was singed; the little fuzzy balls in the fringe shriveled like marshmallows that had gotten too close to the flame. There was soot and white powder on the floor. The back door stood open to help air out the stench, but the screen door was closed to keep out the bugs.

"You're going to need help to clean this up and I'm happy to help," Martie said, leaning the shovel against the back door frame. "The fire must not have been that bad, or they would have cordoned off the room. You won't be able to cook with the electricity off, but then, you said you were doing raw foods anyway, so I guess that won't matter."

Viv nodded and guzzled her tea. Lukewarm tea from a lukewarm refrigerator.

"I'll be right back," she said and left the table. When she returned, the box from Aunt Viv's file cabinet was in her hands and hope was in her heart. Zoe's key had to fit the box. It just had to. It's the only thing that made sense. She glanced at Zoe and nodded. Zoe looked at the box and then back at Viv.

"Why would this key open your Aunt Viv's jewelry box?" Zoe said. "What were the two of them hiding?"

"I don't know," Viv said, as Zoe pulled the keychain from her pocket and held it out, "a love affair maybe, but there is only one way to find out." Viv noticed that Zoe's hands shook, and then she noticed hers were shaking, too. The thought of discovery rattled her so hard her fingers twitched around the key. What if it was just a bunch of trinkets inside—or worse, something really private, something she had no right to see? Like love letters between Zoe's ex and Aunt Viv. Or worse. Her imagination threatened to run free and wild.

She took a deep breath and slid the key into the lock.

The locked clicked. The lid flew open.

"Well, that's a shame," Martie said, peering over Viv's shoulder. "Somebody already beat you to it."

The box was empty. The little mirror on the inside of the lid reflected a tiny ballerina poised in an eternal arabesque frozen in time.

"What are you looking for?" Martie asked. "And why is there

a head of a statue in the middle of the table?"

"It's a long story," Zoe said, her words full of disappointment.

"A long story," Viv echoed and then burst into tears.

CHAPTER TWENTY-FOUR

Viv looked up to see Katarina Becker standing at her back door. It was more than a startling surprise.

"I heard there was a fire," Katarina called from behind the screen. "I wanted to make sure everybody was okay. I tried the front door, but it was locked. Then I heard voices back here. I thought I'd save you a few steps to the front door and back."

"Who doesn't own a scanner in this town?" Viv said and glanced at Martie, who shrugged. The bookworm printed on her shirt wiggled.

"I gotta go," Martie said. "I need to get the bookstore open before the UPS guy gets there." She opened the door and traded places with Katarina, who stepped through the doorway like a star stepping onto a movie set. A set from the 1970s. She looked around as if searching for something, her eyes scanning the room quickly.

Martie poked her head back in the door. "Let me know if you need help to move those statues. My brother will come over with his forklift. I'll take them if you don't want them." She let the screen door slam and Katarina flinched.

Viv looked at Katarina with tear-stained cheeks. "I'd offer you a glass of tea, but I just poured the last of it."

Katarina shrugged and looked around the kitchen. She glanced at the sink and singed curtain, the droopy ball fringe. "Jake said you were accident-prone."

"Jake? Jake told you that?"

"Oh, you didn't know?"

"Know what?" Viv asked.

"We date. On and off. But you could say we're an item."

Viv nearly choked on the air in her throat. Jake never mentioned Katarina. He never said anything about a girlfriend!

"Oh," Viv said thinly. "I didn't know."

"I heard it was always more *off* than on," Zoe said, pointedly.

Viv sensed the discord.

Katarina glanced at Zoe and frowned. "He's way too young for you," she said.

"He's way too young for you," Zoe shot back.

Viv bit her bottom lip. This could go wrong fast.

"Tell us why you're here," Zoe added. "I know you're not here for a welfare check."

Katarina shifted her weight. She was still standing inside the door that led to the patio in the backyard. The screen door was closed, but Viv could see the bright red hibiscus that lined the patio brick. A fountain with concrete fish leaping above the bowl sat nestled in the overgrown hedge, the water pumping apparatus long dead and silent.

"That's not friendly," Katarina said. "That is exactly why I am here. A welfare check. Viv is *my* new friend. I even gave her a ride home the other day. Didn't I, *Viv Marston?*"

Something about the emphasis made Viv's skin turn clammy.

"I even brought you a housewarming gift," Katarina said, thrusting a shopping bag into Viv's hands. Viv noticed the Corks and Curds Charcuterie logo stamped on the front, a fluff of tissue paper spilling from the top.

Katarina's gaze landed on the head of Neptune still sitting in the center of the table and then on the box still nestled in Viv's hands.

"Where did you find that?"

Viv didn't miss more than a beat. "It was mine from when I was little," she lied, not sure why.

"I had one just like it," Katarina said.

"Didn't we all?" Viv added, closing the lid of the box. "And thank you," she added, trying to rouse her enthusiasm over the gift bag. Her nose was stuffy, and her eyes felt hot. The tears had been the tipping point of the tension building all day, and she still felt brittle, like a handful of angel hair pasta before landing in a rolling boil.

She peeked inside the bag and pulled out the items. A box of sesame crackers, a jar of pickled ginger, a tiny box of ceremonial tea, and a miniature jar of hot honey. The sticker on three of the items said, *50%* off and the attempt to remove it seemed half-hearted.

"That's very thoughtful," Viv said, setting the bag aside.

"Of course," Katarina said. "That's what friends are for." She glanced over her shoulder at Zoe. "I know cooks love an odd item in their kitchen. It inspires their creativity."

Viv blanched at the word. She never wanted to be called a *cook*. Not because the word was inferior—because it wasn't, but more because her aspirations were much grander.

"Really, Katarina," Zoe said impatiently. "Why are you here? We were in the middle of something that doesn't concern you."

"Oh, but I think it does," she replied, her gaze landing on the table once again. "I've been meaning to ask why you broke into the museum and tried to kill my father. It's a good thing the alarm went off when it did. I saw you running out of the back door of the museum. You're lucky I didn't have the police arrest you right then."

Zoe glared at the woman. "I didn't do either of those things. The back door was open. I peeked in to see if everything was okay. I never saw your father."

"Likely story," Katarina muttered and turned to Viv. "I really came by because I understand you had a little run-in with the police. I wanted to see if there was anything I could do. Maybe I could use my clout to help."

"That's very kind," Viv said. "But no—"

"Of course," Katarina interrupted. "That's what friends do. My father and I give generously to all the police fundraising events. Fostering respect in the law enforcement community serves everyone."

"But no," Viv repeated, knowing she was about to tell another brazen lie. She glanced briefly at Zoe. "I didn't have a run in with the police at all. Actually, I'm helping Detective Smith with the last investigation before he retires. He and my Aunt Viv were friends."

Katarina shifted her weight again. "Is that so? I guess I heard the wrong gossip, then. Didn't I tell you that you can't believe everything you hear?"

Viv nodded. "Detective Smith and I are doing a deep dive to see if I can remember anything about the crime scene that might be helpful. Like maybe I missed something important."

"You mean like with hypnosis?"

"Not quite that dramatic, but a deep dive for details. Like the wheelchair tracks I saw at the water's edge."

"You mentioned that, and I told you we went to the water to watch the fish last Tuesday."

"It rained all day Tuesday," Viv said. She was bluffing but Katarina wouldn't know that.

"Rain? I—I don't remember it raining last Tuesday," Katarina stuttered. "Yes, I guess it did rain. I guess I'm getting my days mixed up. We go to the park almost every day."

"But you didn't go that day—the day I found the body. That's what you said. You would have found the body yourself if you had."

"That's right!" Katarina nodded, her ponytail bobbing. "We didn't go to the park that day."

"But I did," Viv continued. "And he wasn't wearing his backpack when I found him. He was wearing it in the photo. So how did it wind up at the marina? On a rental boat? Rented by Viv Marston!"

Katarina gasped. "No way! Someone tried to frame you?"

"The backpack had incriminating evidence inside. Evidence even the killer didn't know was there. Like the smell of manatee bait and a message on a piece of paper."

"A message about Viv Marston?"

"No," Viv said, smiling. "A message about the treasure. A clue about where to find it."

Katarina's smile spread slowly, and Viv recognized the curl of amusement in her lip, one corner of her mouth higher than the other. She had seen the same smug smile while locked in Katarina's car for a brief moment, the minty scent of a custom-made scent filling her nose. Katarina had enjoyed holding Viv captive for a few uncomfortable seconds.

"Where is it?" Katarina's voice boomed in the quiet of the

room. She glared at Zoe. "He told you where it was hidden. I know it!"

"Who are you talking about?" Zoe replied.

"You know who I'm talking about. He came strutting into town with his unfinished business. He swaggered into the museum like he owned the place. Bragged about knowing the whereabouts of a necklace worth millions. I saw him talking to you. I know he told you where it was hidden!"

"If he did, I'm not telling you."

"You better tell me," Katarina snarled. "The necklace doesn't belong to you. It's mine. It's my inheritance. Not yours!"

"It's neither," Zoe said, rising from the table to stand between Viv and Katarina, who was still near the door. "The necklace belongs to whoever owns that shipwreck. And that's not you," Viv was surprised by how calm Zoe sounded. Viv's pulse was pounding in her ears.

"It is mine," Katarina declared. "That necklace is *my* inheritance. I want it back! Tell me where it is or you'll wind up just like him!"

"Just like him?" Viv echoed.

Katarina turned a hard gaze to Viv. "You couldn't keep out of it, could you, *Viv Marston*? Just like your aunt. Always trying to wedge yourself between me and my father. Always wanting to be his favorite. His precious pearl. His Bella Dona in the flesh."

Viv tensed.

She saw madness in Katarina's eyes. Not a wild look, not a raving glare—but a glassy stare from two cold, gray eyes in a face chiseled by self-control. Her restraint was breaking down. Her control was dissolving into a sea of loathing, and untenable greed, and resentment for something she could never have. Viv sensed that this was not all about the jewels. That it was never about the jewels. She saw the hard set in Katarina's jaw. This was not about the necklace. This was about a gnawing, frozen need. The unmet craving of a daughter who never got enough of what she wanted. Attention. Acceptance. Her father's undivided love. His love was for the sea. Only the sea. And his sunken treasures.

Zoe's voice broke into the quiet. "What are you going to do with it? Give it to Captain Fred? Are you hoping that if you return his long-lost Bella Dona jewels you will finally win his admiration? His only child. The daughter he shoved aside for something more precious." Her words bit into the moment, harsh and chiding; her tone as acrid as the lingering smell of smoke.

In a whirlwind of motion, Katarina grabbed the shovel where it leaned against the door and swung it at Zoe's head. Zoe ducked, but the blade hit her squarely in the arm, and Zoe buckled under the pain.

"Stop!" Viv yelled. "We don't know where the necklace is! Or where it's hidden! We don't know who stole it!"

Katarina looked up as if surprised by Viv's intrusion.

"I stole the necklace," Katarina said, her breath ragged in her chest. "I took it. I took it so he would blame everyone else. I knew he would drive everyone away. He would shut out everyone he suspected of stealing it. One-by-one he would cast them off like a dead fish on a line. And then he would belong to me. Just me." Katarina took a sharp inhale of breath as if the words had rushed from her mouth without her permission and she could breathe them back in.

"*You* stole the necklace?" Viv asked, her eyes wide.

"And then Viv Marston stole it from me! Viv knew I took it! She tortured me with her silence. She knew silence was more damning than any accusation. He wouldn't believe her anyway. My father would never believe her over me!"

Viv inhaled. "Aunt Viv!" She glanced at Zoe, who was still holding her arm, but she wasn't bleeding.

"The treasure sleeps with Triton," Zoe whispered. "Not the king. Not Neptune. Neptune was the Captain. Triton was next in line for the throne! The treasure was Viv!"

Viv's brow wrinkled with confusion. "You mean there is no necklace? There is no necklace in the statue?"

"In the statue?" Katarina blurted, her eyes wide. "*Viv Marston knows everything.* The necklace is in a statue! That's where she hid it! It's in one of her tacky old statues!"

Katarina turned and shoved the door with her foot. The screen door swung wide.

Viv and Zoe exchanged worried glances. "Are you okay?" she whispered.

Zoe nodded, reached for the phone in her pocket, and Viv

could see she was calling 911.

Torn between hiding in safety with the doors locked and watching the drama unfold on the lawn, Viv followed Katarina outside.

Katarina swung at the leaping dolphin near the tangerine tree and then watched as the pieces exploded in midair. She screamed like a wounded dog, and then moved toward Viv, shovel clenched in her hand. "Where is it?" She screamed as she swung at the pelican statue in her way. The concrete crumbled, but there was no necklace hidden inside. Katarina stumbled with the shovel and then marched toward Viv.

Viv stepped back in terror.

"Where is it?" Katarina bellowed.

Katarina stopped a few feet away from Viv, her eyes caught by the statue on the sidewalk. Turning, she swung with a fury that made Viv cover her head and duck. The mermaid—the tired, chipped mermaid statue that led the way to the front door shattered. White concrete and dust scattered. And there among the shards was the necklace. The missing Bella Dona jewels.

Katarina screamed and dropped to her knees.

The memory of Uncle Floyd's voice filled Viv's ears.

The Million Dollar Mermaid.

The old Esther Williams movie he mentioned in passing. Had he known? He couldn't have. But Aunt Viv must have known of the movie. *The Million Dollar Mermaid* with a secret.

Sirens wailed and whooped, and Viv recognized Detective Smith's car pulling into the driveway, a police cruiser behind it, and a familiar truck bringing up the rear. She returned her gaze to the jumble of gold on the sidewalk at Katarina's feet. The necklace was more magnificent than she could have imagined. What looked like gold and diamonds and emeralds and rubies sparkled in the Florida sunshine.

Viv knew she was looking at a priceless antiquity. A million dollars in gold and jewels and history. A coveted treasure that was lost and found. Stolen. Lost and found again. The jewels in the necklace sparkled, and Viv knew she was looking at something to live for.

Something to die for.

Something she didn't want any part of.

Detective Smith came up behind them with Jake was right behind. Martie Grim stood at the curb.

Martie! Viv thought. She must have known Katarina was up to something. She must have left when she did to call for help.

The detective moved behind Katarina Becker, still kneeling on the sidewalk, enraptured by the tangle of gold and diamonds clutched in her hands.

She didn't resist when he pulled her hands from the necklace and cupped his hand under her elbow. She didn't struggle when he slipped the handcuffs around her wrists, the gleam of the jewels still holding Katarina's attention. And Viv's too.

They stood in a line on the sidewalk at 13 Dolphin Street. Viv, Zoe, and Jake, with shattered concrete at their feet, watching as the hard, controlled mask that was Katarina Becker fell away, and a sad little girl stood in her place. Even her stature seemed diminished.

All that, and she still didn't have what she wanted.

"Wait," Viv said, as the detective turned Katarina toward the car.

"Please! I need to know why," she said, her eyes on the woman. "Why did your father kill him? The guy didn't know where the necklace was hidden. He had clues but didn't know how to solve them! He didn't know where to look! He was just an unlucky kid following an old treasure hunt story. Why did Fred kill him?"

"Fred?" Katarina looked at Viv with vacant gray eyes.

"Not Fred. Not my father. He had already slain his eel. It was me. Me and my enemy. It was either him … or me."

Viv flashed to the tale of the moray eel Captain Fred had told. The eel and the treasure the eel guarded for eons beneath the sea. Captain Fred had said the same thing. The moray or the diver. One would fight to the death. And the other would have the gold.

CHAPTER TWENTY-FIVE

Viv's yard emptied of cops and killers and bystanders. And suddenly, she felt empty herself. What had started out as a stroll in the park on a sunny Saturday had led her on an unexpected path. Murder. Secrets. Unrequited love. Unrequited everything, it seemed, and now, a yard full of concrete rubble. She glanced up and saw Jake standing quietly just out of reach. He smiled and Viv felt her heart flutter. Without even realizing what she was doing, she closed the gap between them and buried herself in his chest. He smelled of a seaside resort. Salt and seaweed and coconut. Maybe a lingering touch of smoke.

"Let's get you inside," he said, pulling her from his chest and wrapping his arm around her shoulder. She could have stood there buried in his scent, but she let him lead her toward the house.

"Katarina," she whispered. "She said you were dating. I didn't mean… I don't want… " Her words fell away. She didn't know what she didn't mean or didn't want.

"There was never anything special between us," Jake answered. "Katarina uses people, and I found myself on that list a few times. There was never anything romantic. There was never anything good."

Viv felt her entire body sigh with relief.

They found themselves at the kitchen table, the place where everyone seemed drawn to gather. Neptune still took center stage, Katarina's gift bag sat beside it. Viv picked it up and dropped it in the trash. Another ruse, she thought. Another manipulation.

"How did Detective Smith know Katarina was at my house?" she asked, dropping herself onto the chair with a heavy sigh. "How did you know to follow him?"

"Martie Grim," Jake said, joining her at the table. "She called it in. She said something didn't feel right and the detective needed to check the situation at an address. I didn't hear the 911 call, of course, but I heard the dispatcher relay the intel. Seriously, if you want to know what's going on in this town, a scanner is the thing."

"I didn't realize Katarina Becker was even on the detective's radar," Viv said. "I figured he had his eye on Captain Fred."

"Even I knew the Beckers were covering tracks. Especially after that break-in fakery," Jake explained. "That looked pretty lame to me. It was an obvious and amateur setup. I talked to one of the EMTs that night. He said the knot on Fred's head looked more like an accident than an assault. Wrong angle. The bruise better matched one of the display cases. Like he had fallen against the edge of the glass. Or maybe even purposefully hit the edge with his head. I wondered then if he was trying to put blame everywhere but on himself or Katarina."

Viv nodded. "I really thought Captain Fred was guilty. There were so many things that pointed to that, and the break-in seemed to clinch it. He looks old and a little feeble," Viv added, "but it's an act like the rest of his show. He certainly has enough power in his hands to shoot a harpoon.

"And then when Katarina reported the harpoon theft, I thought she was trying to divert attention to take suspicion off Captain Fred. But it must have been the other way around. Captain Fred must have known what she had done and staged the break-in to take suspicion off Katarina."

"Detective Smith is no dummy," Jake added. "He was a leap ahead of all of us. Katarina's tour boat is a couple of slips over from the rental bays. A deckhand saw her draw alongside a rental boat and go aboard. She probably thought she was off camera, but she wasn't. He knew something was wrong after they got that weird call for a boat rental." Jake smiled at Viv. "He knew something was up when the rental was for a Viv Marston. He doesn't know you, but he knew Viv Marston had passed."

"I'm pretty sure the speargun in the backpack didn't come off the wall at the museum," Viv said. "I never saw it, but I think that was another one of Katarina's ruses. In the way the detective described the murder weapon, it didn't sound like an artifact. She wanted it to look like someone broke into the museum and took the weapon. She tried to pin that on me and then on Zoe. I'm sure it has prints all over it, but they aren't mine," Viv added quickly. "Even if Detective Smith went through my trash to check."

"He did that?"

"He did."

"Sneaky dude."

"I guess that's why he makes the big bucks."

Jake grinned. He knew better.

"Why were you so cagey about who I saw in Anchor Park that morning?" She ventured, feeling bolder and even more curious.

"Katarina and Captain Fred stroll through the park every morning, weather permitting. It's one of their rituals. He donated the land and the anchor to the city. He's quite proud of that. They go in the morning and sit at the anchor."

"You thought they saw the body and ignored it."

"Something like that."

"She said they didn't go that day. She said Fred didn't want to go. I thought that was because he didn't want to be the one to find the body.

"Maybe she lied about that," Viv amended. "Maybe she didn't want him to go. She didn't want him to see what she had done."

"Oh, I think she did," Jake said. "I think that's exactly why she chose Anchor Park. I know Katarina's tricks. She wanted her father to see the sacrifice she made for him. One ultimate act of devotion. You just happened to get there first."

"That's why she left that ticket stub on the placard," Viv said. "*Veni, Vidi, Vici.*"

Jake look confused.

"It was something Katarina said to me. It means *I came, I saw, I conquered.*"

"Julius Ceasar?"

Viv nodded. "Katarina must have pulled the airline ticket stub from that guy's backpack and then stuck it on the placard near the anchor to deliver one last message. She wanted her father to see it. She wanted him to know what she had done. She thought it would earn his love. I came. I saw. I conquered. Julius Ceasar was stabbed in the back, you know."

"*Veni, Vidi, Vici*," Jake repeated. "You foiled her justice served."

"Except that wasn't justice," Viv said. "Katarina is the one who took the necklace. A jealous teenager with a chip on her shoulder. She let Zoe's diver guy take the fall for the heist. And then three decades later, she let his son take the fall all over again.

"I guess justice has been served in some way," she added after a moment of reflection. "The jewels will get back to their rightful owner."

They were quiet for a moment. Viv appreciated that about Jake. She thought he appreciated that about her too. No need for senseless chatter.

"It's kind of sad, really," Viv said after a while, her fingers mindlessly twirling the box on the table. "All Katarina wanted was his attention. Maybe she thought if she could return the missing jewels to her father after all these years, she would have his adoration. That it would make him love her the way she needed. I think she believed that poor guy knew where the jewels were, but he didn't. All he had was a riddle. Maybe she believed he wanted to steal the treasure for himself. Or maybe she saw her last chance at finding the necklace vanishing like the wink of a diamond in the light. Who knows what was in Katarina's mind?"

Jake nodded. "What's with the box?" he asked, watching as Viv twirled the box in her fingertips.

"Oh, we thought maybe the necklace was in this."

"We?"

"Me and Zoe. Her ex sent her a sentimental keychain with a key attached. It opened the box, but there's nothing in it. Just a tired old ballerina." Viv opened the box to show him.

He grinned. "Don't you know about these boxes?" He gently pulled it from her hands, opened the lid and tugged at the ballerina. "They all have a secret compartment."

The figurine made an anemic musical whine as he tugged. A drawer under her stage popped open. Viv saw that something stuffed inside.

"See?" Jake said. "Secrets."

Viv pinched the paper with her fingertips and pulled it free.

It was handwritten, and Viv recognized the crisp, slanted writing that filled the ledger in the drawer. "It's from Aunt Viv," she said breathlessly, scanning the page to the signature.

"And?"

"And..." Viv began to read.

This confession may never be found, and I am reconciled to this reality. He pulled the jewels from the sea and claimed them for himself. His daughter stole them from her father so he would blame us. No one escaped his rage. So, we made a pact. No one would possess the jewels in our lifetime. Only when death approached would the key and box find their way together again, the truth to be revealed for someone else to carry. The treasure is not lost. She rests in stone. Triton holds her heart, and the Mermaid keeps her safe. That's the sum of it. Nothing more, nothing less. Viv M

"Wow," Jake said. "That's some secret. Nothing more, nothing less."

Viv looked up with tears in her eyes. "They were so noble," she whispered. "Viv held that secret most of her life. She knew the jewels would never be safe in anyone's hands. Especially not in a family like the Beckers. She couldn't return then to the authorities because Captain Fred would have raged against her. Maybe even caused her harm. The only way to keep the jewels safe was to keep them hidden."

Jake nodded. "Family dynamics can be so weird. I got lucky. My family is so sane they're boring."

Viv nodded. "My family is so sane they're boring."

"I knew there was something special about you besides being a pyromaniac."

"Oh, you don't even know the half of it," she said, grinning, the somber nature of the letter shaking free. The mystery was solved, and she had figured it out. Well, almost.

"So, what is your family brand of boring?" Jake asked. "Are they just old or what?"

"You mean my parents?"

Jake nodded.

"They're not old," Viv said. "They're just Charlotte and Reg. They live in a retirement community. She gardens in full makeup and a hat to protect her skin. He volunteers at a nonprofit. They eat dinner out on Saturday. They play couple's golf on Sundays."

Jake laughed. "You call them Charlotte and Reg?"

"Family dynamics," Viv said and shrugged. "Boring as in predictable," she added. "Thanksgiving is always dry-as-bone turkey. Christmas dinner is rubberized ham. Halloween is burnt lasagna and garlic toast. To keep the vampires away."

Jake laughed again.

"Is that why you like to cook? Because your mother didn't?"

"I never thought about it quite like that. Even though my mother was mostly a housewife, meals were, to her, just a necessity. My sisters were a lot older, and no one bothered with dinner family time. I was pretty much left to feed myself. My grandmother is the one who instilled in me her love for the kitchen."

"Mimi," Jake said. "You write about her."

Viv nodded. "I owe her everything. Well, she and maybe Aunt Viv too."

They were silent for another moment, and Viv wondered what Mimi would say about all of this. About a kitchen fire hex on a wanna-be chef. About three ancestors who popped into her food. About a murder over old lies and lost jewels. Even about her dumpy yellow house in Crystal Bay with a dozen statues too heavy to move and one of them full of priceless diamonds. She didn't remember hearing Mimi talk about Viv Marston, the aunt, and she had never given it a second thought until now. She wished she had known Vivianna Martson. Now it was too late.

"Hey," Viv piped up, "Why did Gerry go all weird when I mentioned the harpoon?"

"Oh, that," Jake said and laughed again. "It's not funny, but Aunt Gerry gave me my first and last speargun on my sixteenth birthday. I immediately shot a guy in the butt. It was an accident, and it wasn't as bad as it could have been, but he's still got a scar on his butt cheek, I'm sure. Gerry felt responsible. She's hated those things ever since."

"And you haven't touched a speargun since then?"

"Oh, not even. But that's not why. I'd rather catch my fish the old-fashioned way."

Viv smiled. He was an old-fashioned kind of guy for a surfer dude with wild hair and baggy shorts. He loved his mom. Made a killer ceviche. Fought fires on call. If he was the dude waiting at the crossroads Amelia had mentioned, she was willing to take a chance.

"You got anything to eat?" he asked. "I'm starving."

"Cheese and salami," Viv said and grinned.

Jake laughed. "Got crackers?"

"Boy, do I have crackers!" Viv grinned. "And there's hot honey and pickled ginger in the trash."

Jake made a face. "I'm just going to go for the crackers and cheese."

Viv pulled out plates and two semi-cold beers. The electricity breaker to the appliance was still off.

She heard a familiar *pop* and glanced around the kitchen. The gourmet ancestors must be somewhere about. She wondered if they had been eavesdropping the entire time.

"*Gurrl*, he's as fine as salt on a watermelon and just about as juicy." Floyd's comment made her blush. It wasn't inaccurate, but she didn't need to hear it in her head.

"Floyd, you have no filter," Clara said. "You'd think as old as you are, you'd have learned proper manners by now."

Viv looked up at the jar of dry-roasted peanuts on the shelf. She had left the cupboard door open when she grabbed the box of crackers. Floyd had taken over as Mr. Peanut on the jar, and Clara had taken form on a can of cling peaches in natural juice. Viv grinned, secretly overjoyed to know the gourmet ancestors were still around. They had been lying low since the de-hex spell and the church hymn singalong. They showed up at Denny's swimming like Esther Williams in syrup, but they had been suspiciously absent when Katarina was in the room.

"We owe you an apology," Earlene said, squeezing in beside Clara. "We blew that hex-undo. We didn't think it would catch your house on fire."

"That's not what caught the kitchen on fire. It was that ancient coffee pot," Viv said before she could catch herself.

Jake furrowed his brow. "Who are you talking to? Who said anything about a coffee pot?"

She looked at Jake. "Oh, I knew you were going to ask me about it eventually." She could feel her cheeks burning with embarrassment.

"It wasn't much of a fire," he said, glancing at the wall. "But every fire has the potential to be deadly. You need to install a fire extinguisher. Maybe two. I mean that."

"I really need to toss out all those old appliances," Viv returned. "I think everything in this kitchen is from 1970. Some of it's pretty cool looking, but maybe using the electrical stuff isn't such a great idea."

Jake wolfed down the food and chugged the warm beer. "Hey, I almost forgot! I brought you something." He pulled a wad of tissue paper from his shirt pocket.

"What is this?" Viv asked.

"It's a starfish. Actually, it's a starfish skeleton if you want to be scientifically accurate."

"A starfish!"

"It's a good omen. A lucky star."

"A lucky star," Viv repeated, smiling, remembering her tarot reading with Amelia. "You are a good friend to have around, Jake Palmer. And I hope you are more than a distraction."

Before he could comment, Viv leaned over and planted a kiss on his lips. "Salty," she said and smiled into blue eyes and a tan face and messy sun-bleached hair. "Like salt on a watermelon," she whispered, hearing Uncle Floyd's chuckle echo in her head.

Food for Thought
Citrus Times Culinary Column

Truffles as Good as a Kiss

By Vivianna Marston, The Snooty Foodie

One Valentine's Day, when I had a mad crush on a boy in school and couldn't stop talking about him, Mimi suggested I make him truffles. Truffles, she said, were as good as a kiss. I blushed to my knees!

We spent all of Sunday up to our elbows in chocolate, making enough truffles for the entire class. We wrapped each perfectly round ball in cellophane and tied it with a ribbon printed with hearts. This was my first education in ganache.

Ganache is the accepted French word for chocolate sauce. It is an emulsion of melted chocolate, sweet cream butter or cocoa butter, cream or milk, a pinch of salt, and some kind of sugar. Smooth and shiny, a bit particular about ratios and temperatures, ganache is worth the effort when you want to impress.

The story of how ganache came to be is a fun one. Back in 1850s France, a messy accident in the kitchen gave birth to what would become a culinary disciple, when a pot of boiling cream spilled onto the chocolate. The chef yelled, *"Ganache!"* meaning, *Fool!* The mixture turned out to be delicious. Ganache soon found favor in the pastry kitchen.

The end consistency of a ganache is geared toward its final destination. Thin, smooth, fluffy, or heavy, it's a favorite for glazing a cake with luxurious shine or whipped into a lightweight frosting. It can be piped into pastries or swirled into brownies and muffin batter. Yes, please.

The ganache truffle claims its debut on the Parisian stage not long after this culinary accident occurred, when a playwright- turned- confectioner started selling these treats to his patrons. Rolled in cocoa powder, it resembles a real-life truffle and hence the name.

An easy to eat mouthful of chocolate goodness, the truffle is a rich, velvety, indulgent bite that melts at the temperature of your tongue. One does not chew a truffle, Mimi warned. One lets it melt slowly. Savored. Lingering. Like a kiss.

Ingredients like vanilla, espresso, and citrus zest can also be added.

Like love and messy accidents, there are a few caveats about your ingredients. Use a high-quality semi-sweet or bittersweet chocolate. Dark chocolate is too low in fat content.

Leftover ganache can be used as a dip for fruit, poured onto ice cream, hardened into fudge, or even turned into chocolate gravy.

Leftovers? Who are we kidding?

If you want to impress someone you can't stop thinking about, a tiny box of homemade truffles is a win-them-over dessert surprise as good as a kiss.

CHAPTER TWENTY-SIX

Viv looked up at the smoke circling into the sky. She smiled to herself. For the first time in a long while, she was not responsible for this spire of smoke or the flames shooting upward. Jake stood by the grill, tongs in hand, surveying the controlled blaze.

"I'm almost ready to put the steaks on. You like your steak medium rare?"

"And crispy on the outside," she answered, snuggling deeper into the lawn chair. "Don't let the veggie kabobs burn," she added, her mouth watering with anticipation at the thought of a perfectly cooked ribeye and a pile of grilled squash, onions, and mushrooms.

No one claimed someone else couldn't cook in her presence. It was Aunt Earlene who had that bright idea. "See if he has sizzle," Earlene had said as they were floating in her cereal like three ghostly vacationers on a lazy river float. Floyd had giggled beside her. "It's not your kitchen that's hexed, Viv, it's you. Let Jake cook. See what happens. If the kitchen does catch fire, well, you have an experienced fireman right there and handy to put the fire out."

"Right there and handy," Floyd echoed and giggled again.

"People who love to eat are always the best people," Clara had said, then added, "and of course I'm quoting Julia Child."

Admittedly, the patio was not her kitchen, but it felt close enough as a test. The back patio at 13 Dolphin Street had been weeded and swept, and the old fountain with its concrete leaping fish had a new family of koi residing in the bowl, a solar pump serenading them like a babbling brook. The red hibiscus was as brilliant as ever.

The gourmet ancestors were nowhere to be seen or heard tonight, and she knew they were respecting her privacy with Jake around. Thank goodness they hadn't disappeared altogether. They hadn't found a cure for the hex. The *Book of Nines* spell book was still on Uncle Floyd's ethereal sleuthing agenda, and he had seemed only slightly disappointed that Amelia was not the person they were looking for. The gourmet ancestors seemed resigned to the reality that banishing the hex in Amelia's name had not been the cure. Viv had asked whether the de-hexing didn't work because Amelia was not the hexer, or if they just didn't do the spell right. Or maybe they hadn't sung the right chant. Aunt Clara seemed put out by the suggestion. Viv hadn't pursued the point further.

Don't lose hope, Floyd had encouraged her, his pompadour peeking out of a bowl of fudge ripple ice cream. Earlene and Clara were the cherries balancing on top. Sooner or later, Floyd had said, they would have that hex thing in the bag.

The patio table on Dolphin Street was set and the umbrella angled to make shade, but the sun felt glorious on her shoulders. The sun was low enough to cast golden ribbons across the patio stones, and the air was full of honeysuckle blooms and hot charcoal briquettes.

Viv picked up the Orlando newspaper she had bought from Martie at Tropical Tomes. She turned to the culinary section and then stared at the headline.

Chef Mojo Sparks Flaming Mystery at Saffron Chapel Dinner

Chef Mojo. Viv's favorite culinary instructor. The one who held lavish feasts to raise money for a good cause. What was he up to now? Intrigued, Viv launched into the story.

> What started as a gourmet dining experience and fundraiser for an area food bank turned into what some guests called "a wild trip to Alice's Wonderland," complete with "mild hallucinations and uncontrollable laughter." Culinary professor Morris Brown is known in the community as Chef Mojo

and the originator of the Feast Blessing dinner parties that raise thousands of dollars for charity. At Saturday's dinner of the elite, the chef served a five-course dinner complete with a flame blessing ritual that involved burning spices and herbs he claimed, "opens the palate—and the wallet—and closes the spirit to harm."

Guests at the Saffron Chapel, a historic old church turned restaurant, reported that halfway through the meal, strange things began happening. One diner said it was the most enjoyable meal he had ever had, claiming the "spoonful of knowledge" course was like a "spiritual awakening."

The dinner concluded with a flambe of imported Cuban bananas and rum that reportedly got out of control. The fire department was summoned to the scene after a menu went up in flames and set off the alarm. No injuries or damages were reported. When asked if the fire was intended, Chef Mojo claimed the flames were all "part of the culinary theatre" and that "when you cook with fire, fire cooks back."

Viv laughed and Jake looked up and smiled.

That sounded like Chef Mojo. Fun. Flamboyant. Willing to take a chance. He was lucky no one got harmed.

Lucky. The word echoed in her head. Was he lucky? Or was there something else going on?

When you cook with fire, fire cooks back.

Viv folded the paper and set it aside.

Was the hex culprit someone she knew from the academy? She remembered asking the gourmet ancestors when they first brought up the hex.

"It has all the fat and trimmings of someone who was jealous of your talents. Someone with access to magic."

Someone jealous of her talents.

That wouldn't be Chef Mojo. He was a far better chef than she would ever be.

Someone with access to magic.

That was more likely. Feast Blessings. Flame blessings. Mild hallucinations and uncontrollable laughter. Spices that opened the palate. Flame that rose up but went nowhere.

Was Chef Mojo a witch? A warlock? A practitioner of the black arts? Was he the one who had access to magic? Could he be the one behind the hex? The one who turned her ability to cook with fire into fire?

Viv felt cold despite the warm sun.

"Oh, I forgot," Jake called over, interrupting her thoughts. "I brought you something, but I left it in my truck. Here, hold these while I go get it." He motioned to Viv with the tongs.

Viv's pulse raced. She glanced at the grill and then at the tongs still in his hand.

"Here," he encouraged, clacking the tool at her like a bird beak. "I'll be back in a flash."

The moment the tongs exchanged hands the grill hissed like an angry snake. A green flame shot up and twisted into the tail of a dragon. The ashen coals sparked and re-ignited, and a cloud of saffron-colored smoke billowed above the grill.

"Whoa!" Jake exclaimed. "Get back," he barked, pushing her away as the green flames spiraled higher. "What the hell?"

She dropped the tongs, clattering onto the stones. The grill heaved a sigh. The flamed turned gold.

Viv stared at the grill and then at Jake.

"What is going on?" Jake bellowed. "What is wrong with this grill? What is wrong with you?"

The tears that had welled up spilled onto her cheeks.

"Oh, Viv," he said, concern in his eyes. "This isn't normal. Something is very, very wrong."

"No," she whispered and gulped in a breath of air. The smell of cinnamon and saffron filled her nose. Spices and char. "This *is* my normal, Jake," she said. "And something is *very* wrong."

Jake pulled Viv to his chest. "I'm listening," he said. "Tell me what's going on."

"I can't," Viv muttered into his shirt. "I just can't."

He let her go and rescued the steaks and veggies from the grill, surveying the damage left by the green flame. The steaks might still be edible, but they sure wouldn't be medium rare.

"You want to go out and eat?" Jake asked, plopping into the chair beside her.

"I've lost my appetite," she said and then regretted the sullen tone in her voice. "I don't want to ruin your evening."

"Might be too late for that," Jake said and laughed. "Seriously, Viv, what is going on with you and fire? There is obviously something weird happening and I wish you would tell me."

"I will," Viv said, and glanced into his eyes, hoping to see what she wanted to see. Could she trust him? Was he the one good thing in her life these days? Or was he the test as Amelia and her tarot cards had hinted? The lover at the crossroads? A distraction? Or a test?

"I'm just not ready to talk about it, but soon," she said.

They poked at the steak and vegetables, which were surprisingly more edible than either of them thought they would be. The conversation seemed strained.

What was there to say after all that mayhem?

Jake helped her bring in the dishes, but she refused his help to clean up. Looking like a rejected puppy kicked out of the house, Jake left shortly after. She felt guilty about keeping him clueless, but there was no way she could open that can of crazy just yet.

Viv returned to the patio and sat in the sun, the last rays sinking into a pink horizon. A dragonfly landed on her bare feet. Its wings stilled for a moment, the sunlight catching in the pattern like stained glass. She wiggled her big toe. The dragonfly lifted, hovered a moment, and then dropped back down.

"You again," Viv said warmly. "I bet you have another message I don't understand. I'm still stuck with this horrible hex, and I don't have a clue what to do about it."

Her words sounded so simple. And yet, the situation felt overwhelming. With that one twist of fate, she had lost both dreams and passion. She had lost a ritual she loved more than anything. She lost the connections that feeding others gave her. She even lost her ability to nourish herself. Protein was scarce. Cold food didn't feed her soul. Watching other people cook made her heart ache.

Cooking was what she loved, an act of love born in Mimi's kitchen. She wasn't just grieving the act of cooking, the actual labor behind it, she was grieving all the ingredients that went into the recipe. The celebration and awe. Conversation and community. Nurturing people she cared about. Now she couldn't even offer them a cup of coffee without creating chaos. Her grief felt personal. An attack against her and her alone.

She felt betrayed—not just by whoever was behind the hex but by the very fire itself. Fire being the first gift to humanity, lifting humans from their barbaric ways. Flame that changed the course of humans forever. Fire was changing hers.

She had fought hard to get into culinary school, standing up to Charlotte and her unfounded fears that cheffing wasn't good enough. Not practical enough. Not suitable. And defying Charlotte's wishes, she enrolled in the academy and told Charlotte a lie. What had she gained? Nothing. A degree she couldn't use. A career that had gone up in smoke. Literally. She was losing herself in the hex. She was losing who she thought she would become. Career ashes. Just like Amelia said. A failure. A big nothing. The worst kind of failure: I told you so.

The dragonfly wings fluttered again, and a thought entered her mind as if spoken aloud.

Endings are not empty. Beginnings are not full.

Her heart swelled even as she wrestled with the words and their meaning. Mimi had said that often. Not those words exactly, but something similar. No glass is ever empty. No glass is ever full. The way we see the glass makes the difference between hope and despair. Rainbow sprinkles. There's always a place for rainbow sprinkles.

The air shimmered around the dragonfly. The pink light of the setting sun glowed in its see-through wings. Reality seemed to bend around the creature, like a delicate time warp ushering in a moment of peace. She would find a remedy for the hex. She would find herself again. She would feed the world. Some day.

The wings flickered once more. It was as if the words were spoken in her ear.

Nothing is broken beyond repair. There is night. And the sun also rises.

Viv breathed in deeply, feeling lighter somehow. She was not broken. There was hope. She took another deep breath, and the sweet, cinnamon scent of Chinese five-spice powder filled her awareness. The aroma was fleeting, its origin impossible to locate, and then it dissolved as quickly as it arrived, like a forgotten memory passing through the dark.

THE END

Read a sneak peek from Book 2!

*A Snooty Foodie Mystery with a
Pinch of Magic*

The Rice and Fall
of Food Man Chu

JANE ELZEY

CHAPTER ONE

Vivianna Marston watched as Ah Chu, affectionately known as Food Man Chu, hung his New Menu sign on the door and tapped the pinyin character at the top and then at the bottom.

"For good fortune," he said. "Fu will bring great luck."

"You must be excited," Viv said as he unlocked the ornate wooden door and stepped aside for her to enter. "A new menu is a great way to stir up business and who doesn't need some of that?"

He nodded and smiled warmly, eyes crinkling behind his glasses. At a scant five foot, dressed in crisp black and white, Ah Chu reminded Viv of a penguin as he scurried past the hostess desk and motioned for her to follow.

She could smell the remnants of the cookery lingering in the air, the slightly smoky aroma of sesame seed oil and spices. Garlic, ginger, and five-spice powder left a rich, sweet-salty tang that hung heavy like the red velvet curtains in the windows.

"Please, sit here," he said, pulling out a black lacquer chair at a round table set for one. "Very best seat in the house. I welcome you to Lotus on the Bay."

"Am I the first to sample this new menu?" she asked, as her host drew the curtains with a heavy gold cord. Light filled the restaurant and sparkled on the glasses.

"You are The Snooty Foodie," he answered eagerly. "You should be first." He bowed slightly. Viv bowed her head, hoping it was an appropriate response to an elder.

"I will present a feast," he continued. "Then you can write Food Man Chu's New Menu is most excellent."

Viv smiled at his use of the moniker. She had wondered if he was aware of the nickname. It was an endearing term, not a slight, because Mr. Chu was respected and very well liked in the community. Food Man Chu's food, however, had another reputation. It was not good. Not good at all.

"I will do my best to highlight your best," Viv said with a smile using the expression the editor had suggested when she gave Viv this assignment. *Mr. Chu is a valued customer*, the editor told her. *Be honest but not disparaging. Fair but not unfavorable.*

Viv hoped that would be possible.

Mr. Chu lingered at her elbow. "You like it here?"

Viv nodded.

"Why did you come?"

"To Crystal Bay?"

Mr. Chu nodded. His smile was warm and curious.

"I inherited a house from a relative. And I really needed a lucky break." She could have added that she came to this little Florida tourist town on the edge of the Gulf of Mexico after graduating culinary school and watching her career go up in flames. Literally up in flames. She could have said that writing reviews and selling advertising for the *Citrus Times* was enjoyable—and keeping her afloat financially—but not what she planned to be doing at age twenty-nine. She could have shared that her aspiration was to be a chef in a big-city restaurant with rave reviews, not *writing* reviews about other chefs.

And she could have confessed she was *hexed.*

A chef hex. The victim of a magical jinx that made it impossible for her to cook. Whenever she applied heat, something in the kitchen caught fire.

A chef who couldn't cook.

Lemons. Lemonade.

She was making the best of it.

"I came here many years ago," Mr. Chu announced. "You were not born. I am certain."

Viv laughed lightly. "You don't look a day over thirty."

"I know," he said and giggled like a schoolboy. "I am young fifty-six. Lucky for me. Good genes," he added. "You like Chinese food?"

Viv nodded. "It's always been one of my favorites. I even took Mandarin in college, thinking I might travel to China someday. I can't remember anything but thank you. *Shihtzu*," she said proudly.

He cocked his head. "*Xie Xiè. Xie Xiè*," he repeated, and Viv realized her pronunciation hadn't even come close.

"You will enjoy Chinese food as never before," he said, placing the menu in her hands. Viv glanced at the heavy paper the color of old parchment, bordered with geometric shapes and a lotus flower centered at the top and the bottom.

"I have come to possess a most special book of recipes that create such delight that you will never tire of dining at Lotus on the Bay." He clasped his hands against his chest. "These recipes come from ancient China, only recently discovered while examining my late wife's possessions."

"I am sorry for your loss," Viv said quickly, with genuine warmth.

"*Xie Xiè*," he said, with a nod. "She has been gone ten years now. I did not remember she had this book among her belongings, but when I turned the pages, my memory of such delicious feasts sprang to mind so that I was overtaken with delight. I remembered being served these delicate foods. I remember this banquet of emotion. It was of joy and desire. Of revelry and pure content. It is this banquet is why I married my wife."

Viv glanced back at the menu now feeling awkward. Was he talking about what she thought he was talking about? Courtship was one thing, but joy and desire? TMI. And what did that have to do with food?

He didn't seem to notice her discomfort. "I could not believe my good luck at finding this book so many years gone. Now I am a new man in the kitchen. I have a new menu from old recipes that are like the magic breath of a dragon."

Viv arched a brow. Anything that breathed fire could be a problem.

"I will present the feast, and you will see." He pointed to the menu and nodded enthusiastically. "It will arrive as written."

"Lovely," Viv said, wondering if the fanfare and enthusiasm would make up for a bad meal, a meal she was obligated to write about. Like Goldilocks, she had to find something *just right* she could focus on in her review. "I appreciate your devotion. It's so … so contagious!"

Mr. Chu smiled, turned and then disappeared behind another heavy curtain drawn aside with cords, which Viv guessed was hiding the entrance to the kitchen. She knew from her experience at culinary school how loud, how messy, and hot the commercial kitchen could be. At least the red velvet barrier had a little swank to it. Maybe it was a decade or two out of date, but vintage decor seemed oddly chic in Crystal Bay. Her own house was still full of 1970s decor.

Such drama. Such fanfare, she thought, as she looked over the menu. The last time she ate at Lotus on the Bay, she hadn't even bothered with the leftovers.

The menu declared that dinner began with *The Lotus Awakening*. Her mouth suddenly watered. *Peking Duckling Dumplings.*

Viv pulled out her notebook and made a few notes. She would take the menu with her for reference, but she wanted to keep track of her reactions to each course, deciphering ingredients, technique, and a nuance or two. Even though she couldn't make Peking duck without fire and disaster, she could still approach the experience as a trained chef.

She looked up as Mr. Chu approached, and her breath caught with surprise.

He held aloft a small bamboo steamer basket, two red cloth napkins draped across his forearms, hanging much like the curtains he had just passed through. A golden hue shimmered around the basket, steam swirling above it like visible Chi.

"Oh, my," Viv said, as he placed the basket in front of her and removed the lid. Inside the basket were three dumplings that seemed to float for a moment before settling against the bamboo bottom. She felt a sudden stirring in her ribcage, like butterflies being set free.

"*Ohhhh. Ahhhh*," she breathed, letting the fragrant steam rise. She felt as if her own Chi was being set free as she breathed the warm breath of the dish.

"*Sik fan lah*," he said, motioning to the basket with a nod.

With a suddenness Viv didn't expect, curiosity and anticipation overtook her. Hurriedly, she plucked a dumpling onto her chopsticks and popped it into her mouth. And then, just as suddenly, she felt herself surrender to the soft dough. Her eyes closed. Sweet, salty, spicy, sour, and umami. All were present in that one bite.

She glanced up at Mr. Chu and smiled.

Mr. Chu's eyes were twinkling. "I see you appreciate," he said softly. "It is an awakening of the tastebuds. A Lotus Awakening."

Viv captured the next dumpling from the basket and then closed her eyes again to deconstruct the ingredients. Duck. Cabbage and carrots. Hoisin sauce. Fresh basil. No, not Italian basil. *Thai* basil. Perhaps a tiny mince of bird's-eye pepper.

She glanced up with admiration, but Mr. Chu had left, leaving her to savor the last Peking Duckling Dumpling, her intrigue fully awakened and wanting more.

This was going to be no ordinary meal.

A familiar sound caught her attention, then, like a cork popping from a bottle or a caper bursting in a hot pan. She glanced around the table, noticing for the first time the tea brewing in front of her. Somehow, the steam was still spiraling from the spout as the tea flowers floated in the clear glass of the pot. Viv grinned, recognizing the three faces smiling back at her.

"It's like a sauna in here," Uncle Floyd said, his Elvis style pompadour floating above a pink rosebud in the tea. "I hope this is good for my skin."

Earlene was manifested as a chrysanthemum bud. "You don't have skin, Floyd. You're just a floating head. We're all just floating in the tea."

"It's a very nice tea," Aunt Clara declared. "Perfectly balanced to pair with your feast, Viv. I'm quite certain this is royal jasmine."

"I wondered if you were going to show up," Viv whispered. "I thought maybe you would manifest in the dumplings. They were amazing!"

"You nearly inhaled them, my dear. I don't know that we could have gotten out of your way in time," Clara replied, her face crowned by her tightly curled bangs.

Viv grinned. She nearly inhaled the dumplings. Anticipation, or longing, or something very akin to that had taken over as the steam rose from the basket. The urge to dive in without hesitation had engulfed her. The craving subsided the moment she sank her teeth into the first bite. Now she was left with a tingling, and the minced pepper lingering on her tongue.

She studied the teapot, not at all bothered by this manifestation of two aunts and an uncle from her mother's side of the family, all three of them long, long dead. She knew them as the gourmet ancestors, and they only showed up in her food. And drink. And condiments.

The first time they appeared at culinary school was in a flash and crackle of green sparkles. She had watched as the flame of her kitchen torch sputtered like a Fourth of July sparkler then turned several colors before flaring like a miniature firecracker in her hand.

And then they were there.

Three faces in the three crème' brûlée ramekins where she had been attempting to torch a layer of sugar. That was almost a year ago now, and the gourmet ancestors were still with her. They were still trying to help her find a remedy for the hex. They were still providing gourmet advice. It wasn't always trendy advice, but the ancestors did own a restaurant in their day, and that accounted for a lot. People who fed other people for a living knew a lot about food.

"We took a quick tour of the kitchen," Earlene said, still bobbing around as a flower, her bouffant as stiff as ever. "I believe you are in for a feast like no other."

Viv realized her mouth was still tingling, but the heat of the pepper had disappeared. Now, her tastebuds were awake and anticipating more. "If that first course is par, I agree."

"Par for magic," Floyd said abruptly, his pompadour rocking in the tea. "Can't you feel it, Viv?"

Viv frowned. "Feel what?"

"The magic," Floyd said. "In the food."

Viv frowned. "Magic food?"

Clara nodded. "We suspect your Mr. Chu is cooking from a magical cookbook. We didn't get that good of a gander at it, but the book has all the bells and thistles of spellbound recipes. Magic goes in. Magic comes out. The food enchants, the diner charms, the end result is…"

"We don't know what the end result is," Earlene interrupted. "But we wondered that if Mr. Chu has access to magic, could he be the one responsible for your hex?"

"But I only just met him," Viv exclaimed, then lowered her voice back to a whisper. "I thought we decided that whoever put this hex on me was someone I knew at culinary school."

"We did say that," Floyd agreed. "And I failed you miserably with our first pass at the hex removal remedy. I was absolutely positive we had the right person in our sights. I made a promise to myself that I would not be such a fool again."

Viv heard Earlene snicker. It sounded like a gurgle coming from the teapot.

"Even fools are right sometimes," Clara said. "We don't have much experience with hex magic, as you well know, Viv, so we may pull some doozies until we figure out how to cure this kitchen-hijack hijinks."

"What if we don't?" Viv said, noticing a rustle near the kitchen curtain.

"If we don't, you will need to look for a new career," Clara said, matter-of-factly. "Permanently. I know that breaks your heart to think of it, but have you ever considered teaching? I loved my time in the classroom."

"Did you say loved or loathed?" Earlene asked. "I seem to remember a great deal of unpleasant whining about how horrible the kids were."

Viv was about to respond when her host appeared at the table once again. "Were you talking to someone?" Mr. Chu said, looking around the dining room while balancing a serving tray in one hand. "No one here. You were on the phone?" He *tsked tsked* gently.

"No, I, uh," Viv stammered, "I sometimes talk to myself when I make notes." She glanced at the notebook page, thankful she had managed a few scribbles before the gourmet ancestors popped in.

"*Heart and Harmony*," Mr. Chu announced, motioning to the menu. "That is the name of this course. A soup that warms the soul from the inside out and the outside in. Like Yin and Yang. You have enjoyed your The Lotus Awakening?" His eyebrows rose into his black-framed glasses.

"Incredible," Viv said. "Absolutely delicious. Beyond delicious. I feel like I have experienced… " she stalled, wondering if she should bring up the words *magic* and *recipe* to a stranger.

"The magic breath of a dragon," Mr. Chu interjected. "Is that the feeling you encountered?"

"Uhm. Maybe that was the bird's-eye pepper?"

Mr. Chu laughed lightly, and Viv was struck by its pleasant melody, like a wind chime, and she understood why people liked him.

Viv glanced at the bowl he now placed in front of her. The gold rim sparkled like a pirate's doubloon, and she thought immediately of the treasure hunter's dazzling jewels and his museum on the downtown square. She leaned in and breathed the steam. The scent reminded her of a bouquet, earthy and herbaceous. The broth was impossibly clear, a delicate strand of seaweed floating at the center, visually separating the bowl into two sides. Yin and Yang, she decided, picking up her spoon with anticipation.

Expecting one thing from the clear broth, she consumed quite another. The first sip tasted like a sea breeze—cool and clean and briny. She savored the next spoonful and suddenly felt as if she were drifting on a tide. At dusk. Under a full moon. Something or someone singing softly in the far distance. She opened her eyes, surprised to find herself still seated at the table at Lotus on the Bay. She glanced at the teapot as if it could anchor her to reality.

Floyd as the rosebud nodded. "See," he said. "Magic food."

Viv took another spoonful, and this time the flavor was warm on her tongue. Ginger and lime. A dash of white pepper. The gentle waves from her first bite seemed to crest and then crash with persistence as if against a coastal shore. Yin and Yang. And a feeling of absolute harmony inside and out.

How was she ever going to describe this meal without sounding like an idiot?

Viv added a few notes to her notepad, then drained the bowl, lifting it to her lips with her hands, desperately needing to consume every drop.

"Wow," she breathed, feeling both the cool and the heat on her tongue. Joy filled her as she thought of Jake. She pictured herself standing barefoot on the shore of the Gulf, letting the waves ebb and flow over her toes. Of his hand in hers. Of her hand in his. Yin and Yang.

"Whoa," she said and shook her head to clear the vision. "Let's not go overboard," she whispered to the teapot. "This is not just a meal. This is an experience. Is this what magical food does to you?"

She thought she saw Clara nod from the teapot, and then out of the corner of her eye she saw Mr. Chu approaching. His smile was all-knowing. He knew what *Heart and Harmony* invoked. No wonder he had married his wife after this meal.

"Does everyone experience this?" she blurted. "Does everyone feel this way?"

He clasped his hands in delight. "I cannot say what everyone experiences. Everyone will experience something. And they will never tire of dining at Lotus on the Bay."

"How are you making this happen?" Viv asked. "What ingredients are you using?"

"Only the best ingredients, of course, although nothing uncommon," he answered, his eyes twinkling behind his glasses. "Ordinary ingredients with extraordinary taste. I did say, did I not, that it was a special book of recipes? The book claims the recipes come from the Qing dynasty. That was the last imperial dynasty in

Chinese history. I suggest it came from the palace of the great emperor himself and that is why it carries such power."

Viv reached for her pen. Nice quote to use for the review.

"The recipes may well be from the imperial kitchen itself," Mr. Chu added as he watched her pen fly across the page. "The Ming dynasty preceded the Qing dynasty. Ming is associated with fire. Qing is associated with water, illustrating the triumph of water over fire. Qing over Ming."

Viv scribbled quickly in her notebook. Water triumphant over fire.

"Next course?" Mr. Chu asked. "We have only two more courses. Another, if you count the fortune cookie. No one can leave Lotus on the Bay without their fortune."

Viv glanced at the menu. *The Flame's Embrace served with the Threads of Destiny.* Dessert was *Sweet Enlightenment.*

"I need to get a look at this cookbook," Viv said to the teapot when Mr. Chu returned to the kitchen. "I have to see it. I just have to!"

"We don't have the means," Clara said.

"We don't have hands," Earlene added. "That's what Clara means. We can't pick it up and bring it to you. We don't have the kind of magic that can *poof* something from one place to another."

Viv grinned. The gourmet ancestors were pretty adept at *poofing* themselves from one food to another. They had yet to explain where they went when they weren't in her food, but Viv suspected they didn't really know. Earlene had said once that it felt like an Electrolux sucking them through time to and fro, and Clara had retaliated with a reprimand that made Viv wince like a kid in school. Floyd had added that he had never, *never* felt like he was sucked up through the vacuum. Viv hadn't brought it up again.

"Just ask him," Floyd offered now. "Ask if you can look through his magical recipe book. For reference, of course. To add quality to your review. But I would suggest you don't call it magic. That might scare him off."

"I guess all he can say is *no*," Viv agreed and then waited patiently for her Flaming Embrace to arrive.

It wasn't long before Mr. Chu appeared at the curtain, a curved plate cupped in his hands. The vessel looked more like a Chinese swooping roof than a plate. Viv felt her eyes grow wide.

Nestled on the platter was a noodle nest, which, if she wasn't mistaken, arranged itself into a neat knot as the plate settled in front of her. The meat on top smelled like pork shimmered in a molten amber sauce. For a heartbeat moment, she heard the crackle of fire and the bubble of the sauce simmering. Her chest heaved with happy nostalgia. She remembered sitting with Mimi on the front porch stringing green beans for supper, the smell of pork roasting in the oven drifting through the kitchen window. The peach pie they had made together cooled on the sill, and the sharp tang of peaches and cinnamon sugar hung in the air.

Viv was not truly aware of each bite. She was fully distracted by the noodles, each as delicate as a thread, which seemed to whisper to her as she pulled them from the knot with her chopsticks. The words were not intelligible. Maybe because they were in Chinese. But she felt the words. Honor and tradition, hope and encouragement. Every bite felt like: *You can do it. Keep going. Be invincible. Trust the process. Have courage. Believe in yourself.*

As her chopsticks delivered the noodles and sauce, past, present and future seemed to swirl around her, not in her field of vision, but just on the periphery. She turned her head to catch a glimpse, but she saw only the restaurant dining room, still empty of patrons.

Viv slurped the last thread of destiny and took the last bite of pork. Her heart was as full as her belly. How would she describe this feeling? How would she not sound like a kook?

Viv closed her eyes. It was as if a warm wave of comfort washed over her like a current in a slow-moving river in a deep riverbed. She grabbed her pen. Somehow, she would have to make this make sense.

When the last course arrived, Viv felt she was drifting above the table like a balloon. Or a cloud. Or a bird riding a current no one else could see.

Sweet Enlightenment was mango pudding served in a glowing lantern bowl that had no visible flame and no place for a battery. And it glowed. Sesame seed balls orbited the pudding like moons in space. Smooth and sweet, cool and soothing, she felt a quiet euphoria settle over her. With each spoonful, she felt a content-ment she rarely ever felt. She felt a sense of satisfaction as the culinary journey came to an end. She sighed when she scraped the bottom of the bowl.

"Mr. Chu," she said finally when he appeared at her side one last time, "that was the most incredible meal I have ever had. And I have eaten some fabulous meals."

He beamed as he placed the fortune cookie in front of her.

"Would it be possible for me to see this cookbook? I'm thinking I should describe it to my readers. Could I take a peek inside?"

"Oh, no," he said, shaking his head. "The book is too fragile to share. Besides, it is written in Chinese Hanzi. You are not accustomed to that language." He paused briefly. "Even with your limited studies," he said gently, and Viv knew he was right. She wouldn't recognize more than a single character on the page. But it didn't displace the feeling that she just *had to* see this book, this magical recipe book from ancient China that made the feast feel so… so personal … so alive.

"Could I take a picture of it at least?" she asked.

He paused briefly. He seemed to be considering her request.

"It is priceless."

"What if I took a picture of you holding the book? I need to take a photo for your review, anyway."

Again, Mr. Chu paused. "I will consider it," he said and left the table.

The fortune cookie was freshly baked. She could tell because it was lopsided on one side. The tip of the fortune draped over the fold like a tongue over lips. She perked her ears. Was it humming? It couldn't be. Could it? Maybe that was Food Man Chu humming in the kitchen.

She poured another cup of tea, wondering if the ancestors were gone, and as she sipped the floral brew, she opened her fortune.

"Your words will change everything."

ACKNOWLEDGMENTS

I love food. I love good food. I know that's subjective, but quality, taste, and technique will fill your soul like nothing else. All the women in my family were fabulous southern cooks, so I learned from the best.

Gourmet food didn't come into my life until I was in my twenties. A boyfriend had great connections because of his job, and we often dined at some of Orlando's best restaurants. That was when haute cuisine was still earning a place at the table in Florida, long before High South cuisine became a thing. Lightyears before Bravo and *Top Chef*.

What I learned from the experience was that our palates are broadened when we allow them to be, and every culture offers something unique in taste and presentation. Discovering different ingredients and cooking techniques will make you a better chef. A better chef puts better food on the table, and hopefully great friends to share it with.

Flash forward 30-some odd years, I have since instilled in my daughter (my "Viv" with a top knot) a similar love for good food. She also is a healthy gourmet in her approach, and I am always delighted to sit at her table.

Thanks to Laurence Kahn and Gene Burns for opening that door for me and handing me a plate and fork. Thanks to Jan Brown of *The Dairy Hollow House Cookbook* fame for all those inventive family suppers and salads. Thanks to my Joy of Cooking Club ladies who are enthusiastic about cooking our way around the world. I learn so much from our culinary explorations. And thanks to my beloved Beta readers who said this story made them hungry for more. That was my hope.

ABOUT THE AUTHOR

Jane Elzey is a mischief-maker, storyteller, and bender of the facts. A retired editor and journalist, she now writes southern cozies with a bite. Born and raised in Florida, Jane resettled in the Ozark Mountains of Arkansas more than thirty years ago in a town known for its artists, writers, and creative folk.

The Snooty Foodie Mystery with a Pinch of Magic is Jane's second mystery series. Her first, The Cardboard Cottage Mystery series, began publishing in 2020. The series is about games, friendship, loyalty, and a dearly departed husband. Because in this series the husband always dies. Look for *Dying for Dominoes, Dice on a Deadly Sea, Poison Parcheesi and Wine, Killer Croquet on the Emerald Isle*, and *Ouija and Haints in the Silent City* wherever you buy books. *I Spy a Dead Guy* publishes 2026.

Consider yourself invited to join Jane's Very Important Players Club newsletter for gossip, updates, games, and special offers. Write yourself into one of Jane Elzey's Cardboard Cottage stories by joining the VIP Killer Club, where reader fans can choose an ex for Jane's husband's gotta go list. Visit JaneElzey.com

BOOKS BY JANE ELZEY

and Scorpius Carta Press

The Cardboard Cottage Mystery series

Dying for Dominoes (2020)
Dice of a Deadly Sea (2021)
Poison Parcheesi and Wine (2022)
Killer Croquet on the Emerald Isle (2024)
Ouija and Haints in the Silent City (2025)
I Spy a Dead Guy (publishing 2026)

Snooty Foodie Mystery with a Pinch of Magic

The Bun Also Rises (2026)
The Rice and Fall of Food Man Chu (2026)

Jane Elzey's books are available for purchase wherever you purchase books. Be sure to ask your local library to carry Jane Elzey mysteries.

Visit JaneElzey.com for author gossip, news, and book updates.
Please follow Jane Elzey on Amazon for book release announcements.

www.ingramcontent.com/pod-product-compliance
Lightning Source LLC
Chambersburg PA
CBHW031045310726

48969CB00007B/2119